The Descendant

The Descendant Vampire Series

Book 1

BY KELLEY GREALIS

Copyright © 2013 by Kelley Grealis
All rights reserved.
Cover design by A BCD Creative
Edited by Jenny Bengen-Albert

ISBN: 0-615-61236-9
ISBN-13: 978-0-615-61236-2

For my husband, family and friends - thank you for
your endless support and encouragement.
And for Margo - thank you for the inspiration. I found my joy.

CHAPTER I

*J*knew I wasn't dying. At least that was what the other doctors had said. But what I didn't know, and neither did any of those other doctors, was the cause of my symptoms. In fact, those supposed specialists had all declared me to be perfectly healthy and viewed my symptoms with skepticism. But I knew they were mistaken; there was *something* wrong with me.

I waited for Doctor McNally in the cramped exam room; she was the seventh doctor I'd visited in the past six months. The drab, yellow walls and fluorescent lighting did little to comfort me, but I was still optimistic that this appointment was going to be different from the others. After all, this specialist had run more tests and labs and exams than the others, which gave me hope that she would not only be the doctor to diagnose me, but to cure me.

There was a knock at the door, and Doctor McNally entered the room. She was slender, maybe in her late thirties, with chestnut hair and green eyes. Her blue scrubs were hidden under a white lab coat.

"Good morning, Allison. How are you today?" she asked with a smile.

What a loaded question, I thought. Let's see – depressed, confused, tired, angry, sad, scared, all of the above? I decided to go with something less dramatic. "I'm okay. I'll be better after you tell me what's wrong with me."

The doctor pulled a caster stool from under the counter and sat down. Rolling closer to where I sat on the exam table, she crossed her arms over the clipboard in her lap and looked me in the eyes. "There's nothing wrong with you, Allison."

My heart skipped. Blood flooded my cheeks. Anger boiled in my stomach. Not again. Not another doctor insisting I was well. She couldn't tell me nothing was wrong with me. There had to be an explanation.

"But how can that be?" I pleaded. "Can you look again, please? There has to be something."

"Your blood work is normal, your scans are clean. You are well, Allison. I reviewed the information as it came in and looked it over again before meeting with you. There's nothing here to indicate you are anything but healthy."

I shook my head and dropped my eyes to the floor. What was happening to me wasn't normal. Something wasn't right.

I looked back at the doctor and tried to control my temper. "I don't believe this. You are just like all of the other doctors. There *has* to be something causing all of this. I'm not making this up."

Doctor McNally flipped through my file. "Allison, I'm telling you – according to these results, there is nothing unusual going on with you."

"Then how do you explain my lack of appetite?" I asked through gritted teeth.

"You haven't lost any weight over the past months. Your iron levels are normal…"

"What about my body temperature?" I interrupted. "I flare up at night like a furnace but I'm freezing cold in the morning, like I am now. Just last night, my blistering body heat kept me awake as I wallowed in bed in a pool of sweat. But now? Now I'm freezing, absolutely chilled to the bone. And my sweatshirt, jeans and socks are doing little to warm me. It makes no sense considering it's eighty-some-odd degrees outside. How do you explain that?"

"Allison, your temperature has been normal every time we've taken it, regardless of when it was taken. Even today, your temperature is ninety-eight point six degrees."

"What about my insomnia?" I challenged. "I've barely slept in months."

The doctor pursed her lips and seemed to carefully ponder her next words. "You say you dream, right?"

My mouth parted and my mind went momentarily blank as I stared at the doctor. I had no idea she knew about my dream. I didn't think I'd shared it with anyone. I hadn't even told my husband Matt let alone some doctor I'd only known through a handful of visits. It was my secret, or so I thought. I made no mention of the dream to anyone because it made little sense to me. I knew Matt and Jenna, my best friend since kindergarten, were already worried about my omnipresent sour mood and inexplicable symptoms, and they didn't need something else to worry about – a mysterious dream that somehow imparted temporary serenity upon me.

"I told you about my dream?"

"Mmm hmm. I have it written here from our last visit. You have a recurring dream about a garden."

"It's not just any garden," I snapped, and then immediately felt foolish. For some unknown reason, I was highly protective of my dream. But calling it a simple garden didn't do this paradise justice.

In my dream, the ground is a rich brown and exudes an earthy scent. Large tree roots break through the forest floor, undulating over the landscape like hypnotic waves. The atmosphere is completely saturated with fertility. Abundant, flourishing plant life is everywhere and flowering shrubs cling to the base of trees making it impossible to see where the trunks converge with the ground. Berry bushes are plentiful, as are ferns and thorny hedges.

The trees are a spectacular sight, massive in height and width. If the breadths of the trunks are any indication, these trees have been around for hundreds, if not thousands, of years. The branches soar up into the air, twisting and weaving, creating a sort of jungle gym. Branches kiss the sky where the foliage unfolds into an emerald canopy. Sunlight filters through this ceiling, casting a kaleidoscope of color within the jungle. An ever-present cool breeze sways the leaves, revealing patches of crisp, blue sky.

Beyond the wooded area are lush carpets of grass dotted with flowers in every imaginable color. There are large red blooms, tiny yellow buttercups, tall blue bells, orange lilies, purple puffs, and an array of exotic blossoms. The colors are splendid, so vibrant and full of life. It is as if a luminary is lighting each plant from within, showcasing the flower's beauty. In the distance, wild grasslands dance in the breeze in spellbinding repetition. The air is fragrant, almost overpoweringly so, yet delightful. The individual scents– roses, honeysuckle, freesia, and some unfamiliar ones – blend to form a pleasant perfume.

Other dreams reveal that animals of every kind make this paradise their home. Fluttering birds whistle melodious tunes while monkeys dangle from trees with bananas in hand. Koala bears cling to tree limbs near camouflaged lizards, and toucans perch on branches as they keep a watchful eye over the revelry. Lions, deer, elephants, and other large beasts roam freely, yet there are plenty of smaller creatures, too – rabbits, butterflies and a variety of insects. Friend and foe, hunter and prey live here in magical harmony, making the garden like no other place that has existed before. At least no place I have ever known.

"Allison?" Doctor McNally's voice floated through my ears. "Allison, hello, are you with me?"

I cleared my throat as I realized I had drifted off to my paradise. "Um, yeah. Sorry, I was ah, just thinking."

"Do you want to talk about it? Your dream."

"Not really. It's just um – it's not *just* a garden," I stated, trying to justify my earlier reaction. The last thing I wanted was a suspicious doctor exploring my paradise with me. "It's more of a tropical oasis, of sorts, something like that."

"Allison, is there something else going on?" The doctor stood up from her stool and peered down at me. This was starting to feel like an interrogation and I didn't like it. "Is there something else bothering you besides the symptoms that brought you here?"

"What do you mean?"

"Are you under stress or worried about something? Have you had a major life event like losing a job or a loved one?"

Her questions caught me off guard, but in that moment I suddenly realized something. I wasn't sure what she had asked or how she had asked it, but the doctor's words struck a chord with me. After all of these doctor visits, all it took was one doctor to ask a certain question in a certain way to make me realize the cause of all my ills.

I'm having a midlife crisis, I thought to myself. I was sure the good ole doc here would really think I was nuts if I told her. It did sound ridiculous, after all; I was only thirty-two years old. But somehow, it also made perfect sense.

I'd always had this need to do something great, to have an impact on the world and to leave it a better place. That need started the day I was born when the doctor told my parents that I was special, that he could see it in my eyes. Of course, as it had taken my parents fifteen years to conceive me, their only child, they already knew that. But those words took hold in their minds and they constantly reminded me of how special I was. Though I never felt important or significant, they encouraged me to keep looking for that one thing that would make me truly happy, my life's calling. Dad died six years ago from a heart attack and mom followed three weeks later with a broken heart, but their words still haunted me.

But I couldn't possibly tell the doctor I thought I was having a midlife crisis. Combined with all of the symptoms she apparently thought I was making up, I was sure she'd think I was crazy. Plus, Matt had to be the first person to know what was really going on with me, not her. He had been the one dealing with my sleepless nights, extreme body temperatures and volatile moods, and he deserved to know before anyone else. But I had to tell the doc something and I suddenly knew just the thing. It had to be in my file and was likely the source of her suspicions.

"Well, there is something," I finally said.

Doctor McNally patiently waited.

"Matt and I haven't been able to have a baby. We've been trying since we got married seven years ago. We've seen plenty of doctors. They say the problem is with me but they can't pinpoint what it is."

"Have you talked to anyone about this? About how you are feeling?"

"You mean besides all of the fertility doctors?"

"Mmm hmm."

"No, I haven't," I said tersely.

"Well maybe…"

"Maybe what?" I stood up. I had a hunch what Doctor McNally was about to say and I didn't want to hear it. Another doctor had suggested it years ago; I didn't like the idea then and I wasn't going to like it now.

"Maybe you should see a psychiatrist."

"Excuse me?"

"Well – it's possible that the stress from not being able to have a baby has been causing the symptoms you think you've been having."

"The symptoms I *think* I've been having?" Tears welled up in my eyes and then spilled over. "Listen, *Doctor*," I hissed, "I am not making this up. My symptoms are real. Just because *you* can't figure out what's causing them doesn't make them less real, and I'm not going to go see some quack that will want to psychoanalyze every aspect of my life. Thanks for nothing!"

I grabbed my purse and stomped out of the office and down the hallway. As I used my sweatshirt sleeve to dry my tears, I nearly ran headfirst into a nurse.

"Whoa, are you okay?" the nurse asked. She grabbed me by the shoulders to prevent the collision and a warm vibe flowed over my body. Her skin was pale and creamy, her hair was thick waves of shiny red curls and her eyes were dark lavender with peculiar yellow flecks.

"Oh, excuse me," I muttered. I searched for her name badge but it was hidden under her shoulder-length hair. "I'm, um, sorry."

"It's not a problem." She released me and the sensation left my body. I watched her as she walked away. Her gait was graceful and smooth, quite mesmerizing, and before I knew it, she was out of sight like she was never there at all.

I slammed the door to my Jeep and banged the palms of my hands against the steering wheel. Tears streamed down my face. "Why, God? Why are you doing this to me?" I moaned. I dropped my head to the steering wheel and sobbed.

"Why do I have these symptoms?" I yelled. "And why can't the doctors figure this all out?"

A pang of heat gurgled in my stomach. I moved my hands from the steering wheel and clutched my midsection. This was yet another undiagnosed symptom that had haunted me. The burning wasn't always there; it seemed to come and go whenever it liked. There was only one thing that made it go away – my dream.

My dream had been my only source of comfort over the past months. I treasured it, looked forward to it. The garden felt like home to me, so familiar even though I had never physically been there. I didn't even know where such a paradise would exist. I'd been to many tropical locales, but this jungle, this garden, this paradise far exceeded the beauty of those places. I found myself wishing – hoping – I would dream every night. I looked forward to what the next dream would reveal, how my paradise could become more perfect. Mostly, I anticipated the feeling the dream bestowed on me after I woke. Upon waking I always felt a sense of peace and tranquility and, oddly enough, a sense of belonging. I was a new, content woman with a fresh attitude, my foul outlook gone. I yearned for that serenity for as long as I could hold onto it. Unfortunately, the peacefulness wore off throughout the day, much like a perfume. I had often thought that if I were able to dream of this magical place every night, I would snap out of the unpleasant state of mind I had been in for the past six months. But no matter how hard I tried, I couldn't force it. The dream visited on its own terms.

A knock on the driver's side window startled me. I lifted my head from the steering wheel to find a stranger staring at me. He was a young man, maybe in his mid-twenties, with slicked dirty blond hair, a pointy nose and beady eyes that were as blue as the ocean was deep. He had rudely propped his elbow against the window and was intently peering in at me. His white t-shirt was crisp and he wore a black leather jacket.

"Allison Carmichael?" the voice hissed. I wasn't sure if he was asking a question or making an accusation.

I dabbed my face with a tissue and turned on the car so I could roll down the window just a touch – no need to give this stranger any more room than that. "Who's asking?" I instinctively ensured all the doors were locked.

The stranger stuck his nose in the air and took a deep breath. He rolled his head over his shoulders as if enjoying whatever it was he smelled. I glanced around to see where his car was, or if anyone was with him, but I couldn't spot either. There were several cars in the parking lot and any one of them could have been his. I inhaled, trying to determine what scent he relished so much, but I couldn't detect anything.

"The name is Caz," he said with a southern twang. He settled his eyes on mine. "Caz Devoe."

"Well Caz, what do you want?" I asked.

"I think ya dropped something." Caz pulled his hand from his side and waved what appeared to be my cell phone. He slid his thumb over the back of the device, as if separating a deck of cards. "Says right here on the medical insurance card, 'Allison Carmichael.'

Both were layin' right outside your vehicle. I'm assumin' they're yours."

I paused before answering and looked over to the passenger seat where I had flung my purse. It was unzipped. I rummaged through it and sure enough, no phone, no insurance card. I thought back to how quickly I had stormed out of the doctor's office and supposed it was possible both could have fallen out of my bag.

"Uh," I stammered. Caz held my belongings out to me on the other side of the window. "Um, thanks," I choked out as I pressed the button to lower the window a bit more. I grabbed the items and examined them. There it was – my name on the medical card. I flipped open the phone and found the wallpaper picture of Matt and me. I couldn't believe I could have been so careless. I pressed the button and started to roll up the window.

"What, no thank you handshake?" Caz asked just before the window closed.

I lifted my finger from the button and looked at him. I didn't want to shake his hand. He was a stranger and I didn't like the vibe he gave me; he seemed to be up to something more than what he was letting on.

"Sort of rude after I just returned your belongings, don't ya think?" Caz asked.

I sighed and peered at him. After a few moments, I reluctantly lowered the window, just wide enough to get my hand and wrist through, hoping this would be the end of our meeting. Caz grabbed my hand and a jolt ran through my body. I felt all tingly, like I had stuck a wet finger in an electric socket. The sensation intensified the longer we touched. I tried to pull my hand back but Caz cupped it with his other hand. He closed his eyes and took several deep breaths. It wasn't apparent if he was feeling what I felt.

He seemed to enjoy the moment. My attempts to free my hand were futile as his strength held my arm perfectly straight.

"Mister," I snarled. "What's your problem? Let go of my hand."

Caz opened his eyes and I gasped. His sapphire eyes were rimmed in red and his breathing thinned. He stared at me as if he were in a trance.

"What's wrong with you?" My voice quivered with fear.

He snapped out of his spell and released my hand. The sensation left as quickly as it had come. He leaned his narrow face into my half open window. "Don't let anybody tell ya that you aren't *special.*"

I squeezed my eyes closed, taken back by his word choice. I didn't like how the word "special" slithered off his tongue.

"What are you talking about?" I opened my eyes, but apparently asked the question to myself. Caz was gone. I checked my side mirror but didn't see him. There was no trace of him as I glanced out of the windshield. I twisted in my seat and looked out the rear window but there was nothing. Nobody was walking through the parking lot, no cars were moving. He was gone.

The highway sign announced Buzzard Hill was five miles away, which gave me a few more minutes to think about how I was going to tell Matt about my revelation. It wasn't like I hadn't thought about it for the other twenty miles since leaving the doctor's office. I really didn't know how I was going to say it. The thought alone sounded ridiculous. But a midlife crisis had to be the source of my angst. There was no other reasonable explanation. Part of me wished I could say nothing and that the past six months would just disappear from our memories. But I knew that wouldn't happen; there had been too many mood swings, too much depression, too much anger and despair to chalk it all up to nothing. I had to tell Matt.

I rounded the corner onto my street and admired our home as I pulled into the driveway. It was a Tudor style on a five-acre lot. It wasn't the largest or smallest in the development, but with 3,000 square feet and four bedrooms, it was bigger than we needed. The front of the house was covered in cream stucco outlined in chocolate brown wood, and the lot was decorated with several islands filled with large oak and maple trees.

My eyes slid to the back of our property as I parked the Jeep. Nature surrounded the entire property, including some deep woods behind the house, which often made me feel uneasy. Tall pines and aged oaks stretched for miles, the foliage so thick you could hide an army in there and no one would notice. I sometimes thought someone was tucked in there watching me, but that was just my silly imagination running wild, the result of a sheltered childhood and an overprotective husband always telling me to look over my shoulder. Even now as I stood next to my car, I couldn't tear my eyes from the trees. The foliage swayed as if someone had just run into the woods. But that was impossible; no one was here and even if someone were, I would have seen him. Still, it was unsettling, as the air was dead calm, so a breeze couldn't be blamed.

I glanced up at the sky and spotted buzzards floating amidst the infamous Cleveland gray. The buzzards were no strangers to this town and neither was the gray. Buzzard Hill was known worldwide as the place these scavengers returned to every year. The gray was almost as infamous; any visitor to Cleveland or 100 miles west, east or south of the Lake Erie shoreline was familiar with this phenomenon, the ever-present haze of gloominess, compliments of the weather that rolled in over the lake. I returned my eyes to the woods, still captivated by whatever my imagination thought was there.

"Ali?" Matt called from the garage. "Ali, are you okay?"

I forced my eyes from the trees. Matt leaned out of the door leading from the house into the garage. He wore a white tank, which nicely showcased his biceps, and pajama pants. A wave of apprehension rolled over me, as I knew what I was going to have to tell Matt. I might as well get it over with.

"I'm fine," I muttered as I shuffled into the garage and past the row of motorcycles and ATVs, one for each of us. Since we couldn't have children, Matt and I bought toys. Matt's passion was all things motor. I only tried these things because he wanted me to join him in something he truly enjoyed. I also hoped the activities would distract my mind and make the burning in my belly disappear. That didn't happen.

Matt pecked me on the cheek as he held the door open like a perfect gentleman. I walked through the hallway to the kitchen, placed my hands on the granite countertop and stared out the window at the fall foliage.

"Does that mean Doctor McNally found out what's wrong with you?" Matt asked, his voice hopeful. The poor guy had to have been praying for an answer as much as I had been – if for nothing else than for my mood to improve so we could finally return to normal.

"No," I replied flatly. A pang of heat shot from my stomach to the back of my throat. I grabbed my stomach hoping for relief as my eyes winced with pain. The heat quickly subsided. Matt noticed nothing since my back was to him.

"No?"

"No." I turned to face Matt, my eyes brimming with tears. "She's just like all of the others, Matt. She said there was absolutely nothing wrong with me." I broke down in tears. Matt rushed to me and threw his arms around my shoulders.

"It's okay," he cooed as he rubbed my back. "It's okay."

"No, it's not okay," I sobbed. "She thought I was lying, she even said as much. She said my temperature was normal, my blood count was fine, my scans were clean, my weight was stable, blah, blah, blah. I just don't understand. You believe me, don't you? You don't think I'm crazy, do you?"

"Of course I believe you, Ali. I'm the one lying next to you at night when you're blazing hot. And I've seen your lack of appetite and felt how cold you are during the day. You're not imagining anything."

I felt a little better. Someone believed me and who better than the man who lived with me and who had witnessed all of this first-hand. I gently shifted away from Matt and said, "Thank you."

"You don't have to thank me."

I stared into his hazel eyes. Looking into his eyes, even after seven years of marriage, still gave me butterflies.

"Did she say anything else, Ali? Like where to go from here?"

I let out a heavy sigh. "She asked if anything else was bothering me."

Matt stared back, waiting for me to continue.

"She asked if anything major happened that might be the source of my…*issues.*"

"And?"

"So I told her about our fertility struggles."

"Oh, Ali." Matt sighed and grabbed my hands. "My little Ali-gator, I thought you were good with all of that."

"I am, Matt. I realized years ago that a baby isn't in the cards for us and have made peace with it."

"Then I'm confused." Matt stepped back. "Why would you tell her that?"

"Because I think I figured out what's bothering me, and I thought you should be the first to know."

"Really? You think you know what's wrong with you?"

"Yeah, but if I tell you," I hesitated, "do you promise not to laugh?"

Matt's facial expression relaxed a bit. I could only imagine what he thought was coming.

"Of course," he responded.

A long pause passed. Still searching for the words, I turned to look out the kitchen window, not daring to look Matt in the eyes.

"Ali?"

"I think I'm going through a midlife crisis," I blurted out, blushing at the absurdity of such a statement. It sounded worse in the spoken word than it had in my mind. After all this time mulling over what I was going to say and how I was going to say it, I couldn't believe that this was what came out of my mouth.

I felt Matt staring at me so I turned my head towards him, tensed for his reaction. When I finally looked at his face, I saw what utter shock must look like. His mouth hung open, his eyes were blank, and the color had receded from his cheeks. I couldn't believe I had chosen my words so poorly!

"No, no, no, not *that* kind of midlife crisis! I have no need for a younger boyfriend." I should have seen this reaction coming when I had blurted out the stupid comment in the first place. It hadn't been my intention to hurt Matt. My mood, what I was feeling, had nothing to do with him or our relationship.

A smile spread across Matt's lips when he heard my clarification. "I know what this is all about. You wanna buy that sports car you always wanted and are using this as an excuse, aren't you?" That was my Matt, always up for buying another toy to add to our collection.

I chuckled uncomfortably hoping Matt would take this seriously. "Well the Corvette would be very nice, but no, I'm not ready for it yet, and neither is the overstuffed garage. I'm in a midlife crisis over my career."

"Oh." Matt paused. "That's it?" He crinkled his nose.

"That's it? What do you mean that's it?" I shouted. "Can't you see I'm trying to tell you something important and you're just going to stand there and make a joke of it?" This was one of those times when I could have really used my mother. She would sit and listen and when I was done complaining would have some wise advice to give me. She would know how to handle this situation and wouldn't make light of it.

"I'm sorry. It's just when you first said *midlife crisis* this isn't exactly what I expected."

Silence fell between us. I returned my eyes to the outdoor scenery. I wasn't going to be the next to speak and Matt must have realized this.

"So what's up with your job?"

I whirled around, ready for an argument, but Matt's eyes about made my heart melt. He was so handsome – tall with dark brown hair and a complexion that tanned with minimal sun exposure. It was a stark contrast to my blonde hair and pale skin that agitated with the slightest bit of sun.

I sighed. "Well, you know I've been having a tough time with the recent acquisition of my company. When it was Erie Bank, I was doing a nice job of working myself up the corporate ladder. I had been there over eight years, had a good reputation among my peers and was appointed Vice President when I was still in my twenties, which was practically unheard of. I knew I would be running a division sometime soon, that I'd be moving up. But now with this new company, I've been knocked down a few rungs on that ladder and since the headquarters aren't here anymore, well,

I have limited promotional opportunities." I felt tears welling up again and the last thing I wanted to do was cry over my job.

"Ali, you're smart. If you aren't happy, find something else. I know you can do it."

"But see, that's the thing. This is Cleveland. There aren't many big companies here anymore and there aren't many places willing to match my salary. It's an employer's market right now and they want new hires as cheap as they can get them and there are plenty enough unemployed people who will take a job for less than what I make now. And for some reason, you don't want to move out of Ohio to a place where I could easily find another job. You know my salary needs to stay where it is so we can continue our lifestyle since you took a big pay cut this year." Guilt set in with my last comment. The remark was not meant to be hurtful, but it was reality.

"Matt, I'm sorry. I didn't mean…"

"No, you're right," Matt said. "I did take a hefty pay cut and we can't afford another. But you know what?"

"What?"

"Remember the old adage – watch what you wish for?"

I looked at him, shocked by his response and didn't really know where he was going with all of this.

"Wait, what?" I asked. "I tell you that I feel trapped in a job and a city so we can maintain our lifestyle and you respond with 'watch what you wish for?'"

"Remember when we first met? The game you played? You always wanted to catch up to my salary. And now look; you're the breadwinner! It's not that fun is it, having that pressure on you?" Matt was playful in his tone, trying to cheer me up. It wasn't working.

I snorted. "Yeah, right, watch what you wish for. Whatever."

"Exactly," Matt playfully added.

"It's not just the job, Matt. When I graduated college, I was so full of hope and ambition; I had dreams. I knew I was going to run a Fortune 500 company someday, or open my own business. I was going to be something special."

"Ah, there's that word. Is this about your parents? About how they used to tell you all the time that you were going to be something special?"

"Yeah, sort of. It wasn't just how often they told me, it was the conviction with which they said it, like they knew I was going to be something great. I guess after hearing that so often I thought I was going to do something more than work at a job I hate because it provides the life we want."

"Ali, would you look at what you have and where you have gone in your career? You *have* done something special! We have a beautiful house, food on the table, motorcycles…" he drifted off. "And for what it's worth, you have me."

My heart sank. "Matt, this isn't about you. You haven't done anything to make me feel this way. This is all about me. I feel trapped in my job, trapped in this city, trapped by this crappy economy, but not trapped by you."

"Good," he said. "Because you're stuck with me!"

This conversation didn't make me feel better. I thought sharing my discovery with Matt would lift my spirits but that didn't happen. I wanted to hear that everything would be okay and I'd find what I was looking for and that he would help me in that search. But even if I heard it, I doubted I would have felt any better.

"There's more," I said sheepishly.

Matt chuckled. "Let's hear it. I think I can handle it."

"Well, this whole thing I just told you about is difficult for me to handle because I've always felt that I would be something more."

"Isn't that what we were just talking about?"

"No, this is different. Ever since I was very young, I felt that I was destined for something. It was more than a simple fascination that I would be famous or rich. It truly was…is…something inside of me, an actual burning in my belly, telling me there's something else out there for me. But I don't know what that something is. I don't know how to seek it out. But this craving is there and won't leave me alone. I think if I could just figure out my life's calling, then maybe, just maybe, these damned ailments would go away."

Matt paused and looked at me. "You know what they say?"

"Yeah, yeah," I rolled my eyes, "Watch what you wish for."

"No, the grass is always greener until you get to the other side."

"Very funny," I snickered. "Who is this 'they' I always hear about?"

"Well maybe I snapped your mood." Almost as soon as Matt spoke those words, my aura dampened.

Everything I had said to Matt was true. But based on his reaction, my words failed to relay the depth to which I wholeheartedly knew something was out there calling me. This burning in the pit of my being, or maybe in my soul or subconscious, knew something it couldn't relay to my conscious mind. And there was nothing more frustrating.

"Or maybe, not," Matt said taking in my grumpy demeanor. "How about a motorcycle ride? That'll cheer you up."

"Have you looked outside? It's going to rain."

Matt ducked his head to look out the window. Black, billowy clouds had swallowed the gray sky.

"Okay then. Well, since I have to work, maybe you should call Jenna and hang out with her. You know, a girl's night like you two always used to do."

"No." I immediately dismissed the idea. I didn't need to burden Jenna with my problems, which was precisely what would happen since I couldn't shake this funk. She didn't need me to bring her down. Matt sensed the determinedness in my answer and didn't bother to convince me otherwise. He examined my face as he searched for his next words.

"Well, relax and take a bubble bath and try to cheer up. Remember, we have a party to go to tomorrow and you need to shake this mood, you know, so you don't ruin the whole thing for everyone else!"

I knew he was joking about ruining everyone's time, but he was right. I needed to get my mind straight, but it was hard telling it that when the rest of my body was telling me something else.

Matt kissed me on the lips and bounded across the living room through the foyer and up the stairs. "I got called into work early," he shouted. "I have to get ready."

I walked to the sliding glass door and looked at the woods, then at the black heavens. A lightning bolt cracked across the sky and the rain fell.

CHAPTER 2

I wanted to cry. I squeezed my eyes shut and tried to ignore the fact that it was four o'clock in the morning and I had barely slept a wink. Having tossed and turned for the past six hours, I was now trying to empty my mind of any thoughts about my magical garden, hoping that would be enough to finally let me sleep. But when I opened my eyes again, the clock had only moved two minutes. All I wanted was some shut-eye but it was eluding me. When I was a child, my parents would pray with me before I went to bed and it always seemed to help. I shut my eyes again and whispered several Hail Mary's, hoping the repetition would make me sleepy without waking Matt. That didn't work either. So I lay in bed, watching one minute tick to the next before I finally realized I was drenched in sweat.

I quietly slid out of bed and searched the floor for my pajamas. I had stripped them off several hours earlier to escape the heat they were trapping close to my body. I found them, but there was no use in putting them on now so I balled them up and carefully made my way through the dark and into the bathroom. I flipped on the light and the sudden brightness blinded me as my eyes filled with speckled blackness. As my reflection slowly came into focus, I was pleasantly surprised by what was staring back at me in the mirror.

For getting no sleep, I looked well rested. My skin was smooth, my complexion even, almost radiant, with not a single visible pore. I expected dark circles under my eyes, but there were none. I usually needed foundation for my skin to look so clear. I tugged at my skin in disbelief. It was soft but hot to the touch. Other than my sweat soaked hair, I looked pretty good.

I ran my fingers through my short blonde strands, wrestling with the prior day's hair products. My eyes suddenly caught my attention. Normally a sharp blue gray, they now looked like dull charcoal except for the gold flecks around my pupils that popped with intensity. I shook my head to get any cobwebs out but the tiny teardrop shapes were still there lighting up my otherwise faded eyes. *Harsh vanity lighting at four a.m. sure does weird things,* I thought.

I scanned the bathroom trying to decide what to do with my time. My eyes settled on the closet doors and the work out gear I knew was behind them. If I was up this early, I might as well make the most of it.

I changed into shorts and a t-shirt, tossing aside the nylon running pants that would have been too warm. I clipped my bangs back and tiptoed out of the bathroom, down the stairs to the first level, then to the basement. I didn't know who I thought I was kidding; I wasn't looking forward to exercising. I wished I was more like Matt in this regard; he enjoyed working out and the benefits were quite obvious. I took one look at the equipment and without hesitation started to march back upstairs.

I turned on the television and flipped to a news channel. A pretty blonde reporter in Cocoa Beach, Florida stood in front of a small house cordoned off with caution tape. She was reporting about an attack on the family that had lived there. The parents, three children and one grandparent had been killed for reasons still under investigation. There had been no forced entry and nothing had been stolen. Neighbors were interviewed and they talked about a well-liked family that apparently kept to themselves and had no known enemies. The coroner said a cause of death would be released after full autopsies but leaked references indicated a gruesome crime scene; the victims had been drained of most of their blood. The screen panned back to neighbors who claimed they had heard nothing despite the fact the homes were built close together. This wasn't exactly an uplifting story so I turned off the television and walked back to the kitchen.

Peering out the blinds, all I could see was blackness and a hazy yellow moon that hung close to the treetops. Not a single cloud was in the sky, making every star visible. I had never noticed the sheer number of stars as I did this morning. It looked like a painter had carelessly speckled white paint over a giant black ceiling.

I made a cup of tea and stepped outside to better inspect the stars. The cool air caressed my hot flesh, and I breathed a sigh of relief; it was beyond refreshing. I stood on the patio for several minutes staring at the sky. It was so quiet and peaceful that I didn't even notice the woods.

I settled into the hammock and lay there finding shapes in stars. I located the Little Dipper, Aries and part of the Orion constellation. I also found shapes of my own – a unicorn, a pirate ship and a bicycle. There were so many stars to examine that the options for my imagination were endless. *I could stay here all night*, I thought. But something disturbed my peaceful rendezvous, something at the edge of the woods. I rolled my head to see what it was, but all I caught was a fleeting glimpse of two silvery dots as they faded into the darkness. It was too late in the year for fireflies but before I could think about it, I had drifted off to sleep.

My dream picked up where it had last left off. I am in the middle of paradise smelling flowers, enjoying the songbirds and observing the animals going about their business until a new sound grabs my attention. The distant yet delightful bubbling sound beckons me, so I walk in its direction, relishing the sensation of smooth earth beneath my bare feet. A winding path directs me around immense trees, under hanging vines and up a hill. When I reach the top, I am rewarded by my efforts: the river flows below me, clear and aquamarine, the sun sparkling off its surface.

I scramble down the hill and thrust my hands into the water. My hands serve as a cup ushering the cool liquid to my lips; it tastes as sweet as the air smells. I drop my hands to my chest to let the remainder of the water glide down my body. I stare beyond the glass-like surface and witness fish swishing effortlessly downstream following the river's course through the grassy countryside. The scene is perfectly framed by small hills and the river eventually spills over into a waterfall. The sky is clear and the brilliant orange sun floats in the distance, its rays striking out into the blue heavens.

A sense of calm sweeps over me, like the feeling you get after the first few sips of wine. This is paradise and I never want to leave. And I can tell this place doesn't want me to leave either. I belong here.

I glance around, taking in the breathtaking perfection. My eyes are drawn to a spot off in the distance. A vibrant radiating energy throws off shards of color - reds, yellows, purples - at a frantic pace. The energy's ferocity is too busy for this utopia. I look away, then back. It's still there. I can't imagine what this restless annoyance could be.

I stand and follow the river's path, looking for a passageway. As I walk, I become blinded by light. I throw my arm up to cover my eyes, and in doing so my arm crashes against the cold metal frame of the hammock I had fallen asleep on. I groaned at the realization that my dream was over and the sun, making a rare appearance, was waking me from my slumber.

I dreamily looked around, re-acclimating myself with my surroundings. I was on the hammock, my cup of now cold tea on the ground. The morning air touched my bare legs through the hammock's underside, but thankfully a blanket covered me. My fiery body temperature had disappeared, replaced by shivering coldness.

Matt walked out of the sliding door, a cup of coffee in hand. "Hey, you awake, sweetie?" he whispered in my direction as he closed the door.

"Yeah, why am I out here?" I choked out in my morning voice.

"Ha, um, I don't know why you're out here, Ali. I woke up and you weren't in bed so I came downstairs and noticed the door was open and saw you on the hammock. Rather than wake you, I threw a blanket over you. I hope you aren't upset; I know you have been having problems sleeping. You looked so peaceful; I hoped you were getting some rest."

Matt waited apprehensively for my reaction. He probably expected me to snap at him or yell that he should have woken me and taken me inside. But what Matt didn't know was that I dreamt of my paradise and was now reveling in the benefits. I was calm and happy, and for the moment at least, my mood had snapped back to normal.

"Thank you for the blanket," I said, choking on my words. My throat felt like sandpaper.

Matt's visage brightened. He must have realized I was in a good mood. "Let me get you some fresh tea," he said, and rushed back into the house.

I wiggled myself off of the hammock and wrapped the blanket around me. The thermometer read 74 degrees and I wondered again how anyone could be so cold in this temperature.

Despite my feeling chilled, the sun was shining and the sky was dotted with only a light sprinkling of clouds. It looked like it was going to be a nice day after all. I stretched my neck from side to side, releasing it from the confines of my cocoon-like blanket. The sun scorched the skin on my face and neck. Matt always said I needed to sit in the sun more, to add some color to my fair skin. I preferred to listen to my dermatologist and avoided the sun as much as possible.

Matt returned to the patio with a tall cup of steaming liquid and a lemon perched on the side. "Thank you," I croaked, and took a sip.

"I added honey, for your throat. I hope you aren't getting a cold, that would really suck."

"No kidding. I think I'll be okay though. I'm sure my scratchy throat is from my brilliant decision to fall asleep outside."

"Well I sure hope you're feeling better. Jordana's birthday party is tonight."

I wasn't looking forward to this party. Jordana wasn't an immediate relative; she was Matt's brother-in-law's niece and she was turning sixteen. I knew the party was going to be over the top and packed with people – that's how Leslie and Shawn, Jordana's parents, did everything. I wasn't in the mood to socialize. But I didn't know what I'd rather be doing. I supposed if my mood was cooperating, I might as well make the best of it.

"I'll be fine. I'm looking forward to the party," I lied.

• • •

I gave up trying to style my hair. It wasn't cooperating and no amount of gel, wax or hairspray was going to change that. I threw the pick in the sink and walked to the window. The sun had given way to another gray day just like my contentment was slowly relinquishing to sourness. This constant battle with my mood was getting old, and I was tired of feeling like I had no control over my emotions. I wanted my good mood to last for at least this evening so Matt and I could enjoy the party, but it looked like it was going to be short-lived.

"Ali," Matt called from downstairs. "Are you almost ready? We need to hit the road."

I looked at my watch. It was five o'clock and we needed to start our hour-long journey into Ohio's countryside for the event of the summer. I sprayed my hair one last time, gave myself a once over in the mirror and plastered a fake smile on my face. *Here goes nothing,* I thought.

"You look very pretty," Matt stated as I walked into the kitchen.

He couldn't be serious. My hair was a disaster and I was dressed in jeans and a long-sleeved shirt. "Thank you." I forced a grimace.

Matt opened the car door and I hopped into the passenger seat of the Jeep. There was no need for a discussion about who was driving. Matt knew he would be chauffeuring since I refused to drive on country roads. Growing up in the city, I was accustomed to driving 35 or 45 miles per hour on four lane roads equipped with stop lights and street signs. I wasn't comfortable driving 65 miles per hour on tiny two lane country roads with an occasional stop sign to halt cross street traffic.

Matt backed out of the garage and into the dreary elements. Large rain clouds loomed overhead, ready to burst at any moment. I was trying to be upbeat, but I really didn't want to attend this party and be forced to put on a happy face and tell everyone that everything was fine. I couldn't contain my unhappiness anymore.

"Who does this?" I asked sourly as I flipped the radio to a rock station. My mellow mood was slipping away fast.

"Who does what?"

"This is a bit much, don't you think?" I shoved the invitation closer to Matt so he could have a better look. "I mean, this invite is nicer than our wedding invitations were."

The announcement was crafted on heavy white cardstock and scripted in navy ink broadcasting Jordana's sixteenth birthday party. A beach print served as the backdrop indicating some type of tropical luau theme. The invitation was professionally printed and quite extravagant for a teenager's birthday party.

"Come on, Allison," Matt glared at me. "It's a party; we're supposed to have fun. I was really hoping your good mood would stick around for one night. Can you at least try to have some fun?" Matt grabbed my hand and I met his eyes briefly before he returned his to the road. "Besides, Melissa will be there and I know you love hanging out with my sister."

"Fine," I said. I did love hanging out with Melissa and her husband David. Both had bubbly personalities and were full of life. Plus, Melissa always had a good story or two to share about her hair salon customers. Spending time with her tonight could be a good thing if some of her enthusiasm rubbed off on me, or it could be an utter disaster if I couldn't control my gloominess. I hoped for the former, but knew the latter was going to win out. My aura was getting heavier, a sign I must not have spent much time dreaming about my tropical paradise. It seemed the longer I dreamt about that place, the longer my contentment lasted.

We drove most of the way in silence. I watched small farmhouses and large farms pass us by, and the fields filled with corn stalks ready for harvest served as a reminder that winter was just around the corner. I counted cows in the pastures to pass time and I tried to ignore all of the roadside memorials marking where someone had lost a life in a car wreck on these treacherous roads. Some of the displays were placed at intersections, others on the berm; some were quite elaborate with pictures and flowers, others were as simple as a cross with the victim's name and date of his or her demise. I cringed every time we went through an intersection where we had the right of way but the cross street traffic had to stop. I feared someone would barrel through the stop sign resulting in my own personal roadside memorial.

We drove another mile or two when Matt finally announced, "And here we are."

We turned off the road onto a winding concrete driveway that curved its way past an expertly manicured lawn and led to a mammoth, two-story house. Seeing the house, I knew the invitation wasn't out of place at all. Leslie and Shawn were highly successful owners of a landscaping business, and their clients included some of Ohio's most elite families as well as some lucrative local government contracts.

Matt parked the Jeep in the reserved parking area in the front yard.

"What, no valet?" I asked sarcastically. Matt ignored me.

I climbed out of the car and examined the weather. It was humid and looked like it was going to storm but I, of course, felt chilled. I grabbed my jacket knowing I would need it sooner rather than later.

Matt eyed me. "Really, Allison? A jacket? Everyone here is in shorts, and you're dressed like you're ready for winter."

"Hey, I'm wearing flip flops," I responded sourly, sticking a foot out for his observation. I couldn't imagine why he would care what I was wearing. He should want me to be warm and somewhat happy versus cold and cranky.

"Whatever," Matt replied.

He grabbed my hand and led me around the side of the house, through a wrought iron gate to the pool area. I whistled a snarky tune as I inspected the scene.

Just like the fountain out front, the pool was full of flowers, but these were accompanied by floating candles. Twinkling lights and paper lanterns zigzagged through the air casting a warm glow against the dark sky. Cabanas draped in white flowing gauze provided seating. We were ushered to the back gate where we were given fresh Hawaiian leis.

"This had to cost a good buck," I said, as I toyed with the fragrant necklace.

"Be nice," Matt responded. "Jordana is their only child; you knew they were going to spoil her on this occasion."

The backyard stretched out around us. Candlelit bags anchored with sand directed us to an enormous party tent.

"I'm sure they needed a tent, like they couldn't fit this shindig in their house," I hissed.

"Allison Carmichael, would you please knock off the attitude?" Matt pleaded.

He was right. I needed to knock off the attitude but I didn't know how. This crabbiness emanated from my core and there was nothing I could do to stop it.

We walked inside the tent, which was decorated with the same lights and lanterns that swung over the pool. Tables covered in orange silk and crowned with tropical floral and fruit centerpieces outlined the perimeter of the dance floor. A glittery disco ball hung above. The air smelled vaguely familiar and pleasant but was also overwhelming.

"Do you smell that?" I asked, as I leaned into Matt so he could hear me over the deejay.

"Smell what?"

"All of the flowers. It smells like a damn flower shop in here."

Matt shot me a look. I sensed he was about through with my attitude so I decided to be quiet.

We continued to make our way through the tent. The far wall housed a shrine to the birthday girl. Photos from the time she was born to the present day were displayed in frames and on poster board. Trophies and ribbons showcasing her athletic triumphs and academic achievements were scattered across a table. I mulled over the pictures…cheerleading, homecoming, bonfires and football games. It took me back, reminding me how full of hope and promise I once was at her age. Bitterness swelled inside me. "She better enjoy it now, because she'll be disappointed ten years down the road when life doesn't pan out the way she expects it to."

"Calm down, Ali," Matt scolded. "Here comes Jordana."

Jordana skipped over to us. She looked vibrant in a yellow and white sundress, gold bangles and wedge sandals. Just looking at her outfit made me feel cold. Her long brown hair, highlighted with golden tones, swung just beneath her tanned shoulders.

"Hi guys," Jordana gushed as she hugged me. "I'm so happy you could make it!"

I forced another fake smile. "Happy birthday, Jordana. Thanks for inviting us. We're so happy to be here."

Jordana hugged Matt and pecked him on the cheek. "Mom and dad are over there talking with guests." She pointed towards the front of the tent, clear on the other side from where we were standing. "I gotta greet more guests. Please, grab something to eat and drink and have fun!"

"Enjoy your night, Jordana!" Matt yelled as she bounded away.

"Very nice," Matt said.

"What?"

"Nice fake smile. It was passable, but I could see right through it," Matt smirked as he kissed my forehead. I rolled my eyes. At least I was trying.

We walked across the tent and said our hellos to Leslie and Shawn before finding an empty table where we waited for Melissa and David.

"You want something to drink?" Matt asked. "A Mai Tai or Pina Colada?"

"Corona, please." Maybe a beer would take the edge off my disposition.

Just as Matt went off in search of a bartender, I was tackled from behind. It was Melissa and David. *Thank goodness*, I thought.

"How *are* you, my sweet sister-in-law?" Melissa gushed as she ran her fingers through my hair, rearranging the pieces. "Your hair looks awesome," she added. "Maybe next time, we'll take a little off the back. Ya know, for something different." I was glad she thought my hair looked good. The hour-long struggle in front of the mirror must have paid off.

"I'm fine, Melissa," I said, trying to muster enthusiasm. I hugged David. "So happy to be at the event of the year." I waved my hand at the festivities around us.

"Oh, I see." David stepped back. "In a gloomy mood, huh?"

"Matt warned us about this," Melissa said, winking at Matt as he returned with our drinks.

I looked at Matt and playfully punched him in the arm. "What? Are you telling everybody my problems?" I feebly joked. I was mortified that Matt would do that to me. It was enough that he and my best friend had to put up with me; I didn't need to bring my in-laws down too.

"No, no, you know I wouldn't do that. But I couldn't let my sister walk into a lion's den without any warning!" he joked back.

"Fair enough," I responded. It was probably better this way. At least I wouldn't have to endure questions from Melissa and David since they already knew something was wrong. Maybe I could even drop my front.

The four of us sat at the table and made small talk about work, the latest news headlines and the local sports team. I halfheartedly listened to the conversations and barely spoke. I wished I were someplace else but where, I didn't know. This party and my presence at it felt forced and awkward and I wanted out.

"Let's go get something to eat. It smells delicious in here," Melissa suggested.

"Looks like Ali needs another beer," David said, nodding his head at my empty beer bottle.

"Geez, Ali, you thirsty?" Matt asked. "I just got you that beer."

My cheeks flushed. I felt parched but that was no excuse to guzzle a beer in a few minutes. "Um, yeah, I guess I am a little thirsty," I stammered and threw everyone a sheepish grin.

The food smelled delicious, but I wasn't hungry. Nevertheless, I joined everyone in line. Like the rest of the party, the buffet was overflowing with excess. The plates and flatware were one step below fine china. The table was staffed with servers in fancy chef jackets and silly hats. The food was over the top...spiced veggies, bacon wrapped scallops, shrimp cocktail, coconut breaded shrimp, meat rolls, sushi, chicken kabobs, Po Po, spare ribs, and Poi. And of course, no luau would be complete without a roasted pig and a chocolate fountain.

"Aren't you going to eat anything?" Matt asked.

I looked at my plate and sighed. I hadn't eaten breakfast or lunch today and my plate was a sorry excuse for dinner with a handful of veggies and one scallop. I didn't want to make a fuss about my appetite, or lack thereof. I looked up at the server I was standing in front of, prepared to take whatever he offered so I wouldn't draw any more attention to myself.

"Would you like some Mahi Mahi?" the server asked in a velvety voice.

He was deliciously handsome, tall with a muscular build. His shoulder length blond hair was pulled back into a low ponytail that accentuated his angular jaw and high cheekbones. His chef's hat looked too average for his beautiful face. This man could be a model; I couldn't fathom why he was serving food. Stitched into his shirt above his heart was his name - Lorenzo. The name struck me as uncommon but his eyes captivated me more. Lorenzo's eyes glowed like emeralds, polished and smooth as glass. The lights from the dance floor played off of them like a mirror in which I could see everything going on behind me. The golden speckles around his pupils were bright and full of life, like how mine looked earlier this morning. But his were different; they danced in circles. I couldn't help but stare.

"Um, Ali?" Matt's words broke my gaze.

I cleared my throat and looked at the buffet table, then back up at *those* eyes. Lorenzo looked at me with a crooked smile as he pushed a piece of fish on my plate. *He must get this all the time*, I thought. Women probably gawked at him wherever he went, especially if he routinely worked out here in the middle of nowhere.

"Uh, thank you," I whispered. I turned in embarrassment and walked toward our table.

"Are you okay?" Matt asked, balancing his plate in one hand while wrapping his arm around my waist. He glanced over his shoulder at Lorenzo.

"Um, yeah, I'm fine. I was just about to say something to Melissa while we were in line but the thought left my mind," I lied. "Like you say, your memory goes out the window after thirty, right?"

"Right," Matt replied suspiciously.

I flushed again with embarrassment. What was I doing? My husband, the love of my life, was standing at my side and I couldn't help but stare at the wait staff? Where were my manners? Where was my self-control?

Matt pulled my chair out for me, my back to the buffet. I was sure that wasn't a coincidence. My napkin fell to the floor and as I bent to retrieve it, I couldn't help but look back at Lorenzo. He wasn't looking in my direction; he was busy doing his job. I didn't know what I was hoping for, but a little glance from him would have been a nice ego boost. I pushed the thought from my mind and returned to the conversation at our table.

I was quiet during our meal. Matt and David talked cars and work, but neither subject interested me. Melissa chatted in my ear about all the town gossip she had heard the past few days at her hair salon. I didn't care to hear it but threw in the occasional "uh huh" and "mmm hmm" to appear politely interested.

"Ali?" Melissa's voice broke through my haze.

"Yeah, I heard you. The Johnston's barn burned down and the police suspect arson."

"No, not that. Aren't you hungry? I don't think you had a bite of food all evening."

Melissa was right; I had only played with my food throughout dinner.

"Actually, I don't feel well."

"Well you must be thirsty because you sucked down your other two Coronas."

I looked at the table and sure enough, there were two empty beer bottles. I wasn't sure what my problem was tonight. I typically didn't drink this much and definitely not this fast.

"I have a sore throat," I replied. "I fell asleep on the hammock this morning and woke up with a sore throat. The cold feels good against it."

"Well you better switch to something a little less potent if you're going to drink like that," she smiled.

"Ha, yeah, you're right. I'll grab some punch from the fountain. Who has a chocolate fountain and a punch fountain at a birthday party?" I lamely joked, trying to divert attention from me.

The evening wore on and I had to admit it was a nice party. The rain held off for most of the night; heavy drops had just started to tap on the tent's roof. The lanterns swayed in the breeze casting a hazy light. The deejay turned tunes and every kid, young and old, was on the dance floor. I stuck to my seat the entire night as my social butterfly husband and in-laws went off to converse with others. I couldn't blame them. It was probably uncomfortable sitting around me with my moods fluctuating from semi-sociable to completely petulant.

I also stayed in my seat for another reason. I wanted to look for him...Lorenzo. I had felt so drawn to him in the buffet line. I didn't know why, but I craved another inappropriate stare into those eyes. There was something there, pulling me towards him, but not in a romantic way; I only had eyes like that for Matt. It was like Lorenzo's eyes were calling me, but I couldn't decipher the message. I glanced around the room, but the buffet tables were gone. I thought Lorenzo was, too, but I finally caught a brief glimpse of him where the buffet line had been set up. It appeared he was looking in my direction, but that was silly of me to think. There was no reason he would be looking for me.

I stood and walked towards Lorenzo. His back was to me as he packed the last of the serving utensils. I had no idea what I was doing or what I was going to say to him. I didn't know why I felt the need to meet this stranger, to figure out what his eyes were trying to say. As I crossed the dance floor, Lorenzo turned and looked in the direction of where I had been sitting. He noticed I wasn't there and his eyes nervously scanned the room until he spotted me. He stared at me for the briefest second before he tucked the box under his arm and turned around the corner of the tent. I quickened my pace, reaching the spot where he had just stood. As I carefully peered around the side of tent, two teen-agers collided with me.

"Excuse me," I said, flustered by the unexpected guests.

"Sorry, we didn't see you there," the girl said. I recognized her as one of Jordana's friends from the pictures I looked at earlier.

"Yes, excuse us ma'am, we were just makin' our way to the dance floor," the boy said in a familiar twang. I examined his face; narrow nose, dark blond hair spiked with gel, and the bluest of blue eyes. He had on a white t-shirt, jeans, black Converse sneakers and a leather jacket flung over his shoulder.

"I know you," I blurted out.

"You know who?" the girl asked and rolled her eyes.

"Him. You're Caz Devoe."

"Sorry ma'am, you must have me mistaken for someone else. My name is Bill Smith. This here is my girlfriend Tammy Styles. We go to high school with Jordana."

"No," I stuttered. "I met you yesterday morning in the parking lot at the hospital. You found my phone and insurance card by my car."

"I was in school yesterday morning," Bill replied. The expression on his face seemed to question my sanity, but there was no mistaking his sapphire eyes or the narrow nose. Sure, his hair was styled differently, but this had to be Caz.

"Come on, Bill, let's go dance." Tammy tugged on Bill's arm. I stood there and watched them pass. As I turned my head to finish my original mission, I caught a glimpse of "Bill" looking over his shoulder, but I was too slow in turning my head to catch him. I would swear on my parents' graves that Bill Smith was Caz Devoe. But it didn't really matter. I returned my attention to my original goal.

I grabbed the tent pole in an effort to hide behind it and peered around the corner. Lorenzo was nowhere to be found. I wasn't sure where he could have gone. I didn't hear any cars start when I ran into Bill and Tammy. There was one catering truck left but it appeared locked and was dark inside.

"Hey," someone said behind me and taped my shoulder. I jumped. It was Melissa. "What are you looking for over here?"

"You scared the daylights out of me!" My hand covered my heart as I tried to compose myself. I glanced around the corner one more time. "I'm not looking for anything in particular; just checking out the backyard."

Melissa eyed me up and down. "Matt mentioned you've been in a funk lately but didn't really tell me what's going on. I don't want to pry, but if you need someone to talk to, you know I'm here. And my lips are sealed." That was Melissa's assurance that my problems wouldn't become the talk of her hair salon.

"I know Mel," I said and stared off for a brief moment. I wondered if I could really tell her I was going through a mid-life crisis and how she would react. She would probably laugh just like her brother had. And I didn't want to recount all of my physical ailments; not here. That conversation would take all night.

"I don't know what it is," I started. "But everything just seems to be catching up to me these past few weeks. I feel like I'm trapped in a job I hate in a town that doesn't offer any opportunity. I feel somewhat trapped in my life."

Melissa's eyes narrowed when I said the word *trapped*. I spoke before her mind could wander too far in the wrong direction.

"This is about me, Mel, not Matt. You know I love him more than anything in this world. This is me, realizing I'm not going to be anything more than what I am today…an average, ordinary middle manager. No glorious CEO position, no ritzy Hollywood lifestyle, no going-down-in-history moments here, you know?"

Melissa squeezed my hand and looked into my eyes. "You know Ali, you have a wonderful life. You might think it is average or boring, but do you know how many people would trade places with you? To have the house, husband and life you have?"

Yep, that was it. I knew she would make me feel foolish, though I knew that wasn't her intention. "I know," I said and fought back tears. "It's just I feel like there is something else out there for me. I've felt it for quite some time. I guess I should chalk up this recent spell to frustration in not knowing how to go about finding my calling."

"Well Ali, you know what? If something is meant to be, it will find you."

Her statement took me off guard. I had never thought about it that way; that my calling would find me. I figured I had to actively pursue it, even though over thirty years of trying had never yielded results. Plus, this burning in the center of my core wouldn't let me rest, wouldn't allow me to not look. The prospect of something finding me instead of the other way around was quite appealing. Maybe, if I let my mind believe I was relaxing and anticipating *it*, the burning would realize this and grant me reprieve. I could sit back and enjoy life and let *it* find me. Why hadn't I thought of this before?

"Maybe you're right." A smile spread across my face as the idea lingered in my head.

"At least I got you to smile," Melissa said, and we both broke out in laughter.

"Hey, what time is it?" I asked, changing the subject.

"It's around eleven thirty, getting kind of late. We should probably head out soon."

"Yeah. Let me find my hubby and we'll follow you out."

I ran to the Jeep, my jacket serving as a makeshift umbrella shielding me from the downpour. Matt scrambled behind and we yelled our goodbyes to Melissa and David.

"Hey, heads up," Matt shouted and tossed the keys in my direction. I caught the keys, briefly dropping my jacket. Rain soaked my hair. I climbed into the driver's seat, not thrilled about having to drive.

"Really?" I asked, but couldn't help chuckling. Melissa's insight was front of mind for me. It was such a relief to think I could give up my search and wait for my calling to find me. And the burning in my stomach must have liked it, too, because the inferno had subsided. All of this good news zapped my sour mood.

"Yes, really," Matt responded in a goofy voice. "I had more adult beverages than you and besides, you quit drinking hours ago. At least quit drinking alcohol. Boy, you sure sucked down the punch tonight."

"Yeah, well, my throat is still scratchy. I think I'm getting that cold you mentioned earlier. Thanks for jinxing me!" I said, and winked at Matt.

I slowly drove down the long driveway towards the road. The wipers were on high speed, but barely cleared the rain enough for me to see for a second.

"Some time with my sister seems to have put you in a better mood," Matt observed.

"Yeah, well, I love hanging out with your sister. It's hard not to be in a good mood after chatting with her." I leaned closer to the radio and flipped to a classic rock station as I pulled onto the road. I didn't feel like sharing Melissa's words of wisdom with Matt tonight. I wanted to enjoy this newfound mood I was in, and I hoped Matt would see how happy I was and that we could simply enjoy the rest of the evening without having to discuss my midlife crisis.

"You know," I continued, "I really hate driving on these roads, especially in a torrential downpour."

"I know Ali-gator, but you'll be fine. Just keep your eyes on the road." Matt pointed straight ahead, a purposeful distraction so he could flip the radio back to his favorite country station.

"You just won't compromise on the radio, will you?" I laughed.

"Nope! When you get old like me, you'll learn to appreciate country music."

"Ha, that's laughable considering you've only got two years on me. I highly doubt my musical taste will change in the next couple years."

I neared an intersection and gently pushed on the brake pedal. I didn't have to stop, but the cross traffic did. I wanted to slow down just in case someone else wasn't paying attention.

"What was that all about?" Matt asked. He knew how I handled these roads and insisted on teasing me every time I had to drive them.

"That's me, playing it safe, just in case someone blows through the stop sign." I flipped the radio to another rock station.

"Come on Ali, these roads are no more dangerous than the city roads you grew up on. Hey, you always said you wanted a little more adventure in your life, why don't you take the next intersection at the speed limit?"

"Oh yeah, smarty pants? Game on!"

I approached another intersection and took my foot off the gas; I couldn't help my instincts. At least I didn't brake.

"See? That wasn't so bad, was it?"

I rolled my eyes and laughed.

The rain refused to subside and the sky was as black as a witch's brew. Occasional bursts of lightning lit the road, but I was depending on my high beams to navigate. As we curved up the hill, we saw a brief flash of oncoming headlights and I turned down my brights. As I did, I saw Matt, out of the corner of my eye, reach for the radio. I took my eyes off the road and slapped his hand.

"Oh no you don't," I playfully chided.

"Look out!" Matt yelled.

I jerked my head up in time to see our car veering towards a ditch. I pulled the steering wheel sharply back to the left, slipping in front of the oncoming traffic, then pulled the wheel to the right to get us back in our lane. The passing car laid on its horn.

"Okay, no more music the rest of the way," Matt demanded, turning off the radio. "Be careful! Driving into a ditch like that could be the end of us."

"I know, I'm sorry," I whispered. My heart was beating a million times per minute and my legs felt weak. I felt so foolish about almost wrecking. I was only trying to be fun and happy. I never intended to hurt us.

"I'm really sorry…" I started as we passed through an intersection. I took my eyes from the road to look at Matt, and that's when I saw my worst fear coming true.

A pickup truck was barreling down the cross road and didn't appear to be slowing down or stopping. I couldn't see the color or make of the truck. All I saw were two headlights and two shimmering spots on the windshield at about the height where a driver would be sitting.

"Noooooooooooo," I yelled.

Everything played out in slow motion. Matt stared at me with a startled expression, not realizing what was about to happen. I had no time to brake, not that it would have mattered. I watched the truck approach until it t-boned Matt's side of the Jeep. I heard metal crunching and tires screeching over wet pavement. The Jeep skidded through the intersection. The weight of the car was too much for the driver's side tires to handle and we flipped once, maybe twice. Glass shattered. I heard crashing and hissing and metal scraping the road and as soon as it happened, it was all over; the motion, the noise, it all stopped. Blackness settled around me.

Only seconds passed but it felt like eternity. The constant blare of a horn rang through my ears. I realized my head, resting against the steering wheel, caused the annoyance. I pushed myself back into my seat and the horn silenced. I couldn't see anything, not even my headlights. I moaned, though I felt no pain, and squinted in an attempt to adjust my eyesight, but couldn't see a thing. The silence was deafening.

Panic flooded my body. Matt! Where was Matt?

I opened my mouth but nothing came out. I outstretched my right arm but felt emptiness. Then I heard something; splintered glass moving over pavement. Maybe the car we had just passed saw us crash and stopped to help.

The noise grew louder. Yes, someone was approaching the car.

"Help," I croaked, barely audible to me let alone someone else. Tears stung my eyes.

Someone tugged at the passenger door, which, from the sound of it, appeared elevated, somehow higher than where we were stuck. The car must have landed in the very ditch we had some-how avoided seconds earlier.

Metal peeled on metal as someone pulled the door open. Some-one was trying to rescue Matt, or so I thought.

I raised my head to see what was going on and to scream for help, but before I could utter a word, the Jeep jerked from its resting spot. The car trembled as it was violently pulled from the ground. It felt like we were being dragged up a mountain. I braced myself, not sure what to expect next. The jerking ceased and all four tires settled on even ground as the car came to rest. My perception was blurred and my voice still failed me. Hazy visions flicked across my mind. An intense heat swept over my nose and mouth. It felt like a hand but was much too hot to be human. I slipped into unconsciousness.

CHAPTER 3

I'm back in paradise walking along the river's edge, seeking passage to the other side. A small bridge crafted of sun-bleached wood seemingly pops out of nowhere. I quickly cross it and immediately look to the horizon. The prism is still there, wildly reflecting rays of color, and it seems to beckon me forward. I can't comprehend what sort of disruptive display could be radiating from this serene garden. The only way to solve this mystery is to pursue it myself.

I walk for what feels like an eternity navigating up hills and through thick brush. All the while, my eyes are fixed on the finish line. I haven't anticipated or seen these obstacles, and I begin to hope that this marvel isn't a mirage or a figment of my imagination. This mystery better be worth it.

I approach what I hope will be the last hill. As soon as I reach the summit, I'm blinded by light. Intense rays of red, yellow, orange and violet cut through the air. I hold one arm in front of my eyes as a shield, the other arm outstretched in an effort to guide me through the jungle I'm about to reenter.

I stagger, run into trees and trip on stones as the rainbow dances all around me. The light whizzes around at an incredible speed, and it's making me nauseous. As if the flickering light isn't bad enough, the air is also filled with a shrill clatter. It's a mystical sound, one that couldn't possibly subsist in any earthly existence. It sounds like a thousand pixie fairies singing in piercingly high-pitched voices. The clatter shimmers through the air, wreaking havoc on my ears. The light and sound are definitely misplaced in this perfect paradise. Or maybe they are precisely placed. Maybe they are here to keep intruders away, to protect whatever it is trying to hide. But I can't turn around now. I've traveled too far to turn back, but I'm unsure if I can endure these conditions much longer.

Just when I think I can't take much more, I break through into an opening. The insanity of the light and sound stops and is replaced by a beautiful vision. Before me stands a tree, but not just any tree.

The trunk is narrow and covered in a smooth, gray bark. The branches start low, maybe shoulder height, and extend toward the sky in a perfect bell shape. The leaves are translucent green, and every vein of every leaf is visible. The branches are decorated with apples, oranges, bananas and pears, and it is now apparent what is throwing off the light.

Each piece of fruit is a dazzling display of tiny crystals. There are no other trees in the clearing shading it from the sun, so it is completely bathed in sunlight. A gentle breeze causes the fruit to dance, sending shards of color all around the atmosphere. I stand there, absorbing the beauty of the tree and the light bouncing off of my surroundings. The breeze picks up and the fruits' aromas waft toward me, filling my nostrils with a beautiful, intoxicating scent that creates an urge deep in my core. I need to see this tree up close, to touch it, to verify the fruit is real. But most of all, I need to taste the bounty of this tree.

I walk toward the tree, my eyes never straying from the bejeweled fruits. As I get closer, a snapping noise breaks my concentration. I freeze and dart my eyes to the right, searching for the source of the disturbance. The snapping grows closer and louder, and my annoyance intensifies. I can't imagine who or what is about to ruin my moment. Possessiveness washes over me. I don't want to share this treasure with anyone.

A man slowly emerges from the jungle, one arm held over his eyes to shield them from the tree's intense radiance. He wears a long tunic, cinched at his waist with a rope. The cream fabric is ripped in several spots and the hem is tattered. His hair is long and brown and, like his outfit, looks like it could use a good washing. As I watch, the newcomer drops his arm and surveys the area. He looks in my direction and appears to look right through me. Then, the stranger's eyes settle on the tree. He stares at the fruit, observing its beauty as it sways in the breeze. He appears content to just stand there and stare.

The breeze shifts almost purposefully, redirecting the sweet scent away from me and toward the stranger. The thick aroma swirls through the air at a leisurely pace until it reaches him, and he inhales deeply, drawing in a breath of perfume. His eyes close and he rolls his head across his shoulders. After a few moments, he opens his eyes and his expression changes. His eyes narrow, focusing on the fruit before him. He rolls up on his toes, as if to take a step, and then pauses in hesitation.

Anger overcomes me. How dare this stranger, who found this place after me, ignore me and think he can approach the tree and eat its fruit. I know this is his intention; it is the same reaction I had when I first saw the tree and smelled its perfume. I have to stop him. I should be the first to taste the fruit of this magnificent tree!

"Hey," I yell. But the stranger doesn't seem to hear me. He continues his trancelike approach to the tree.

"Hey, you," I shout again. I try to step forward, but can't move. My feet are cemented to the earth as if I'm a planted tree. I try determinedly to move them, but they aren't going anywhere. I try to shout again, but nothing comes out of my throat.

The stranger is in front of the tree, both hands at his sides. His head is cocked as he stares intently at a piece of red fruit dangling in front of him. Movement around the trunk of the tree catches my attention. It is a massive black serpent. The creature appears well fed given its girth and is several feet long. I can make out each individual scale on its body, and its underbelly is the same color as its back – pure black. The only other color on the animal is a strange marking on its head. It appears to be a crest of some sort, in a deep red hue, the shape of a diamond but with curved lines.

The creature quietly slithers up the trunk and disappears under the thick covering of leaves. The selfishness I felt a moment earlier is now gone, replaced with concern for what is about to happen to the man. I want to warn the stranger of the impending danger, but my voice fails again. The serpent's head reemerges inches from the man's face. The stranger straightens and stares at the snake. The two appear to be in deep conversation but I can't hear a word. Several minutes pass. It appears the beast is trying to convince the man to eat as it nudges the glittering fruit with its head. The man finally plucks an apple from the branch and holds it to his eye. I am not envious, but rather awash with curiosity. I wonder how he would react to the fruit and if it would it be soft and juicy, the crystalline flesh only a decoy. The stranger slowly

raises the fruit to his lips, pauses to say something else to the creature, and takes a bite. Juice rolls down the side of the apple and
the man licks his lips as he swallows. I watch in amazement. So the
most beautiful fruit *is* edible.

Moments pass as I wait for the stranger's reaction. But the man
stands still, expressionless. I wonder why he does not take another
bite. He suddenly flings the fruit to the ground and drops to his
knees. I gasp in horror. The stranger falls to his hands as he tries to
catch his breath. The serpent slithers down the tree so quickly that
I can only see a black blur. It approaches the man and says something to him, but I still can't hear anything. The serpent draws
back like it is going to strike. Why would the creature do this? Not
in this garden, this is paradise! As it prepares to strike, I notice its
eyes. The black beady eyes are now red, the same crimson color as
the marking on its head. They glow like rubies, casting rays of light
just like the fruit. The creature's mouth curls back, revealing a pair
of long, thin fangs that are dripping with what I presume is venom.
The creature moves swiftly and strikes the man on the throat. The
man lies on the ground, writhing in pain.

"What in the hell," I shouted as I jolted awake, my breathing
labored and my heart pounding. I felt sweat on my brow. The
dream frightened me and left me with so many questions. How
could my perfect paradise turn into something so horrible? Who
was the man in my dream and what happened to him? What was
the conversation between the serpent and the man? And why had
the serpent bitten the man? All of these questions ran through my
head as my eyes adjusted. *Where am I*, I wondered.

I could tell I was lying in bed but it wasn't my own. The mattress was
less pillow top and more like a vinyl padded cushion. I could smell
copper, antiseptic and stale air. Stark fluorescent lights overhead

hurt my eyes. Through the blurriness I could see that the walls were a bland yellow; I definitely wasn't in my bedroom. I heard the ticking and beeping of machines, and I was apparently hooked up to them by something stuck in my wrist and taped to my chest. A TV hung on the wall, and I used it as an object to refocus my vision. It was set on a news station, the volume muted. I could decipher pieces of the closed captioning; something about a car accident in Tennessee. An entire family of six was killed. Someone who looked like a nurse fluttered about the room.

"Where am I?" The nurse walked to my bedside. Her name badge read Marlo.

"Allison, you're okay," Marlo replied, her voice soft and soothing, almost reassuring. "You're in the hospital." Marlo held my gaze and I felt my anxiousness fade away, as if her eyes were pulling it out of me. She was a pretty woman, tall and thin with thick wavy red locks that flowed to the middle of her back. Her eyes were most captivating. They were a beautiful shade of lavender, deep and intense in color, with gold specks. They reminded me of irises that bloom in early spring.

"I'm in a hospital? What happened?" I asked in disbelief as I tried to sit up. Marlo gently but firmly pushed my shoulders back toward the mattress.

"You're at Medina Memorial Hospital. You were in a pretty bad car wreck a few nights ago, but you'll be fine."

"Car wreck?" I tried to think back to a few days ago, but my mind was a blank slate. There was nothing there. I couldn't recall anything...not what I had been wearing, or where I had been going or even the accident itself.

"Yes, and you are very lucky. You've been unconscious for a few days but you didn't break any bones and there was no internal bleeding."

"Accident," I whispered to myself, still in disbelief and still trying to recall something.

"Now that you're awake, let me get Doctor Frid so that he can examine you." Marlo turned towards the door and before exiting added, "And you also have a visitor."

I didn't fully grasp Marlo's last words. My mind was still wandering, searching for a memory to fill in all the blanks about the accident.

"Wait," I half shouted, but Marlo was already out the door. "Where's Matt?" I whispered to myself. Surely the visitor she mentioned must be Matt. He would definitely be here at the hospital waiting for me to wake. It wouldn't be like him to not be here by my side, unless...

No, I couldn't think of that. Matt must be with the doctor. I was sure they were discussing my injuries and what I needed to do next and my follow up doctor appointments. Matt was here, I was sure of it.

The doctor knocked on the door and stepped inside. He was an older gentleman with salt and pepper hair. He wore thin spectacles that sat on the edge of his nose and the requisite white lab coat and stethoscope. A hospital tag hung around his neck identified him as Doctor Jonathan Frid.

"Good morning, Allison," he said, "How are you feeling?" He reached into his lab coat searching for some instrument I was sure he was going to inspect me with.

I looked at him and back at the door and wondered where my visitor was.

"I'm fine. Where's Matt?"

Before the doctor could speak, the door cracked open. I strained my neck to see who it was. It wasn't Matt; it was my best friend Jenna. Panic set in over me.

"Would somebody please tell me what is going on?" I said through clenched teeth, tears welling up in my eyes. "Where is Matt?"

"Allison, please take it easy," the doctor said. Jenna walked over to the other side of the bed, opposite Doctor Frid. "You were in a serious accident and I need you to stay calm."

My eyes flitted back and forth between the doctor and Jenna. They exchanged a glance that made it apparent they knew something I didn't.

"Oh God," I said. "He was in the car with me, wasn't he? Was he hurt? Is he okay? Is he…" I couldn't finish the sentence. I couldn't bring myself to say the word.

I fell back in the bed, covered my face with my hands and sobbed uncontrollably. Through my bawling, I could make out bits of the conversation going on around me.

"I guess it's confirmed," Jenna stated. "She doesn't remember making me her emergency contact, or…"

"Yes, she has memory loss," Doctor Frid interrupted, cutting off Jenna's statement.

"How bad do you think it is?" Jenna asked the doctor.

"Hard to say until she calms down…"

"Should we say anything about…?" Jenna's voice trailed off.

I stopped sobbing long enough to choke out, "Would someone *please* tell me what is going on? What are you talking about?"

Jenna pulled a chair up to the side of the bed and handed me some tissues. Her face was blanketed with concern. She looked different to me. Her brown hair was shorter than the last time I saw her, which I couldn't recall when that was.

"Ali," she started in a soft tone, almost a whisper. "Matt died three years ago."

I froze. My tears stopped as did my breathing. My heart may have even stopped for a second. I stared into Jenna's dull brown eyes, searching for answers or some explanation. I had no idea what she was talking about. Matt didn't die three years ago. I forced my mind to go back in time and thought about where was I three years ago, where Matt was and what possibly could have happened to him. I could picture our house, with the cream and brown front, and the yard with the woods all around. I could see my Jeep and a motorcycle. But I couldn't see Matt.

"I don't believe you," I whispered.

Jenna grabbed my hand. "Ali, it's true, he was at work and…" I tuned her out.

I forced my mind to think about my accident. Surely if I thought about it hard enough, I would recollect something. Jenna continued talking. I could hear her murmurs, but I couldn't hear the details. I had to think hard, bring something out from the depths of my mind.

And there it was – a brief flash. It was instantaneous, but it was what I was looking for. I could see me sitting in my Jeep with Matt in the passenger seat, rain beating down on the windshield. As quickly as I saw it, it was gone. But it was vivid and more importantly, it was real.

"No, you're wrong," I shouted. "Matt was with me! I was driving and he was in the passenger seat. I just saw it! I *can* see it. He was with me!"

Jenna stood up still holding my hand. "Ali, that's not possible." Her eyes were filled with sympathy, her face with concern. She slowly shook her head from side to side and she seemed pretty convinced she knew what she was talking about.

Doctor Frid spoke. "No one else was with you in the car, Allison. I read the response team report; you were the only passenger."

"No, no, that's not true! Matt was there, I'm telling you!" I felt myself coming unglued, launching into hysterics. Tears flowed freely. "Why won't you believe me? He *was* there!" I shouted. The machines behind me beeped at a frantic pace.

"Nurse! Nurse," Doctor Frid yelled. "Please give her something to calm her down."

A different nurse, rotund with tanned skin and dark hair, entered the room. I backed myself into the bed trying to escape the needle headed in my direction. "No, I don't need a shot; I need to see my husband! Somebody please tell me where he is!" I felt the shot of whatever the nurse poked into my IV start to work its magic. I was calming down, but my mind was still racing for any memory of me and my husband that would prove Jenna and the doctor wrong.

"Where's Matt?" I asked Jenna in a sleepy voice. "Where...is... Matt?"

I drifted off to sleep.

CHAPTER 4

It wasn't a bad dream; this was my new reality. I had hoped to open my eyes to Matt lying next to me, but instead, I woke up still in the hospital. The prior day's events came crashing down like a boxer's left hook to the jaw. I had been in an accident. My husband was dead.

My head and eyes were killing me; it felt like I had cried all night. I rolled over and found Jenna sitting on the couch in my hospital room. "Hey," she said, and walked over to the side of my bed. She gently brushed the bangs out of my eyes.

"Hey," I muttered back.

My last memories rushed back into my conscious with a vengeance. I couldn't believe Matt was dead. It didn't seem possible, but the alternative was also unlikely; Doctor Frid and Jenna wouldn't lie to me about something like this. My heartbeat quickened and my breath shortened as I became more alert. I tried to compose myself, to hold it together in front of Jenna; a shot of whatever the nurse gave me yesterday would really help right now.

"How are you doing?" Jenna asked.

"About as okay as can be expected, I suppose." I shifted my position in an attempt to depress the anxiousness I felt creeping up on me.

"The doctor said you can go home today."

"Yeah? Great," I responded flatly. *And what exactly would I be going home to,* I wanted to ask. I wasn't in any hurry to rush back to an empty house.

"Jenna?" I asked. "Is it true? About Matt?" I couldn't help myself. It seemed so unreal that he could be gone. Maybe if I asked the question again I would get the answer I wanted.

Jenna glanced out the window, then back at me, and sighed. "Yes, it's true. I wouldn't lie about something like that."

That wasn't the answer I wanted.

"Then why don't I remember? If he's gone, why can't I recall what happened? Why don't I remember his funeral?"

"The doctor said you hit your head pretty hard in the accident. He suspected you would have some memory loss, but he wasn't sure how bad it would be."

"Hmm." I supposed that made sense. I lay there for a few minutes taking in the gravity of my situation. My husband *was* gone. What would life be like without him? I apparently knew the answer in the depths of my memory since I'd lost him three years ago, but it felt like I was living through this for the very first time. "What about the vision I had last night of me and him in my Jeep? I was driving and he was in the passenger seat; it was dark out and it was raining heavily. It was so vivid, so real."

"Doctor Frid said that could be your mind recalling some other time the two of you were together."

Tears welled in my eyes and I scrunched my face in an effort not to cry.

"Hey, hey, hey," Jenna said, and sat on the edge of my bed. "You're going to be okay. You've managed without Matt for the past three years; you'll get through this too."

"Yeah, but Jenna," I said, tears streaming down my cheeks. I could taste the salt at the corner of my lips. "It feels like I just lost Matt, like right now or yesterday when you told me. I don't remember how he died. I don't remember the funeral. I don't remember the past three years without him. It's like my mind is this big black hole and everything you are saying is new to me. Hearing the news last night, or yesterday, or whenever it was, was like hearing it for the first time."

"I know, Ali," Jenna said quietly. "Maybe when we get you home some things will start to come back to you. Let me get Doctor Frid so he can clear you for discharge."

I was escorted to Jenna's car in a wheelchair. It seemed unnecessary but the nurse insisted it was hospital policy. Besides my tear-induced headache, I felt amazingly fine. I didn't have any scratches, sore muscles or broken bones.

The crisp October air greeted me as I was wheeled outside. I pulled my sweater tighter in an effort to keep me warm. Sunlight filtered through a sea of gray clouds. It wasn't enough to warm me but it nonetheless shocked my eyes. The combination of fluorescent hospital lighting and hours of crying had taken their toll, and my eyes were not prepared for the natural light. Jenna offered up her sunglasses and I quickly put them on as the nurse helped me into the passenger seat.

We sat in silence as Jenna drove. I tried to wrap my head around the last three years' events.

"Can you tell me what happened?" I asked.

Jenna glanced at me. "According to the police report, you hit your brakes hard, even though you didn't have a stop sign. You flipped through the intersection and landed in a ditch."

"Doesn't sound like it ended well for the Jeep."

"Nope; it's totaled."

I strained my mind, trying to imagine my Jeep flipping through an intersection in an attempt to recall the accident. I came up empty. I didn't remember where I was driving to or from, or hitting my brakes, or anything for that matter. "That's not what I was asking about, though." I wasn't really interested in the details of my accident; I was thinking about my husband. "What happened to Matt?"

"Oh," Jenna said. She stared straight ahead at the road, almost concentrating too hard on driving. "Um, well, he was working at the stamping plant repairing one of the presses which stamps out car parts. Apparently the machine wasn't locked out properly. He was rushed to the hospital but there was nothing they could do for him."

I winced as she recited her abbreviated version of the accident. I appreciated her sparing me the gory details. I could only imagine that he was working inside the press when someone accidentally started it back up. It had to have been horrific. I bit my lip and closed my eyes, not wanting to think about the pain he must have been in. If there was a God, hopefully He took Matt without much suffering. I looked out the side window, trying to hold back tears. "Oh," was all I could say.

So he was really gone and I couldn't remember any of it. I knew my best friend wouldn't lie about this, but it still seemed impossible. Even with a serious injury to my head, I should have been able to remember something of my husband's passing. And if I couldn't recall it on my own, I should at least remember something as Jenna spoke of it. A significant event like that should be recallable no matter what.

"Can you do me a favor?" I asked, still staring out the window.

"Sure, what?"

"Can you take me to the cemetery? So I can visit Matt?"

Jenna continued staring straight ahead, focused like a laser beam.

"Please?" I asked.

"That's not possible."

"What do you mean, that's not possible? He's dead, isn't he? He must be buried somewhere."

"Yeah, Ali he is. But after Matt died, you insisted on cremating him."

"Okay, so where are his ashes?"

Jenna tossed me a look that said I wasn't going to like what I was about to hear. "Well, you decided to have a private service. Very private. It was just you and the captain of a boat you chartered. You threw the urn overboard into Lake Erie. You insisted it was what Matt would have wanted since he loved boating and fishing."

"What!" I exclaimed. "How could I have done *that?*"

"You weren't exactly yourself after his accident and none of us could talk you out of it. You insisted on it."

"Good grief," I whispered. "It's like I don't even know myself or my life." I sat there and stared at my fingers resting in my lap. Several minutes passed. My thoughts drifted from Matt's accident to my life without him. "What have I been doing these past three years?"

"I'm not quite sure," Jenna responded tentatively.

"What do you mean?"

"Well, after Matt died, you shut out all of your friends and were practically a recluse. Other than the occasional phone call to let me know you were still alive, I have no clue what you have been up to. You haven't been working though, that much I do know. You quit your job after receiving the settlement from Matt's accident."

Settlement, I thought. The more details Jenna shared with me, the more this story came to life. I was like a child listening to a story for the first time, but instead of being in awe over an exciting tale, I was in awe of the fact that this story was my life. It didn't seem real, but it had to be true. My mind was empty and Jenna had all of the answers. My best friend wouldn't lead me astray, but this was all a bit much to absorb.

"I'm sorry," I said, though I didn't know what I was apologizing for. I was sorry that I gave my friends the cold shoulder. I was sorry that I was asking so many questions. I was sorry that Jenna had to take care of me. I was sorry that I appeared to be getting on Jenna's nerves. It felt like we had been through this before. Nothing was more frustrating than not being able to recall any of this. But Jenna was my only source of information and I needed to know what she knew so that I could start putting my life back together. So I could stop being a sorry basket case.

"No Ali, I'm sorry. I shouldn't be upset with you. It's just been really hard seeing you in so much pain for so long and you shutting everyone out of your life. All of our other friends kind of gave up on you. They tried to help but you shut them out."

I sat there not knowing what to say so I started picking at my fingernails. I couldn't imagine shutting out my friends. Since I had no family besides Matt, my friends *were* my family. I must have been in a terrible amount of pain and turmoil after Matt's death to choose to lead a life without my friends. My fingernails held my attention for a minute until I noticed the sun was irritating my neck. I rubbed it, hoping to relieve the irritation, and as I looked up I saw a familiar highway sigh. "Hey, isn't that the exit to my house?"

"Yeah, your old place."

"My old place?"

"Um, yeah. You sold the house on Peace Eagle after the accident. You said you couldn't stand living in the house you and Matt shared; it was too big for you to keep up with and too painful to be there without him."

"Fantastic," I said and threw my arms in the air. "Is there nothing familiar left in my life? Matt is gone, my friends are gone, my car is totaled and now I live in a different house? Well, you're still here, so thank you for that. I was at least looking forward to going home where I could hopefully still feel Matt's presence!"

"Hey, give it some time Ali. You were just in a major accident and have amnesia. It will all come back to you. You'll settle back into your life."

We drove for another thirty minutes or so in silence. Jenna finally exited the highway onto a country road. I wasn't sure where we were. The two lane road was lined with trees and thick foliage in shades of crimson, marigold and copper. Few houses were around and the landscape was mainly dotted with farms and woods. We approached an intersection with a two-way stop and I sunk down into the seat, fearful that another car wouldn't stop as we zoomed past. I relaxed once we were clear. The road twisted and fell into steep dips and rose back out of them. The motion, combined with the sunlight flickering through the trees, made me sick.

"Where in the world are you taking me," I muttered, one hand on my stomach, the other blocking the sunlight from my eyes. My head was cocked to shield my neck from the sun.

"Home," Jenna replied. "We're almost there."

We passed a weathered wooden sign that had seen better days. Carved letters filled with chipped black paint read 'Welcome to Ridge Hollow.'

"Really?" I asked.

"Really," Jenna replied.

I was a bit surprised that I apparently moved to Ridge Hollow. This sleepy little town was miles away from where I had lived in Buzzard Hill, deeper into the countryside than I ever thought I would move. The landscape was blanketed with trees, pines and wildflowers and there were more farms than there were in Buzzard Hill. Houses were few and far between. I doubted that there were more than fifty homes in the entire town. I recalled passing through this area years ago with Matt. There was absolutely nothing here; no grocery stores, gas stations, bars, malls, nothing. This was a place where Matt would have loved to have lived.

Jenna slowed the car and turned off onto a gravel driveway. Trees lining the path formed an arch overhead, shielding the area from any sunshine. The tires rolled slowly through the twisting gravel corridor leading to a blacktop driveway. After a few more twists, the trees broke and there stood a quaint little cottage. It was a one story home with white siding and green shutters. It was tiny but the perfect size for one person. I saw an attached garage to the left and a separate building, possibly another garage, in the backyard.

"It's cute," I said, "but I certainly don't remember buying this place."

"You apparently took up gardening over the years," Jenna pointed out.

"Geez, no kidding."

The front of the house was bordered by a white picket fence. Tall orange lilies and multicolored zinnias filled the bed in front of the fence. Beyond that was a small walkway leading to the front door with flower beds on both sides of the porch filled with short pines and burning bushes.

I got out of the car before Jenna even had a chance to put it in park. I stood in the driveway and stared at the house, hoping that something would trigger my memory, but nothing did. I walked around to the back of the house and Jenna followed. The back-yard was spacious, a huge green area with a fenced-in garden a few yards back. Tomatoes, peppers and corn were ready for harvest.

"Clearly I have a green thumb I don't know about," I murmured under my breath. Jenna chuckled. "Seriously. I never gardened before, so how on earth did I pull this off?"

"Well," Jenna said softly, "I did mention you had a lot of time on your hands."

We walked further into the yard and came upon a good sized lake with a paddle boat and a bench in the perfect spot to watch the sunset. The lake stretched out to the edge of the ridge where the land steeply fell off into a hollow, rocky abyss. The town was aptly named Ridge Hollow for the many rocky ridges and valleys it had within its borders. The rest of the property was surrounded by dense woods, the fall foliage a bright contrast to the gray backdrop.

"It is beautiful," I whispered. I looked around at the back of the house and the ridge and the lake. It truly was a beautiful, serene place, but it just wasn't me. I was an urbanite. I would have guessed I had moved to the city or even a beach house; just not here, in the complete middle of nowhere. This property might have been as close to nowhere as anything. Then again, it did have a beachy vibe. Maybe I opted for this rather than the shores of Lake Erie, which could be brutally snowy in the winter. Or maybe, since this was the type of town Matt wanted to move to, I had moved here to feel closer to him. "But it doesn't feel like home."

"Let's get you inside," Jenna said. She wrapped her arms around my shoulders and redirected me towards the house. "Maybe some-thing in there will spark a memory."

We entered through the green front door and were greeted by a casually decorated foyer. The walls were painted light blue and the floor tiled in a rustic tan stone. A picture of the sun setting over the lake in the backyard hung on the wall.

A staircase to the right led to the loft bedroom. It was a small room but plenty enough space for one. A large wrought iron bed anchored the room, topped with a sea foam green comforter and oversized pillows. A white wooden dresser was tucked into a corner. The room was open to the living space below.

Back downstairs, the foyer stepped down into the living room which was open to the kitchen. A white sofa sat across from the fireplace and a TV was mounted on the wall. Jenna walked into the kitchen but I broke to the right towards a door.

"Let's see what's behind door number one," I said to myself.

The door creaked open and I felt around for a light switch. Soft lighting blossomed from the ceiling illuminating a room filled with wooden bookshelves. I stepped into the middle of the room and looked up and all around. Every square inch of wall space was filled with books or CD cases. I had always wanted a den filled with books and music, and had begged Matt to build one for me at our house in Buzzard Hill, but I had never gotten it. I must have indulged myself. I ran my finger across a row of books. All were bound in black, brown or burgundy leather, some with buckles on their spines, but none had titles or authors. I pulled out a book and flipped through the yellowed pages. They were filled with beautiful calligraphy that appeared to have been written by a person, not printed by a machine. I started to read a line when Jenna walked in.

"What's in here?"

I placed the book back on the shelf. "Looks like I got that den I always wanted."

"Boy, you aren't kidding. How many books are in here?"

"Who knows? Enough to occupy all that free time you told me I have." I cracked a smile which Jenna returned.

"So whatcha been reading?" Jenna walked over to a desk and switched on the lamp. She tilted her head to look at the book on the desk. "Wow, Ali. The Bible?"

"The Bible?" I asked. That was one book I would have never have guessed I was reading. I walked next to Jenna and chuckled when I saw the words 'Holy Bible' pressed in gold leaf on the cover. "After twelve years of Catholic schooling, you'd think I'd have had enough of that book."

"No kidding. Hey, it doesn't look like you got very far," Jenna said as she flipped through the pages. "Your bookmarker is at the story of Adam and Eve."

"Geez, not far at all. Well you can bet with all of the other interesting books in this room, I'll be reading something else before picking the Bible back up!" We both chuckled.

We left the den and walked back into the living room. I stopped at the sofa table topped with picture frames and examined them. There was one of me and Jenna in our college sweatshirts; another of me with a big group of friends (most of whom I had apparently deserted); a picture of my parents; and several panoramic shots that looked like they had been taken on various vacations. I paused as I came upon a picture of Matt. It was a small bronzed frame, and Matt was sitting on his Harley with a huge smile on his face. This must have been taken when he first bought the bike; the bike still had all of its stock parts and showed no signs of any of the customization Matt had done. I stared at the picture, my heart not believing he was gone but my mind telling me that he was. I set it down when another picture caught my eye. This one was of me and a stranger. It was a man, an extremely attractive man, who had his arm around me. He was taller than me with thick black hair and piercing blue eyes. He was slender yet muscular. I searched the background of the picture looking for some sign of where we might have been but I couldn't figure it out.

"Who is this?" I asked Jenna.

Jenna peeked over my shoulder. "Whoa!" she exclaimed. "I don't know but he sure is a looker."

"Apparently we know each other by the way he has his arm around me. I haven't mentioned anything about him to you?"

"Ali, you and I haven't talked that much and when we did, it was brief. You never mentioned if you were seeing someone new." Jenna winced as she delivered the news, as if trying to break it to me softly.

The words sliced through me. *Seeing someone new.* It seemed so surreal that I could be dating anybody when I felt like I had just lost Matt.

"But it's okay if you are," Jenna quickly added. "Matt has been gone for three years; it's understandable that you've moved on by now."

Jenna's words echoed through my ears as I stared at the picture. I must have met this stranger sometime during the last few years if I couldn't remember him at all.

I set the frame down and flung myself on the couch. "This sucks!" I yelled at the top of my lungs and punched a cushion. "This not remembering stuff is for the birds. I feel like my life has been flipped upside down, that I went to bed and woke up living someone else's life!"

"Oh Ali, I'm so sorry," Jenna said. "Doctor Frid said it would take some time for your memory to come back. It *will* come back. And now that you are home, maybe that will happen sooner rather than later."

I looked Jenna in the eyes; she was trying to reassure me that I would be okay, but it wasn't working. I felt tears welling up in my eyes and I really didn't want to cry anymore. I rolled my eyes and clenched my jaw to make the tears stop.

"I can spend the night here if you want," Jenna offered.

I let out a large sigh, trying to decide if that was what I wanted or if I wanted some time to myself. My thoughts were interrupted by a frantic knock at the door. I sat up and looked at Jenna.

"Who could that be?" I asked.

Jenna shrugged her shoulders.

I got up and went to the front door, cracking it just enough for me to see outside. A man in a leather riding jacket stood there fumbling to remove his motorcycle helmet. Beyond him, parked in my driveway, was a motorcycle. It was a sharp, red sport bike but a make and model that I didn't recognize. I found this odd since Matt taught me quite a bit about motorcycles and I could usually quickly identify most any bike.

"Allison," the voice called out from under the helmet. "Are you all right?"

The stranger pulled off his helmet and ran his fingers through his dark hair. "Are you okay?" he asked again.

"Um," I stammered. I squinted to make sure I was seeing things clearly. The man in front of me was the same man from the picture.

"I'm, um, I'm fine," I stammered.

"I'm sorry I didn't get here sooner. I was out of town on business but as soon as I heard about your accident, I flew back."

"Uh huh," I responded, hoping my mind would start connecting some dots.

"Ali," Jenna called from the living room, "who is it?"

I opened the door wider to allow the stranger to enter. He was more beautiful in person than he was in the photograph. He was definitely taller than me and his hair was different than it was in the picture. His dark locks were long and spiky on top and short on the sides and perfectly held in place even though he had just removed a helmet. His features were chiseled and defined, his cheekbones high, his jaw strong. His skin appeared smooth and flawless, pale like mine, and his eyes...well, they were breathtaking. They were a beautiful shade of aquamarine with several yellow flecks.

I stood in the middle of the foyer staring at the stranger and he stared back, holding my gaze.

"Well are you going to introduce me?" Jenna asked politely as she walked into the foyer, clearing her throat.

"Um, err, this is Jenna Wintourly, my best friend," I said to the handsome stranger, pointing over my shoulder without moving my head. "Jenna, this is...um..." I trailed off.

The stranger cocked his head and narrowed his eyes. "Allison, do you know who I am? Do you remember me?" He placed a hand on my arm and affectionately rubbed it.

"She, uh, hit her head," Jenna fumbled. The stranger looked at Jenna, and that look apparently took her voice away because she didn't finish her sentence.

I continued staring into his eyes as my mind scanned through what must have been memories. Picture after picture of the two of us together flew through my mind. They were mostly head shots of the two of us in various poses, the backgrounds indiscernible. I concentrated, hoping I could freeze on one scene and that it would give me some concrete information. I squeezed my eyes shut, willing the memories to stop at one and they finally did. We were in an embrace staring deep into each other's eyes. The stranger mouthed *I love you, Allison* and I mouthed *I love you* back to him.

I opened my eyes. "Yes, I remember you."

The stranger stepped closer and bowed his head as if to get a better look into my eyes. "What is my name?" he whispered. He smelled so delicious that I wanted to wrap my arms around him and not let go, but I fought the urge. He grabbed both of my hands and a wave of energy ran over me, a warm numbing feeling. Images flew through my head like a flip book, more scenes of the two of us together.

"Vincent," I whispered. A smirk drew across the stranger's face as he raised an eyebrow waiting for me to speak his last name. "Vincent Drake."

I pulled my hands away from his and turned to look at Jenna. "This is Vincent Drake," I said assuredly.

"Oh Ali! This is great," Jenna gushed. She ran over and gave me a hug. "Your memory is coming back already! That's so promising."

"Very promising," Vincent echoed, his smooth voice soft and pleasant.

"Nice to meet you," Jenna said to Vincent. The two shook hands. Jenna smiled like a little kid in a toy store. She couldn't stop staring.

"The pleasure is all mine," Vincent replied, turning Jenna's hand to kiss it. "I've heard a lot about you."

"I wish I could say the same," Jenna blurted out.

There was a pause as Jenna and Vincent were caught in a brief gaze before Jenna shook her hand loose. "I uh, should get going and leave you two alone. Unless you need me, Ali."

I looked at Vincent, and while I couldn't remember the details of our apparent relationship, I felt that I had known him a long time; long enough that I could be alone with him. It felt like there was depth to our relationship in the visions that flashed through my head and I felt safe in his presence now. This man was part of my life. I could feel it if even if I didn't remember it.

"I'm fine Jenna, thanks. Thanks for everything."

"Okay, well I left my phone number on the fridge; I figured you wouldn't remember it."

Jenna grabbed her jacket and purse and headed for the door. "Call if you need anything. Take care of her," Jenna said pointing a finger at Vincent.

"There's nothing more I'd rather do," he responded.

CHAPTER 5

I couldn't get the image out of my mind. *I love you, Allison,* Vincent whispered to me. *I love you,* I whispered back. The vision had been so vivid I had actually felt Vincent's arms around me and heard the words we both uttered. I replayed the scene in my mind like a skipping record, still not believing that I was with another man who wasn't my husband. Realizing Vincent and I were together was made easier by the emotions accompanying the vision; the words were sincere, the feelings true. I felt it as I saw it. I could practically taste the passion in those spoken words. Now I just needed the memories to make all the pieces fall into place.

I sat on the couch mulling over this particular vision as Vincent dashed around the house tending to my every need. He had been doing this for the past several hours, ever since Jenna had left us. I thought it was a bit much; I was a big girl and could take care of myself. But I figured I'd let him spoil me if that was what he wanted.

"Do you want me to get you a book to read?" Vincent asked, pointing to the den.

"No, I'm not in the mood for reading."

"Are you sure? It's getting late and it might help you fall asleep."

"I'm sure."

Vincent looked towards the den and back at me. His mouth parted, as if he were going to ask again if I wanted a book, but I cut him off. "I really don't want a book," I stated. I had no idea why he wanted me to read something so badly.

"Well how about a blanket?"

"No, I'm…" I trailed off. There was no point in finishing the sentence. Vincent was already up the stairs, in my bedroom retrieving a blanket. A blanket I didn't need. I was hot and seemed to be getting hotter by the second. I took off my sweatshirt and socks and straightened my t-shirt.

"Here you go." Vincent unfolded the blanket and swept it across my lap, tucking it in under my feet.

"Thanks." I didn't want to fight it.

"How about a fire?"

"Fine," I resigned. Even if I said no, I was sure he'd still build it.

I watched Vincent stack wood in the fireplace and shove newspaper between the logs. So this was my boyfriend. The boyfriend I couldn't remember. *He is quite handsome,* I thought as a smile spread across my face. He stood, grabbed some matches from the mantle and bent over to light the fire. I had to admit, it was a nice view.

"Do you know what happened, Allison?" Vincent turned to look at me. I darted my eyes away from his rear view. The corners of his mouth turned up. I was busted.

"They say I was in an accident," I responded, shrugging my shoulders. "I don't know where I was or what I was doing. Apparently the road was wet, I hit my brakes and here I am missing part of my memory."

"The doctor said your memory would come back." He sounded so sure of it that he almost convinced me.

"Yeah…" I drifted off, staring at the flickering fire.

"What is it?" Vincent asked and sat next to me on the couch. "Do you not feel well?"

"It's not that. I feel fine. Too fine maybe. Not a bump, scrape, bruise or sore muscle here."

"Yes, it is a miracle you weren't seriously hurt. Physically, that is."

"Yeah, miracle," I muttered.

"Then what is it? I can tell something is disturbing you."

"I don't want to upset you. It's silly. It's just my memory or something."

"It's not silly, Allison. You can tell me anything."

I gazed into Vincent's beautiful blue eyes. *I love you,* flashed across my mind again. I inhaled and his scent filled my nostrils. It was refreshing like a spring day, but warm like autumn and all around scrumptious. I resisted the urge to get lost in his eyes or his presence.

I took a deep breath before I began. "When I woke up in the hospital, I, um, was looking for Matt. I didn't remember you. I didn't ask for you. I swore that I was driving and Matt was in the car with me when the accident happened. Silly, huh?" I cringed in anticipation of Vincent's response.

"You thought you were with Matt the night of your accident?"

Vincent sounded surprised, but that wasn't the part of my confession I had expected him to react to. I thought he would have been upset that I didn't remember him.

"Yeah, but Doctor Frid said it was just my mind recalling a past memory, some other time when Matt was with me. The doc figured

I was going to have some memory loss but wasn't sure how much."
I paused and stared at my hands, feeling foolish for not remembering my boyfriend. "I'm sorry," I muttered.

"What are you sorry for?"

"I didn't remember you. I *don't* remember you." Tears swelled
behind my beleaguered eyes. "I mean, it's strange, Vincent. I have
no memory of you and yet I feel like I have known you my entire
life. I feel comfortable with you, like I know you and you know
me. I just don't have any of the memories to back these feelings."

"There's nothing to be sorry about," Vincent said as he wiped
my tears with his thumbs. His flesh was exceptionally hot.

"You're so warm," I said. A gentle smile spread across his lips.

"Well if you can't remember, Allison," Vincent said, ignoring my
observation, "I'm just going to have to help you remember."

"Right," I mumbled and rolled my eyes. "Good luck." If my best
friend from kindergarten couldn't jog my memory, I doubted my
boyfriend of only a year would get me to remember anything.

"Do you remember how we first met?"

"Come on Vincent." I didn't want to play this game. I just
wanted to relax.

Vincent placed his index finger to my lips, hushing me. "Humor
me," he requested. I stared into his eyes, which gave my stomach
the butterflies, and resigned.

"No," I replied. "I don't remember how we met."

"Think back to about a year ago."

I shook my head, already giving up.

"Allison, clear your mind and concentrate. Think back to last
fall. You drove into town and stopped at a café. Do you remember
the café? You frequented the place."

Vincent placed his hands on my leg and a jolt of energy ran
through me. I shivered but he didn't seem to notice. My attraction

to him, everything I felt when I looked at him or inhaled his scent, came to life with his touch.

"Do you remember the couch you usually sat on? The one next to the bookshelves?"

I stared harder at the fire and a vision began to flicker in my mind, just like the flames in the fireplace. It was like watching a television show with bad reception. Visions and blackness intermingled. The visions became slightly longer until I could finally make out a scene. It was a charming little place with weathered wood floors and heavy curtains that made the space feel more like a parlor than a coffee shop. Coffee machines were stationed near the front door next to a glass counter filled with gourmet sandwiches and sweets. Mismatched tables and chairs filled most of the dining area and a handful of people were sipping their caffeinated beverages. The air was saturated with a heavy coffee aroma and the sound of an acoustic guitar. A plush couch faced the fireplace and a wall of bookshelves. And there I was, sitting on the couch with a cup of tea and a book. But I wasn't reading the book; I was captivated by the music flowing from a dark corner in the back of the room. I strained to see who was there but couldn't make much of the shadowy silhouette. The music faded and the figure emerged, his head hung low. The man went to the counter, retrieved a cup of coffee and turned to face me.

"Oh my gosh," I gasped. I whipped my head around to look at Vincent. The man in my vision was him. "We met at the Buzzards Brew coffee shop?" I asked in disbelief.

"That's right," Vincent responded, pleasure evident in his tone.

"You were playing the guitar and I was reading by the fire," I stated, still not believing my mind was able to recall a memory.

"Yes, you used to say you sat there pretending to read but you were actually watching me play." Vincent smiled again. "I thought that was sweet."

"Huh," was all I could muster.

I was flabbergasted. Not only was I able to remember something that had happened in the last three years, but the memory was of Vincent. This man was incredibly handsome, but he apparently was also a musician. I'd always had a thing for musicians but had never dated one. He also rode a motorcycle, which meant that he had some sense of adventure, both of which were incredibly sexy to me. And on top of all that, in the few hours he'd been with me, he'd been very attentive to my needs. If it hadn't been for his hand on my leg, I would have thought that I was dreaming.

"Come on, Allison," Vincent whispered. "See if you can remember something else."

I closed my eyes again and strained my mind. I was willing to play along now since I was getting results. If I could recall one memory tonight, maybe I could recall another. I concentrated so hard that I barely noticed Vincent's hand on my leg; the heat of his skin seeped through the blanket and my sweatpants and flowed over my skin. The flickering resumed. My mind ran through the coffee shop scene again as if in fast forward, and then everything went blank. I frantically rolled my eyes behind my eyelids searching for something, anything, but it was all gone.

"I...I can't. I don't see anything," I said, frustrated. I opened my eyes and looked at Vincent. In that moment, I was consumed with fear that I couldn't remember anything else and my memory would never fully return.

"Concentrate," Vincent instructed. "Let it come to you."

Vincent's calm demeanor was enough to calm me, for the moment at least. I shut my eyes and after a few seconds the blankness turned into static and more broken visions.

"Wait a minute," I whispered.

"Shhhh, just concentrate."

I saw a snippet of a beach but it wasn't the ocean. It was Lake Erie, maybe an island rather than the coastline. It was night and the moonlight casted its hue on a small cottage. My memory skipped forward; there was a fire in the fireplace and a table set for two. My vision skipped again; Vincent and I were outside in a hot tub sharing a bottle of red wine. The bottle markedly jumped out of the scene like it was glowing. It was a green bottle with a black label and crimson monogram of some sort. Then my mind flicked through the entire scene again.

I jumped off the couch.

"What did you see?" Vincent asked, springing to his feet with excitement.

"You, me, some cottage at night and a hot tub." I ran my fingers through my hair, not believing what I just saw. I wanted my memory to return, but this was almost too much. I was confused why certain memories were returning before others and why I couldn't recall losing my husband or the grieving process I must have gone through to get to the point where I felt comfortable going on a vacation with another man. I guessed I had really moved on – life goes on. If these memories were filling in, it must be only a matter of time before I remembered everything else, including Matt's accident.

"Do you know where we were?"

I stared at the floor as more broken pictures flickered through my head at a frantic pace; I couldn't keep up. There was kissing – and more – and other scenes; the two of us at the zoo, us grocery shopping, Vincent cooking dinner for me and another vacation but I couldn't place the locale. I shook my head hoping to make the images stop, but it didn't work.

"Allison?"

The pictures flashed through my mind like the sun through the trees on the drive to my house this afternoon. It was making me dizzy. How could I go from having no memory of the past three years to this? I finally understood that Vincent and I were dating. I'd moved on. Got it. But it still didn't feel right. Everything felt odd because I still couldn't remember Matt's passing. I felt like I wasn't honoring Matt's memory because while I couldn't remember his last years, I was remembering all of these fun times with my new boyfriend.

"Allison?" Vincent called out again. He stepped towards me and I stepped back.

"No," I shouted at him.

"Allison, what's wrong?"

"Everything's wrong!" I yelled. "All of this! I wake up with no memory, thinking I'm still married and that my husband is alive only to discover that he's been dead for three years. My best friend tells me I shut out all of my friends, quit my job and moved to this place." I waved my hand around with dramatic flair. "This isn't my home. This isn't me! Why would I move to the middle of nowhere? Why would I move away from anybody that could help me?"

"You said…" Vincent started.

"Stop," I commanded, holding my hand up. "I don't feel like I belong here. That's the truth. Then there's you." I paused; Vincent didn't say anything. I calmed down a bit and softened my tone. "You appear in my life in what seems like out of nowhere. I'm having memories *of* you, but I don't *remember* you. Vincent, I don't think I could dream of someone more perfect than you. It's like my fairy godmother granted me my every wish in a man…you are irresistibly handsome, ride a motorcycle, you're attentive, you play the guitar. I mean come on! And all of a sudden all of these memories flood my mind at once. It's a little overwhelming." I broke down in tears, my shoulders trembling. Vincent wrapped his arms around me.

"It's okay Allison. It's okay," Vincent purred as he rubbed my back, trying to calm me down.

"Is it?" I asked as I pulled away from Vincent's burning embrace. "Because it doesn't feel okay. I don't know who I am or whose life I'm living. Something's just not right here."

Vincent rubbed my arms and stared at the floor, as if he were contemplating something. "Well maybe you need a change of scenery," he suggested.

"Come again?" I was baffled by his suggestion.

"You said this doesn't feel like home to you, right?"

I nodded my head in affirmation.

"Well, maybe you need to go someplace else, a place you really enjoy. Maybe that will make you feel more comfortable and help your memory."

It was an interesting thought. Some place that felt more homey, maybe a place where we had created a lot of memories. "Feel free to share any ideas about where that might be, because I can't seem to think of any," I said sarcastically.

"I know just the place," Vincent smirked.

"Okay, where?"

"Oh no! I want this to be a surprise."

"Great," I sighed. "Another surprise. Feels like I've had quite a few of those over the past few days."

"I promise you Allison, you will know this place when you see it."

"Fine," I resigned. "How are we getting there?"

Vincent's brow creased. "What do you mean?"

"Well, you showed up on your motorcycle, and I probably shouldn't ride on the back of it with a head injury. My Jeep is totaled. So how are we getting to this mystery place?"

"Look in your garage," Vincent said with a smile. I studied his expression for a moment, hoping he would just tell me what I was going to find, but he offered up no clues. "Go on," he said with a wink.

I walked through the kitchen over to the door leading to the garage. When I opened the door and turned on the light, my jaw dropped in shock.

"You have *got* to be kidding me!" I exclaimed.

Sitting in the middle of my garage was my dream car, a canary yellow Corvette. Not only was it a Vette, but it was the ZR1 model, an extremely rare car capable of going over 200 miles per hour.

"This is a ZR1," I gasped.

"Yes it is," Vincent whispered in my ear as he snuck up behind me. "It's one of a kind, just like you." He wrapped his arms around my waist and the heat radiating from his body was very noticeable. I broke from his embrace.

"But how did I get my hands on this?" I asked, circling the car.

"Let's just say I have a few connections."

"You didn't buy this for me, did you?" This was way too generous of a present. I could never accept it, despite the fact that this was a car I had always dreamed of owning.

"No," Vincent chuckled. "You bought it. I just helped you find one. But I did convince you to upgrade to this model."

"Wait," I gasped. "I bought this?" I walked around the car again, staring at it in amazement. I was afraid that if I touched it, it might disappear.

Vincent nodded.

"But this car costs over $100,000!"

Vincent raised his eyebrows. He didn't have to say anything because his expression said it all. Of course I bought the car and of course he knew how much it cost. I apparently had enough money from Matt's settlement to not have to work and to buy a car that cost more than what most people make in a year. But I didn't really want to think or talk about all that now. I wanted to know what Vincent had in store for me. My newfound excitement over my car had me looking forward to a little adventure.

"So where are we going? What do I need to pack?"

"Grab some warm clothes," he responded with a sly grin. "And a bathing suit."

I packed my bags in five minutes flat. I had seriously upgraded my wardrobe in the past three years. I felt like I was going through a stranger's closet stocked with name brand and custom made cloth-ing. I couldn't help but slip into a pair of tight black jeans, a red sweater and tall black boots. I felt like a rock star. Vincent packed some things from a drawer in my dresser. According to him, we didn't live together but he did spend some nights at my place.

I rushed downstairs and into the garage. "You drive," I said, and Vincent jumped behind the wheel. I had no idea where we were going and the idea of driving didn't really appeal to me, even if it was a ZR1. The anticipation of what was to come was more than I could take; I was never one who liked to be in suspense for too long. Though only a few memories popped back in my mind, they were enough to let me know that Vincent and I were together, and when we hung out, it was always an adventure.

"So what kind of motorcycle do you have? I didn't recognize it."

Vincent grinned. He was casually in control of my Corvette with one hand draped over the steering wheel and the other on the shifter.

"It's an Agusta. It's a special production model."

"Hmmm," I mulled. "I've never heard of an Agusta and I thought I knew a thing or two about bikes. What makes it a special production model?"

Vincent's grin got larger. "It's a fairly rare bike, limited in production."

"Sounds expensive."

"It is."

"I bet it didn't cost as much as my car," I laughed.

Vincent chuckled as well. "Actually, more."

I stopped laughing and stared at Vincent's profile. *Are you kidding me*, I thought. I had never known anyone who could afford a motorcycle that expensive.

"Um, what is it again that you do for a living?" I asked. "I can't quite remember."

Vincent glanced at me, humor awash on his face. He seemed to enjoy the fact that I was learning all of this for the first time, even though it was technically the second time.

"I own my own medical supply company," he said.

"Oh," I responded.

We drove for a bit in silence. My car easily hugged every curve of the road as we eventually found the highway and headed north. Vincent sure had a lead foot. I looked over to see the speedometer somewhere over 100 miles per hour.

"Um," I cleared my throat. "I think you'd better watch your speed. You know…cops?"

Vincent let out a laugh. "They couldn't catch us in this car," he responded cockily.

"Okay, then can you slow down for me?" I asked more seriously. "I was just in a car accident."

Vincent turned his head towards me and studied my face. His eyes were so bright in the darkness and the gold flecks seemed to circle his pupils. I could have melted there, just staring into his eyes.

"I'm sorry," he said. "That was inconsiderate of me." He returned his eyes to road and reduced his speed.

We traveled to a two lane highway that ran up the coastline, passing highway signs with the names of the many islands that dotted the lake.

"I'm guessing we're going to an island?" I asked, breaking the silence.

"Yes, but which one?" Vincent playfully responded.

"Why don't you just save us some time and tell me," I joked back.

Vincent looked at me and examined my face. "Rattlesnake Island."

I paused again and couldn't help but stare at Vincent. This time, I wasn't in awe of his looks; I was shocked by our destination. "Are you kidding? And keep your eyes on the road." I gently pushed Vincent's face forward.

"No Allison, I'm not kidding. I have a place there."

"But isn't that the island that's like a private club?"

"It's not *like* a private club, it *is* a private club."

"Yeah, right, there're only so many members and you have to wait for someone to leave, which usually means you have to wait for someone to die, to even have a chance at getting in there?"

"That's right," Vincent responded coolly.

Rattlesnake Island was a mystery to everyone except those select few who were invited to be members. The island was owned by a group of unknown investors and only those investors, members and their guests were permitted on the island. Guests had to be approved in advance before setting foot on the island, and private security guards made sure of it. To become a member, you had to wait for someone to give up their membership and then be nominated by at least two current members, a nearly impossible feat since no one knew who the members were. It was a secretive club run by an elite group of people who had lots of money. The secrecy caused plenty of speculation as to what went on at the island.

"How did you get invited to be part of that?" I asked.

Vincent smirked again. "You know I can't talk about that."

"Yeah, but it was worth a try." I paused, thinking about the many rumored rules of the island. "So, am I able to get on the island?"

Vincent laughed again, though I didn't think the question was funny. "Of course, Allison. You have been fully vetted. They know who you are. You're allowed on the island with me."

The word *vetted* gave me the chills. I couldn't imagine who these people were and why they were so secretive or what, exactly, they knew about me. All would have been good questions, but I didn't bother asking any of them because I knew I wouldn't get any answers.

I looked down at the clock. It was eleven o'clock at night and we were headed for an island. Car ferries didn't run to Rattlesnake Island and it was too chilly for a boat ride, although my hot flesh would probably enjoy the reprieve.

"So how are we getting over to the island?"

As I asked, Vincent turned off the highway. A street sign indicated that Erie Island Airport was just five miles away.

"Never mind," I said. Vincent smiled. We were flying to Rattlesnake Island.

CHAPTER 6

I'd seen the Lake Erie shoreline from the air before, but not like this. The black sky wrapped around us and the yellow moon's hazy light created a magical feeling. Below, city lights twinkled like light bulbs on a switchboard. Downtown skyscrapers towered to the east and smoke from a power plant billowed to the west. And before us was the lake, its gentle ripples ebbing toward the shoreline. I'd seen snippets of this view from commercial airliners' tiny coach windows, but those views paled in comparison to the full view I had from the cockpit windows of Vincent's five-seater Maverick jet.

I was initially shocked when Vincent said he was piloting the plane but felt reassured once he showed me his license. We took off in silence and didn't say anything for some time. I was too petrified about distracting Vincent from flying the plane even though he assured me he had flown thousands of miles, some even with me, and could handle talking and flying at the same time. Nevertheless,

I opted for silence and his concentration. The view was enough to captivate me.

"Allison," Vincent's voice broke through my headset. I took my eyes off of the beautiful view only to have it replaced by another, his face. "Look there," he said, pointing straight ahead.

Off in the near distance, I could see the outline of an island bathed in the pale moonlight. It was a black mass planted in the middle of the shiny lake. A beacon of some sort lit the eastern tip but no other ground lighting was visible and no other islands were in sight.

"Is that it? Rattlesnake Island?"

"Yes. I'm going to circle it a few times to see if it helps you remember."

Vincent maneuvered the plane to the left, headed west, and then turned back to fly over the island. I stared down and all around but nothing in the black shadows below was jogging any memories. I looked over at Vincent, who was staring at me, and shook my head.

"Come here." Vincent waved me over in his direction and I leaned as far as the seatbelt would allow. "Do you see that?" His finger made a circular motion at the western most tip of the island.

"Yeah," I responded, not exactly sure what I was looking at.

"We've hiked there many times on the rocky cliffs." Vincent patted my leg with his hand. "Do you remember any of our hikes?"

I strained my eyes, trying to make out the terrain. The moonlight illuminated some of the rock but also casted long shadows. I could see some valleys and peaks and noticed that the rock spiraled upwards, giving the appearance of a rattlesnake's coiled tail.

"No, I don't remember our hikes, but I do remember this view."

I followed the line of the island down the rocky elevation and looked east. The land dipped sharply south then gracefully curved north where it jetted out into the lake, almost like a head. The lit beacon I noticed earlier sat just north of the edge, illuminated like an eye.

"It sure is aptly named, isn't it?" I said with a chuckle.

"I figured this view would spark something for you. Now let's get you on land and see what else you remember."

The lights on the landing strip weren't visible before but they were now. It was almost as though someone knew we were coming and had flipped on the light switch. Vincent landed the plane smoothly, and I wouldn't have expected anything less. After parking the plane, we made our way to a storage building and slipped inside in search of Vincent's car.

The building was long and narrow with a high domed ceiling lit only with dim security lights. Vincent grabbed my hand and walked purposely; he seemed to know exactly where he was going. My head turned from side to side as I looked around at all of the expensive cars parked on either side of the structure. The catalog of cars was quite impressive; every type of luxury and sport car imaginable was parked there. Cadillacs, Bentleys, Lincolns, even a Ferrari. I couldn't fathom being rich enough to be able to afford keeping cars like those on the island, and I wondered again who exactly belonged to this secretive club. Suddenly, something caught my attention out of the corner of my eye. Tucked away, between a red Audi and silver BMW was a black Harley Davidson motorcycle. I stopped dead in my tracks.

My sudden stop took Vincent off guard and our hands broke free. He turned and looked at me, then took a few steps closer.

"What is it, Allison?"

I stared at the bike for a few more seconds before answering as thoughts and memories raced through my head. The bike looked exactly like the one Matt had owned; the same one that he was on in the small picture frame at my house. Before turning my eyes away, I noticed a chrome decal on the side of the bike. It was a large chrome cap over the air filter, an aftermarket part, with a skull and crossbones punched into the metal. Matt had had the same cap on his bike. He had bought it the same day he got the bike because he said he thought it was cool. I shook my head again. *This is ridiculous*, I thought to myself. How many other people out there have the same bike, in black – the most popular color – with the same after market part? I couldn't let the sight of this bike, some stranger's bike, get into my head and ruin my getaway with Vincent.

"It's nothing. Let's go," I said, and tugged at Vincent's hand.

Vincent's eyes flickered between me and the bike, and for a split second his clear blue eyes seemed to turn black with a tinge of red. I wasn't sure if it was confusion, worry, concern or something else, but I definitely hadn't seen it before. It felt like something sinister, almost evil, had literally clouded over his beautiful blue eyes for the briefest of moments and then disappeared like the fall clouds floating over the moon. I shook my head again. The lighting wasn't good, and I was probably just imagining things.

"Come on," I said again.

Vincent turned on his heels and walked with a briskness his stride didn't have before. I hoped he couldn't tell that the bike reminded me of my dead husband. Matt was part of my past, and Vincent had to accept that, but I didn't want anything to ruin this trip. Especially after I already admitted to Vincent that I didn't remember him or call out for him in the hospital after my accident.

We climbed into Vincent's black Mercedes, and by this time I wasn't surprised that this was his island ride. After the Agusta, the private jet, the island and all the other cars I had seen, I would have been foolish to expect anything different.

The island's one main road ran down its center through a thick, dense forest of pines, maples and oaks. The foliage, still holding strong before giving way to the snow and biting cold of winter, drenched us in pure blackness, the car's headlights providing the only light. There were no visible road signs, street signs or other roads or driveways. I had no idea where we were going and I didn't want to ask. Vincent hadn't said a word since we left the garage. I wasn't sure if he was mad at me for my reaction to the motorcycle or if he was just tired. Vincent slowed the car as if to turn but where, I wasn't sure. All I could see were voluminous tree trunks and no road.

"Whoa, where are you going?" I asked. It appeared we were headed directly towards the thick woods. I didn't think this car could handle the rugged terrain and there was no visible sign of any path.

"To the cottage," Vincent simply replied.

I turned my attention back to the road and couldn't believe my eyes. The trees parted like a curtain being drawn at the start of a play, revealing a dirt path that I hadn't seen when Vincent had first turned the car. My jaw dropped as I looked out the rear window. A solid wall of trees stood behind us.

"Uh – what just happened?" I asked.

"What do you mean?"

"The trees. Did you see…I mean, I didn't see this path from the road."

"It comes up on you quickly, Allison. You have to pay attention or you'll pass it."

I looked out the rear window again. I had been paying attention to where Vincent was driving and hadn't noticed any other roads including this one. It had appeared out of nowhere. I rubbed my eyes. Trees couldn't move like that. I sat back and stared ahead. It had been a really long day and everything had to be catching up to me. I had obviously just missed seeing the path.

The path was a long, straight shot that gave way to a small clearing. Trees and vines littered the property with the exception of the clearing where the cottage rested. The headlights illuminated the front of the cottage. It was a one story, gray stone structure with a wooden wraparound porch. A swing for two and Adirondack chairs sat on the porch with tiny tables, enough to hold a few drinks. Smoke lazily drifted from the chimney and the lake could be heard lapping against the shore just beyond the house.

"Look familiar?" Vincent asked as he grabbed my hand to help me from the car.

"It does," I responded. "I think I remember this place." The cottage appeared in my vision earlier this evening when Vincent first tried to help me regain my memory.

"Well let's get you inside and see what else you remember."

We held hands as we walked up to the dark cottage. Vincent grabbed his keys and unlocked the door. An entry light came on.

"After you," he said and waved his arm across the threshold.

As I stepped forward, Vincent swept me off my feet.

"What's this all about?" I asked.

"I'm carrying you over the threshold. I did this the first time I brought you here but I'm guessing you don't remember."

I stared into Vincent's eyes as he said this and a memory slowly popped into my mind. It was of us, in a similar moment as this, but we were wearing different clothes and my hair was a different cut and color. It was clearly a different time.

"I actually do remember. It was Christmas when you brought me here for the first time, right?"

"Yes, Allison. It was Christmas last year." Vincent set me down and walked around turning on more lights. "I knew this place would help your memory."

I turned to view the rest of the house. The vaulted ceilings were filled with wood beams that crisscrossed the space. The kitchen, dinette, and living area were one giant room separated only by furniture and two bedrooms and a bathroom were off to the side.

Vincent placed a hand on my shoulder, a warm tingling sensation ran over my body. "Does this look familiar to you?" he whispered in my ear.

"Yes," I said with a smile, pleased and relieved more memories were coming back so quickly.

The memories started to flood my mind again, quickly flipping from scene to scene.

"We decorated a Christmas tree over there," I said, pointing across the room at the long window that framed the lake. "And the hot tub is on the porch, covered by the awning just out the door and to the left."

"That's right. What else?" Vincent encouraged.

"Um, stockings! You had them hung over the fireplace. And you had mistletoe hanging, well, hanging right here," I pointed up above me at the doorway where we were standing.

Vincent chuckled at my last recollection and spun me around. "And do you remember what I did when you spotted the mistletoe?"

I felt giddy, like a little school girl with her first crush. I had a pretty good idea what happened and couldn't wait for the replay.

"I don't remember," I coyly replied. "But I have a feeling you're going to remind me."

Vincent smiled and stepped towards me, wrapping his strong arms around my waist. I could feel the heat of his body against the blazing temperature of mine. I went weak in the knees with anticipation. Vincent stared into my eyes, and that crystal blue abyss was something I could get lost in very easily. The gold flecks were no longer dancing as I thought they had been earlier; rather, they were perfectly still. "Let's see if this brings back any memories," he whispered.

Vincent pressed his lips to mine. They were scorching hot, as I imagined mine were too. But they were soft and smooth and perfect, just like him. The kiss was delicate and sweet; it took everything I could do in my power not to throw my arms around his neck and throw all of my passion into this kiss. Vincent pulled his head away and I reached for another kiss but couldn't quite reach.

"I take it that sparked a memory," Vincent stated rather than asked.

"It sparked something," I responded.

Suddenly my mind was filled with various memories of the two of us from the past year. There were scenes of the two of us at my house, the place we left this evening because I said it didn't feel like home. I saw snippets of me in the garden, of Vincent cooking dinner, of the two of us watching the sunset and even driving around in my Corvette. There were other visions of us at this cottage. It appeared we frequented Rattlesnake Island and enjoyed the many perks the exclusive membership offered from private covered cabanas on the beach in the summer, to full access to a gourmet chef, to cruising around the lake on Vincent's boat, to staying up all hours of the night gazing at the stars and talking. I even had visions of us hiking on the cliffs we saw earlier this evening and swimming in the lake.

"I think this is working, Vincent."

"What's that?"

"You bringing me here. It's working; my memory is coming back."

"I knew this place would help you; you always loved it here."

"And why do I love it here so much?" I couldn't help but ask. Back at my house, Vincent had indicated this was a place I enjoyed and figured I would be more comfortable here.

Vincent paused. "You said it was a place for you to escape from it all. When you are here, you can forget your past and look forward to your future."

I let the words sink in. I guess I could see how this island was an escape. Very few people could get on it and there was nothing around but nature.

"Well it seems you know best. How can I ever thank you?"

"Oh I'm sure I'll think of something," Vincent toyed. "But for now, it's late; let's get you to bed."

I wasn't really tired, but Vincent was right; it was late and I should try to get some sleep. After all, I did have an exhausting day coming home from the hospital, learning that I had a new home and boyfriend and the trip to the cottage. Not to mention I was imagining moving trees.

I excused myself to the bathroom, dug through my bag and found a pair of black silk pajamas. I washed my face and stared at myself in the mirror. My reflection looked different to me but I couldn't quite pinpoint exactly what was different. The color of my hair seemed more vibrant as did the yellow flecks in my eyes. Then my mind turned to what could potentially happen next when I went back to the bedroom. Would Vincent let me sleep or would he try to bring back more memories – intimate ones? I had flashes of the two of us together like that but wasn't confident I was ready to relive that right now.

I walked back into the bedroom and Vincent was in bed, eyes closed, apparently already asleep. Guess I didn't have to worry about his intentions. It had probably been an exhausting day for him, too. I gently slid into bed so as not to wake him and turned out the light. It was twelve forty-seven in the morning.

I lay there for what felt like forever. I didn't want to roll around and risk waking Vincent so I stared at the ceiling and found shapes in the wood grain on the beams and hoped this mundane task would eventually knock me out. It didn't. On top of my sleeplessness, I was also burning up. I felt like a coal furnace pumping out intense heat. My silk pajamas were soaked and uncomfortable and I couldn't stand it any longer. I slid my legs over the side of the bed to remove the sweaty mess. I reached in my bag and found a cotton shirt that I slid on. I went back to the bed and looked at the clock. It was four seventeen in the morning. *Terrific*, I thought, *I'm never going to fall asleep.*

"Troubles sleeping?" Vincent called out, his bare back to me.

"Sorry, I didn't mean to wake you. I can't sleep."

"You didn't wake me," he said and rolled over. "I wasn't sleeping either."

"Really? You appeared out."

"No, I've been up since we went to bed, I think. I didn't want to toss and turn to find a comfortable spot and wake you."

"That's funny," I said, "because I was doing the same thing."

Vincent stretched out his arm towards my face. He gently grabbed it and pulled my head towards him.

"Oh," he cooed, "you're burning up."

"I know, right? But so are you," I whispered back. But unlike me, Vincent was just hot, not a sweaty mess. His hand was extremely hot against the side of my face. We lay there and stared at each other for several moments. Vincent seemed to study my face.

"What?" I asked, embarrassed by all of the attention.

Vincent sighed. "I was just thinking how odd it was that we both can't sleep and are burning up. But I suppose it's nothing, just a coincidence. Let's get some breakfast."

He was out of bed quicker than a blink of the eye and pulled a shirt over his bare chest, much to my dismay. He was quite the eye candy with perfectly chiseled abs and arms. I pulled on a pair of pants and a robe and followed him into the kitchen as I pondered Vincent's observation.

"Tea?" he asked.

"Yes please, but hold the breakfast."

"Tea but no breakfast?" Vincent questioned inquisitively.

"You heard me," I jokingly said.

"But you didn't eat dinner last night. You must be famished."

"Nope. I'm not hungry...for food at least."

Vincent stared just a bit longer, as if not believing what he heard. I almost couldn't believe I made the suggestive comment. "Okay," he resigned, and placed the eggs back in the refrigerator.

"What do you want to do today?" I asked.

"That, my dear, is up to you," Vincent said as he sat down across the table from me. He handed me a mug as he sipped his.

"Jog my memory; what is there to do on this island?"

"Well, we could go hiking, or take the boat out, but it's a bit chilly for that."

"No kidding," I interrupted. "The cold air might feel good on my hot skin now but I'll be freezing cold later!"

Vincent smirked and looked at the ground for a moment before returning his eyes to me.

"Yes, me too," he added.

I thought it was an odd comment since no one seemingly got as cold as I did during the daytime. "Or," he continued, "we can walk the cliffs, or..."

"Or what?" I asked.

"Or we can just stay in," he replied with a wink.

I gasped, not knowing how to respond. The proposition was tempting…staying holed up inside with this flawless person and do who knows what all day…but I wasn't quite ready for that. Though my memories were coming back and I felt comfortable around Vincent, I wasn't ready to go *there*, something inside me told me to wait.

"Um," I choked out, flustered. "How about hiking?"

"You sure about that?" Vincent asked with a raised eyebrow.

"Yes, why?"

"Just checking. We have to leave tomorrow so I want to make sure we do something you *really* want to do."

"Why do we have to leave tomorrow?" I quickly asked, ignoring his suggestive tone.

"Work. I left an important client when I came to see you after the accident." Vincent was uncharacteristically tense in his response.

"Oh, I see. Somebody more important than me?" I joked.

"No one is more important than you, Allison." Vincent's tone turned serious then softened a bit. "But it is something important nonetheless that I have to take care of."

"Okay, that's not a problem," I playfully toyed. "I get it. You have work to get done and can't spend all of your time entertaining me."

Vincent got up and walked behind me and wrapped me in an embrace. His touch was noticeably cooler than it had been when we first woke. "I would love to spend every waking minute with you and have you all to myself."

Vincent took me to his favorite spot in the woods on the east side of the island to watch the sunrise. This area was particularly dense with pine trees and shrubs that ever so slightly thinned as we neared the shore. It was apparent that Vincent knew the spot well as he walked directly to our destination without the assistance of a path.

"Here we are," Vincent said looking up the trunk of a tall pine. The tree looked like a staircase with branches spiraling from the base up into the sky.

"Here we are," I repeated looking around. The horizon was hidden by the landscape and didn't appear to be the best spot to see the sun rise.

Vincent chuckled at my sarcasm. "I'm telling you, this is the perfect place to watch the sunrise."

"I could see how it would be perfect...if only we could see the horizon."

Vincent laughed harder. "Oh Allison, come on," he beckoned as he leapt onto a branch, extending his hand to me.

I gawked at his hand. "You can't be serious?"

Vincent shook his hand towards me and nodded his head in encouragement.

"You want me," I paused in disbelief, "to climb a tree, to watch the sunrise?"

"Mmm hmm."

"Me? Clumsy little ole me?"

"Yes, Allison. Trust me, you can do this. And the view is worth it!"

I scoffed at the ground, not knowing what to say. Vincent was patiently waiting for me to grab his hand. He looked confident in what we were about to embark on, his chin strong, his eyes glowing with excitement.

"Well, all right. But if I break an arm, you have a lot of explaining to do to Jenna."

We both laughed as I grabbed Vincent's hand. He pulled me up to the branch he was standing on. His touch sent a tingling sensation over my cold skin.

"Just go slow," I pleaded.

"You don't give yourself enough credit, Allison. You can keep up."

Vincent bounded to a branch above us and then to another above that. I cautiously grabbed the next branch which looked like it could snap under my weight. I hoisted myself up and then grabbed the next branch and lifted myself onto it. Vincent peered down at me from his perch with an approving nod.

"I know you can move faster than that," he teased.

He then took off, appearing to hop about ten feet up vertically, but I knew that was impossible. His motion was fluid and graceful, quite the opposite of my guarded ascent. But I was up for a challenge. If he was going to showboat, then I was going to try to give him a good performance as well.

"All right smarty pants," I whispered.

I crouched on the branch and grabbed it with my hands, launching myself at the next branch. But instead of landing on the next branch, I landed next to a beaming Vincent. His smile stretched tightly across his face, his eyes almost beckoning me to follow him. Before I even had a chance to contemplate what I had just done, or figure out how I had done it, Vincent was gone. He moved up the tree at a steady pace and then disappeared from sight. I stared up the tree looking for any sign of him.

"You better hurry or you are going to miss the sunrise," he called.

I scoffed, again not knowing what to make of this situation but didn't think about it too long. I hunched down and sprang up a few branches, bouncing off of those to the next and then another. I felt like I was flying, like nothing could stop me.

"Hey, where you going?"

I stopped and looked around. Vincent was a few branches below me.

"You keep going to the top of this tree," he warned, "and you'll tip it."

"Oh," I sighed, perplexed about how I had just sprung up the tree so fast. "How did I pass you?"

"Must be the adrenaline," Vincent joked. "Come here."

He held out his hand and assisted me down to where he stood. A sense of calm and relaxation washed over me, and I chalked it up to the beautiful view. I looked out to the east over the treetops and spotted the horizon. The blue gray sky had a hint of purple and seemingly stretched on for miles. The lake was calm and smooth like a piece of polished glass. Seagulls drifted through the air. The slightest hint of yellow began to peek over the water's edge.

"This is amazing," I breathed.

We sat there and watched the sun slowly rise as if it were emerging from the water itself. The yellow tinge turned into a perfect half circle, then into a brilliant orange ball. It rose high into the gray autumn sky, casting its warmth over the lake. Birds gleefully danced through rays that slowly skimmed their way over the lake, reaching the island's shore. A welcoming warmth landed on us. It was a brisk, cool morning and the sun's heat felt good against my cold skin. I closed my eyes and inhaled deeply, taking in the moment. What a perfect way to start off the day. I looked over at Vincent.

"What's wrong?" I asked. The side of his face was covered in a rash.

"Oh, just a little sensitivity to the sun, you know. It makes my blood boil."

I noticed my neck had started to burn like it had yesterday when Jenna drove me home from the hospital. I rubbed and scratched at it hoping for relief but it only made it worse. "I know what you mean," I responded.

"Let's go," Vincent said.

"Yeah, before we both get sunburns!"

Vincent chortled, "Yeah, something like that."

It was an ideal day to hike the woods on Rattlesnake Island. The gray sky was frosted over with a thin layer of clouds that shielded our sensitive skin from the sun. The temperature was cool, typical for this time of year, with a chilly breeze blowing in over the lake.

Vincent and I talked about everything; it was like meeting him for the first time. In fact, he told me so much about me that if felt like I was meeting *me* for the first time. We talked again about how we met and several of our dates thereafter. Vincent had flown us to New York on our first date to see a Broadway play. I learned more about Vincent's medical supply business. He was a very hands-on business owner traveling all over the world to meet personally with his clients. He explained that when he was gone, I frequented the coffee shop where we had met. It was there that I sat curled up on the couch by the fire reading. He also insisted that I did take up gardening to help pass the time, and my yard was living proof of that.

We talked about family; me being an only child, he having four siblings. Both of our parents were deceased and family was very important to us both. Vincent was close with his siblings, three brothers and one sister. They were so close that the siblings joined Vincent in his business. I asked if I had met his siblings in the past year but Vincent explained that they lived all over the world supporting the family business and I hadn't met them yet. I commented how close I used to be with Matt's family, since I didn't have any siblings. Vincent didn't seem to mind that I brought up Matt's name. In fact, we talked about Matt, at least what I could remember. However, Vincent was already aware of most of what I told him...how Matt and I met, when we got married, where we lived in Buzzard Hill. Of course I didn't remember sharing any of this as these memories were buried somewhere in my mind, blocked by the impact of my accident. Vincent was even able to fill in a few details for me, mostly around Matt's accident.

It really was a good day and I felt like I had made a lot of progress. Sporadic memories popped into my head, even some of the phone calls that Jenna and I shared over the past few years. Quite a few memories came to mind of my recent travels with Vincent; he had apparently turned me into quite the world traveler. Together we had visited Paris, Rome, Egypt and New Zealand. It appeared I had assumed a bit of a fairy tale lifestyle over the past year.

It was all starting to come together, and much more quickly than I had ever thought possible. I loved what I was learning about this life I could not remember. I was still sad when I thought about Matt's passing, but the more I talked about it and the more my memory came back, I felt that time had healed my wounds and that I had moved on. I would always keep Matt in my heart; he was my one true love, but I had to move on with my life and I couldn't think of anyone more perfect to do that with than Vincent.

We arrived back at the cottage as the sun was setting and were greeted with a dinner table set for two complete with candles and chilled champagne.

"How did you manage this?" I asked.

"The island's personal chef. I called him before we ran out this morning. I hope you're hungry."

I wasn't hungry at all, though I couldn't remember the last time I had eaten. I thought that I should probably eat something so Vincent didn't worry about me.

"It smells delicious," I said as Vincent pulled out my chair. He grabbed the champagne and poured me a glass but returned the bottle to the chiller before pouring his glass.

"Aren't you having anything to drink?"

"I am," he responded. He opened the wine refrigerator. "But not champagne."

Vincent pulled out a dark green corked bottle with a label I vaguely recognized. It was a black label with a crimson red diamond created out of curved flowing lines and some sort of crest in the center.

"Red wine?" I asked.

Vincent smirked and let out a little chuckle. I wasn't sure what was so funny about my question.

"Yes," he responded.

"Can I have some?" I would much rather drink wine than champagne.

"Allison, please. That's a $750 bottle of champagne I just opened for you. You can't let that go to waste."

I didn't think I was much of a champagne drinker and I certainly had no idea I had acquired a taste for such expensive champagne. But Vincent's comment made me feel silly and ungrateful and apparently this came through in my expression.

"Besides, you don't like this *wine*," Vincent stated, apparently trying to make me feel better. "It requires a...well, let's just say an acquired taste."

We dined on filet mignon and perch which was fresh from the lake. I didn't have much of an appetite and picked at my food. It appeared Vincent didn't have much of an appetite either as he barely ate anything off of his dish. He was quite thirsty, though, finishing off four glasses of wine. Somehow, the alcohol didn't have any effect on him, but then again, the champagne wasn't really affecting me either. After dinner we enjoyed a dip in the hot tub with more wine and champagne. Our conversation continued to flow freely, mostly Vincent telling me about our escapades and me chiming in when a memory popped in my mind. We concluded the conversation with things we still wanted to do with our lives.

"I want to travel more," I said.

"And where would you like to visit, Allison?"

"Seeing as I don't remember Paris, Rome, Egypt or New Zealand, I would like to revisit those places. But I would also like to go to Australia. And Russia. Oh, and a trip to the Arctic Circle might be fun!"

"All of these things are possible," Vincent said.

"Really?"

"Really."

"Well what about you? What do you want to do in life?"

"What do I want to do in *life?*" Vincent's voice faded on the last word he spoke as if contemplating the meaning of it. "All I want is to spend every waking day and sleepless night with you, no matter where it is."

I stared at Vincent, taking in his comment. How did I deserve this man, this life? He was so perfect – handsome, mannered, a hard worker and he apparently wanted to spoil me. I couldn't understand how someone like him would want to be with someone like me. Not that I didn't think I was deserving; after all I had been through I definitely deserved happiness! But it was like we were cut from different cloths. He was a world traveler; before meeting him, I had never ventured beyond the Caribbean. He was a very rich business owner; I had means but only due to my tragic past. We had so many similarities yet we were still so different. I had no idea how our social circles ever crossed.

"Come on, let's get to bed. We have to leave early in the morning."

• • •

I was actually tired and the comfort of the bed was welcoming. Vincent tucked me in and gave me a gentle kiss, ever the gentleman, returning to the living room to log on to his computer to get some work done. I lay there for only a few minutes, once again making shapes out of the wood grain, before I fell asleep.

The dream is back, but it isn't the beautiful garden I had previously dreamt about. No, this forest is different. It is dark and cold and not welcoming at all. The air smells putrid; it is rank and vile and sour...everything I would imagine death to smell like if death had a scent. The trees are barren, the brown leaves matted against the ground. Only twisted, contorted branches fill the space above me, stretching out into the black, starless sky. There is no color here; the landscape is drab in various shades of black, brown and gray. There's no sign of life.

I look around, not knowing where I am or where I am supposed to go. And then, a pain in my stomach knocks me to my knees. It is a burning sensation like nothing I have ever felt before, as if someone has set fire to my stomach and a burning fireball is rotating within me. I let out a howl, hoping the pain will subside, but it only gets worse. The fiery pit throws out sharp pangs as if trying to claw its way out of me. I throw both clenched fists into my stomach in an attempt to detract from the pain to no avail. The fiery rays climb their way up my throat, leaving behind a scorching trail of pain before it settles in the back of my throat. The heat dries my mouth and gives me a thirst like nothing I have ever experienced. The pain is unbearable. I open my mouth to yell but nothing comes out.

I reach a hand up to my face and instinctively feel my skin. It's rough and wrinkled and my cheeks are sunken. I pull my hand back and my fingers curl, yellow raggedy fingernails springing from the tips. I dig my elbows into the ground and pull my body over the rough surface towards a puddle. I hoist myself up as I near the edge so I can use the water as a mirror. I stare at the person looking at me in the puddle. *That's not me,* I think.

It is an old lady, but not just old, something is wrong with her. Her skin isn't that of an old person, it is more like that of a mummified body, hardened and aged in color. Her hair is short, like mine, but a gray mess which is falling out in patches. Her eyes are devoid of all color, black pits with tiny yellow specks that revolve in a circular motion. I pull a hand closer to the water and dip a finger. The reflection does the same. I jerk back and grunt before easing myself back over the pool of liquid. I cock my head; the reflection does the same. I reach a hand to my face and pull at my cracked lips. I stick a finger in my mouth and cut it on something sharp. I grunt again and pull myself to my knees so I can push my face closer to the makeshift mirror. I slowly curl my lips back and two sharp dagger-like eyeteeth emerge. The fireball in my pit throws another burst of flames up my throat. I throw my head back in pain and wither on the ground.

I hear something which sounds like a voice. It is faint at first and seems to quell the burning flames inside of me. The voice is soft and smooth and floats through the air filling my ears. It is calling my name.

"Allison………..Allison."

The sound is enchanting and intriguing but I don't know where it's coming from. It calls my name again so I stand and walk in a circle looking for the source. I settle on a direction and start walking, the voice leading my way. I walk several paces before the voice stops me at the trunk of an enormous oak tree.

"Ah, Allison," the voice calls out from behind me.

I slowly turn to see the source of my guiding voice but all I can see is a black figure with glowing eyes hidden in the shadows of this sterile forest.

"You are not well, are you?" it asks me. I shake my head.

"Do you know what will make you feel better?"

I shake my head again, my eyes fixated on the two shimmering blue specks cloaked in darkness.

"I know what will make you feel better. Do you want to see?"

Another burst of fire bellows up my throat, singeing my mouth. I quickly nod my head in affirmation; anything to suppress this burning in my pit.

"Follow me," the voice says from the darkness, outstretching a pale hand for me.

I walk forward and grab the hand and feel instant relief, like the flames have been extinguished. The stranger pulls me forward, pressing his body into mine, his face now visible. The man oddly resembles Vincent yet looks nothing like him. He has the same strong jaw line and the same dark hair, but his complexion is lifeless and his eyes black, like the ones I saw in the puddle, gold specks recklessly spinning at a frantic pace.

"Do you trust me?" the man asks.

I don't know why, but I feel I can trust this man and nod my head. The scene changes in a flash. We are still in the forest, darkness all around, but beyond the forest's edge, there is sunlight, music and laughter. It's a party. Where we sit, the forest is still barren, but on the outskirts the trees are filled with green leaves and swags of red material interlaced through the branches.

I'm sitting on a couch beneath the barren trees, the partygoers out of sight but still within hearing distance. The Vincent lookalike sits on the other end of the white L-shaped couch, a woman swooning in his embrace. She has her head buried in his neck but he does not appear interested. I am not alone either. A man sits behind me, his arms wrapped around me as he nuzzles my neck.

But my eyes never leave the man that brought me here. I see my morbid, mummified reflection in his eyes.

"You know what to do," he whispers to me, our guests oblivious to his words.

I don't quite understand what he means. What am I supposed to do? A flame flickers in my stomach and I turn to look at my suitor. My reflection in this stranger's eyes paints a different picture. I am beautiful with porcelain skin and vibrant blue eyes. Gone is the dead, decaying flesh and gray hair. There is a glimmer in this man's eye; he is happy to see my sudden interest. And I am interested too. I want him but in a way I never felt before, in a way I do not quite understand. I am not physically attracted to this man; rather, I am hungry for him. The thought of him calms the beast that roars in my core. I look back at Vincent who nods at me in encouragement.

"Do it," he hisses.

As he says these words, he curls back his lips revealing a set of sharp dagger-like teeth that emerge from his gums. I watch calmly, like I know what he is going to do, like I should expect it. He sinks his teeth into the woman's neck and she seems to notice nothing as she falls backwards, panting in the heat of the moment. The fool has no idea she is dying. I turn and look at my would-be victim as he inches his face closer to mine. The boiling cauldron in my stomach bubbles over in anticipation. I feel my fangs emerge and my mouth fills with venom. My prey leans in for something he doesn't know is coming. My teeth penetrate his flesh and his warm blood trickles down my throat, cooling the burning sensation. The satisfaction is overwhelming; the more I drink, the more I want. I press my mouth harder against his neck trying to capture every last drop to satisfy the evil within me. The man does not realize what is happening to him. I feast until there is nothing left, finally feeling fully satisfied, the fire in my pit extinguished. I toss the body aside like an unwanted newspaper. I look over at Vincent, who looks different. His cheeks are full and his color is back. The reflection in his eyes reveals color flooding back to my skin in place of the petrified flesh that was there before. My nails retreat and I feel blood rush to my face. I am strong and satiated. I am what I should be.

I woke screaming, Vincent already by my side.

"Allison, what's wrong? What is it?"

I sat up panting, trying to catch my breath. I was sweating bullets but that wasn't too odd these days.

"Nightmare," I gasped.

"It's okay," Vincent stated, wrapping his arm around me as he sat on the bed. "Do you want to talk about it?"

"No, it was just a meaningless nightmare."

I couldn't tell Vincent about this dream. It felt so real, like we were both actually there witnessing and performing those heinous acts. I didn't know what was more disturbing, the fact that Vincent, in my dream, seemed to know what we both were or my feeling at the end of the dream. What I did felt right. It felt like second nature. I didn't feel remorseful about what I had done; I felt good and full of life as my body returned to its normal appearance. This just wasn't right.

"Well maybe some breakfast will make you feel better."

"No," I sternly responded, "I just want to go home."

CHAPTER 7

ure relief. That's what I felt when I was finally back on the mainland. After waking from my nightmare, I took a long, hot shower, quickly dressed and packed my bags even more quickly. I wanted to get off of Rattlesnake Island, and fast. But Vincent apparently had other plans. He insisted he needed to finish work but the only thing he accomplished was annoying me to no end. He kept probing for information about my nightmare even though I told him sternly more than once I had no desire to talk about it. I had to take myself outside for him to get the picture that I was mute on the subject. Vincent seemingly dragged his feet all day until we departed in the late afternoon.

I sensed that Vincent could tell something was bothering me. Not that this was difficult to figure out; I had barely said a word since leaving the cottage. I just couldn't shake the nightmare because it was incredibly disturbing on so many levels. I had always believed that dreams were the mind's way of jumbling a bunch of real memories together and regurgitating them in a different way, but this dream was no jumbled mess of memories. I couldn't imagine how my mind could conjure up such a disturbing scene of us as vampires in a forest with two unsuspecting victims. Even worse was how real the vision had felt; the pain in my stomach, the hardened skin on my face, and the overwhelming feeling of satisfaction and fullness when I drank the man's blood. I shuddered at the thought. The dream felt so lifelike it was threatening, and that kept me from talking about it. I had no idea how to explain it all to Vincent. It was unfathomable to me how my mind could present something so horrendous.

I stared out the passenger window of the Corvette hoping the passing scenery would erase the appalling images and feelings. It was early evening and the sun was setting against a sky rich in shades of gray and purple. The steady stream of rain seemed to be subsiding and raindrops glistened on the baring tree branches. On a normal day, the scene would be quite tranquil, but today it wasn't enough to expunge the ugliness trapped in my mind.

"Are you sure you don't want to talk about your dream?" Vincent insisted.

"Yeah, I'm sure."

"You know, sometimes talking about it helps." Vincent threw me a reassuring glance.

I sighed heavily, realizing he just wasn't going to give up. And unlike the cottage, where I could go outside and avoid Vincent, I was trapped here in the car. I had no escape, at least not until we got back to my house. And if his antics at the cottage were any indication, he was going to badger me all the way home.

"It was just a disturbing dream that I don't know how to explain."

"Well why don't you tell me and maybe I can help figure it out with you."

I rolled my eyes. "Why do you want to know so badly?"

"I don't like to see you like this. You aren't yourself. I think if you talked about it, you would discover what the dream was trying to tell you."

"Kind of like a hidden message?"

"Something like that."

It was a good point, but Vincent hadn't a clue about what I had seen and felt last night. There was no way this dream had any kind of hidden message.

"Fine, but I'm warning you, it's a weird one." I smiled at Vincent and he returned the gesture.

"I'm all ears."

"Well, we were both in the dream," I started.

"And you consider that a nightmare?" Vincent joked.

I smirked and continued. "We were in this strange place. It was a forest of sorts. It was dark and colorless, lifeless for that matter. The trees were gray and leafless and blended into the black sky and the place smelled terrible. Anyway, I was there and in tremendous pain. It was the worst stomachache I've ever experienced times a thousand. It was this awful burning that churned in my stomach. On top of that, I looked horrible, like a mummified monster. My skin was hard and discolored and my hair was falling out. I heard what I thought was your voice calling me so I followed it and found you. Only you didn't look like you. You looked ill too, but not mummified like me. You looked malnourished, I guess. You took my hand and the scene changed to where you and I were sitting on a couch with two strangers, a man and a woman, who were clearly unaware of the danger around them."

"Danger? Because you weren't feeling well and looked awful?" Vincent teased.

"Yes, danger," I replied, ignoring his attempt at a joke. "You, uh, went first and then I followed."

"I don't quite follow you."

"You, um – bit the woman," I said, discomfort clearly apparent in my voice.

"I bit the woman?" Vincent asked with a raised eyebrow.

"Yes. Like a vampire," I confessed before rushing into the rest of my explanation. "But then I bit the man and it was horrible. I cast him aside like he meant nothing but I felt great about what I had just done, like I was reborn. I felt better physically, and my appearance changed back to normal. It felt so real and so right. It was quite disturbing."

There was a long pause as I stared straight ahead through the wet windshield. I was afraid to look over and see Vincent's reaction. I could tell by the peaks and valleys in the road that we were getting closer to my house. That was a good thing. After my ridiculous revelation, I was planning to lock myself in my room and duck my head under the covers and hide myself from Vincent. He had to think I was a complete lunatic after hearing my dream.

"Hmm," Vincent purred from the driver's seat as he downshifted around a corner.

"Excuse me?"

"Huh? What?" Vincent asked. He apparently was deep in thought over something.

"What are you mulling over?" I couldn't possibly believe he could be thinking that hard about my ghastly dream. There was no way to interpret it, to make sense of it. It was just a bunch of nonsensical stuff.

"Your dream," Vincent responded matter-of-factly.

"First, it was a nightmare. And second, what could be so interesting? It means nothing!"

"If it means nothing, then why do you suppose it bothers you so much?"

I threw myself back into my seat. "Because it was disturbing on so many levels." I paused. "Yet it felt so real."

Vincent was quiet as we rounded another corner. He looked like he was thinking about something again.

"What?" I asked. I was getting irritated that he was making so much out of nothing at all.

"It's nothing."

"Oh no, come on…what is it? You made me tell you my ridiculous nightmare; you can surely tell me what you are thinking." I couldn't wait to hear his interpretation of my horrific dream.

"Okay," Vincent said, turning his head to look at me. "What if it's true?" He narrowed his eyes as he asked the question with intense sincerity.

"What if what's true?"

"Your dream, of course." Vincent was serious and wasn't giving any signs that he was joking.

"Oh come on! You can't be serious?"

"But I am. What if we are vampires?"

His comment was so absurd I almost didn't respond. "I'd have to say you need to get your head examined. There's no such thing as vampires."

"Have you ever thought about it?"

"Thought about what? Being a vampire?"

"Yes."

"Yeah, that's something I think about all the time. Come on Vincent, knock it off. Are we really having this discussion? Vampires aren't real."

Vincent chuckled softly as he turned into my driveway.

"Oh, but they are my dear."

I couldn't believe what I was hearing, the nonsense that was coming out of Vincent's mouth. He had to be pulling my leg, but he had one heck of a poker face going on. Vampires? The thought was beyond ludicrous.

"What are you looking for?" Vincent asked.

I pushed my face closer to the passenger window, pretending to look for something. "A full moon. That's the only explanation for your wacky behavior right now."

"There's nothing wacky, as you say, about my behavior. Allison, have you ever really paid attention to the world around you? Vampires do exist."

I had had about enough of this garbage. We had spent a couple of wonderful days together, and now he was pulling this weirdo act on me. I couldn't imagine why he would be doing this to me, especially now. I felt like my life was finally falling back into place after my accident and now I was going to find out that my companion was off his rocker.

Vincent parked the car in the garage and I immediately jumped out and grabbed my bag out of the back. I snatched the keys from his grasp and hurriedly unlocked the house door, flinging my bag inside.

"What's wrong, Allison?" Vincent called after me.

"Seriously? Get out of my house!" I shouted at Vincent as I stormed into the kitchen.

What's wrong, I thought! He couldn't be serious. He wanted me to consider that vampires actually existed and he had the nerve to ask me what was *wrong*?

"Please consider it," Vincent stated.

"Excuse me?" I stopped in my tracks and twirled around.

"Just let me explain," Vincent calmly beseeched in his smooth voice as he followed me into the kitchen.

"Explain what?" I felt a rush of blood go straight to my face as anger swelled inside of me. "You expect me to believe that *you* are a vampire? That *I* am a vampire? Do you know how ridiculous that sounds? Vampires…do…not…exist!" I snarled each word individually, my nostrils flaring. "Why are you doing this to me? Why now? I was starting to feel normal again, to understand my life and everything that has happened over the past three years and you spring this absurd consideration on me?" I broke down in sobs.

Vincent ignored my questions and spoke in a calm voice. "The dreams you have been having, they are trying to tell you something."

I paused and took a few short shallow breaths. "How do you know what I dream about?" I asked coldly.

"Look at me," he gently commanded in a soft voice as he grabbed my arm and pulled me close to him.

"Look at me, Allison." Vincent placed a scorching finger under my chin and lifted my head to meet his gaze. His touch was much hotter than it had been earlier. He placed his other arm around my waist. "This is what you dream about."

Suddenly, the dream flashed before me in broken segments, but I could make out enough to realize that it was indeed my dream, the one I craved each night when I went to bed. There was the garden with all of the tropical flowers, the canopy of trees and the animals roaming freely. Then the scene fluttered and I saw the stream and a bridge. The vision flickered again and I was floating over flat lands and valleys filled with tall grasses. Then the tree appeared, with its glittering fruit swaying in the breeze, throwing off prisms of color. The final scene showed the stranger biting the fruit and the serpent attacking the man.

I gasped as I pulled away from Vincent. "What in the hell…" I stared in disbelief, my breathing labored. *How did I just see that,* I thought. I searched Vincent's face for an answer but didn't find it. He just stared into my eyes, waiting for my reaction.

"If you won't leave my house, then I will!" I exclaimed.

I grabbed the first set of keys my hands came upon in the drawer and charged out the door into the garage. I rolled my eyes as I realized I grabbed my motorcycle key. I guessed I was going for a ride in the wet elements. I threw my leg over the motorcycle and stuck the key in the ignition. I had no idea where I was going, but I needed to get away from Vincent, whoever he was. Or whatever he was.

"Allison, where are you going?" Vincent yelled over the roar of my engine.

I threw on a pair of clear riding glasses but didn't bother putting my helmet on; I just needed to get away. Fast.

I laid a patch on the garage floor, spinning the bike towards the door and released the clutch. I was out of the garage on my way to nowhere very fast. I didn't even stop at the end of the driveway to see if traffic was coming as I turned onto the country road. Anger burned inside of me. Vincent had to be out of his mind. How dare he tell me such nonsense and expect me to believe it.

My entire being was so consumed with anger that I didn't even realize how easily I was navigating the twisting, wet road ways. The ground, still moist from the earlier rain, was way too treacherous for a motorcycle. Yet I leaned into each turn, my motorcycle hugging the wet pavement as if the riding conditions were ideal. I broke to the right and to the left and then up a hill and found a straightaway. I pulled in the clutch, shifted into fifth gear and opened the throttle. The cool, damp air felt pleasant on my skin which was starting to burn, probably from the anger and contempt I now felt for Vincent. The faster I rode, the less I thought of him. It was as if the wind against my face removed any thought of him.

A severe right turn approached and I down shifted, still taking the turn with too much speed, but easily rolled through it.

Lights in my side mirrors caught my attention. I looked down at my speedometer. I was doing 85 in a 55 mile per hour zone. *Better slow down,* I thought; *could be a cop.* The light drew closer and I realized there was only one headlight – a motorcycle headlight. It was late in the evening, and there was only one other person who would be out in the dark, in the middle of nowhere and in the rain on a motorcycle. Vincent.

Anger swelled in me again so I sped up. I saw a sign in the far distance that I easily read. It said 'Whipps Ledges.' In the summer months, Whipps Ledges was a favorite spot for many locals. It was a forested park filled with caves and cliffs that attracted hikers, rock climbers, nature lovers and the occasional group of high school kids looking for a spot to smoke some pot. But no one would be there at this time of night or at this time of year. It would be much too dangerous to try to navigate the rocky terrain in the rain and dark.

I sped to the sign, down shifted and took a hard left into the parking lot. I shifted my bike into neutral, pocketed my key and took off for the woods.

I again didn't think about what I was doing. It was pitch black and I was entering the woods, a place that frightened me enough during the daylight, let alone this time of night. And a lunatic, who claimed that both he and I were vampires, was on my tail. Leading him into the woods probably wasn't the brightest idea.

I quickly ascended the wooden stairs built into the earth. The staircase turned into a dirt path that I somehow climbed without much difficulty and without winding myself. The path led to a tall wall of conglomerate rock carved by glaciers millions of years earlier. The whole wooded park was full of rock ledges and outcroppings of the same stone, hence the park's name. I paused and pushed my hot body against the cool, moist wall. It was a welcome relief against my searing flesh. I listened but couldn't hear anyone behind me. Maybe Vincent didn't see me turn off the road. Or maybe he was waiting for me in the parking lot.

I kept climbing up the path which eventually turned into smooth stone surrounded by crevices cut deep into the earth and rock formations protruding toward the sky. I effortlessly leapt over a wide crevice, walked a few feet and found a clearing in the trees. The moon shone brightly above, not quite full. The sky was dark with scattered rain clouds looming low. Stars dotted the clear patches of sky.

I sat down and let my mind wander. I couldn't understand why Vincent would make such a statement, why he would claim to be a vampire and tell me I was one too. He had to be nuts. That was the only explanation. Then again, over the past few days, he had been trying to point out similarities between the two of us. Was it just coincidence that we were both cold during the day and boiling hot at night? He was much colder and hotter than me though, so what did that mean? Surely it was a coincidence how pale we both were. We lived in Ohio after all, not the sunniest of locations. And considering the weather this summer, it was near impossible for anyone to catch any sun. There were also the strange sleeping habits, but we weren't the only two in this world with insomnia. And why would he do this to me now, so soon after my accident? My life was starting to feel normal again and I was falling back into my life and my memory was returning. Why would he want to disrupt that with such an offhanded story?

My mind drifted, and drifted, and drifted until I thought of nothing at all. I lay on the cool stone, hands behind my head and lost track of time as I stared at the craters in the moon.

"Allison," I heard Vincent whisper from the dark. My body stiffened. Maybe if I didn't move or say anything, he would go away.

Moments passed, and then I heard, "I can see you."

I tried looking around without moving my head. Maybe he would think I was asleep.

"I know you are awake."

"Lucky guess since I don't sleep much these days," I responded sarcastically.

Vincent emerged, his blue silvery eyes beacons against the darkness. His eyes reminded me of fire flies that fill the air of summer nights.

"Allison, let me explain please. Let me tell you your story."

"My story?" I sat up. "You talk as if you have known me my whole life."

"I have," he replied. "And I knew your mother Mary, her mother Camille, your great grandfather Peter, his mother Eleanor, her father Cyrus…"

"Great, so you did a little digging on my family history. What's your point?" I snapped.

"I know them because my brothers and sister have watched them, and the rest of your lineage for…well, let's just say a very long time." His voice was calm and smooth, his eyes steady.

"I have had enough of your bull!" I shouted and stood up. "What do you want from me?"

"I don't want anything from you. But you do need me. Do you want to know what your dream means or how it ends?" Vincent's eyes glowed as he slowly approached me. He appeared quite confident and the cockiness rubbed me the wrong way.

"Oh, yes, please clue me in on what my dreams are trying to tell me," I sarcastically responded, flailing an arm in the air.

"Allison, please sit down and I'll tell you the rest of the story."

Though it was dark outside, I could see all of Vincent's features in perfect clarity. His high cheekbones were illuminated by the moonlight; his clear blue eyes glowed like gemstones, the glints of gold slowly dancing in circles around his pupils and his lips rosy red against the pale canvas of his skin. As much as I wanted to, I just couldn't resist him right now.

Vincent held my arms as I slowly descended to the ground. "You feel quite feverish," he whispered as he knelt next to me. "Are you feeling well?"

"I'm fine," I muttered. "Tell me what you think you know about my dreams."

"What do you recall from your dreams," Vincent asked.

"You tell me; apparently you already know what I dream about."

"True." He paused. "Then tell me what you know about vampires."

I huffed. "Well, let's see, Vincent. Vampires are mythical creatures that don't exist in reality," I said, staring straight into his eyes. "They prey on humans to sustain themselves and don't like garlic, holy water, stakes through the heart, sunlight or holy ground. Did I miss anything?"

Vincent chuckled, a low growl billowing in his chest. "I see you've watched one too many vampire movies; your facts are all wrong."

"Yeah, well enlighten me, please," I responded flatly.

"Let's try this. What do you know about how the vampire came to be; how the first vampire was created?" Vincent asked as he looked sternly into my eyes. He was serious.

I mockingly placed my index finger on my chin and looked up in the air. "Hmm, let me see…I got nothing. Apparently Hollywood hasn't covered that topic."

"Hmm," Vincent hummed as he looked my face over with amusement. He was so beautiful in the pale moonlight. "I'll just start at the beginning. Do you know where you are in your dream?"

"No."

"Any idea?" His face hovered close to mine and a rush of desire ran over me, but I restrained myself. I couldn't figure out what it was that drew me to him. I had to turn my head and look away from his captivating eyes. "The perfect garden, filled with every type of vegetation possible. Every animal exists there in peace." He whispered the words close to my neck, sending a chill over my otherwise blazing hot skin. Vincent studied my face, looking for a sign that I had some inkling that I knew what he was talking about.

"I haven't the faintest idea," I whispered, "but can you please get to the point?" I stated with slight irritation hoping he would back away. It didn't work.

"Ever hear of the Garden of Eden?" He was still searching my face, still breathing on my neck.

I turned to face him. "Of course I have. Twelve years of Catholic school will teach you a thing or two about the Bible," I snipped. "Are you trying to tell me that I'm dreaming about the Garden of Eden? The place doesn't exist." I scooted away, attempting to put some distance between us.

"Actually, it did. But the Bible doesn't tell you that; it allows you to believe it is a contrived place, created to illustrate the point of man's original sin. There are other things that have been left out of the Bible as well."

"Oh yeah? Like what?"

"Well, since your education versed you so well on the book of Genesis," Vincent smirked and moved closer, "I'll just give you some of the highlights. You know the story of Adam and Eve and how they ate fruit from the Tree of Knowledge of Good and Evil, which the Lord forbade them from doing, right?"

"Yes, of course. The Lord came down and kicked Adam and Eve out of the garden."

"That's right," Vincent said. "When doing that, the Lord also damned the serpent that had tempted Eve. Do you recall what that damnation entailed?"

I strained my mind, but the details weren't there. "No, I don't remember that much."

"So much for that pricey Catholic education." He was obviously amused. This was fun for him. "The Lord damned the serpent to a miserable life on earth and placed a permanent rift between it and man so that the serpent could never use its persuasion over mankind again."

"Yeah, that sounds familiar," I said, still trying to recall my days of Bible study.

"Adam and Eve forfeited eternal life, for themselves and all of mankind, and were forced to toil in the field for survival. In this new *home*," he dwelled on the word, "they had two sons."

"Yeah, yeah – Cain and Abel."

"And do you know their story?" Vincent asked, raising an eyebrow, clearly pleased I recalled their names.

"Cain was jealous of the success Abel was enjoying in his labors and the praise he received from the Lord and Cain killed Abel. But this is all written in the Bible."

"You are right on both points. But the story omitted from the Bible is what Cain did next," Vincent snarled close to my ear.

My curiosity peaked. I shifted my body to face Vincent.

"Cain was so wrought with guilt over killing his brother that he didn't know what to do. He asked the Lord and his family for forgiveness, and it was granted, but he couldn't forgive himself.

He did not know how to live with himself for what he had done and yet he didn't have the courage to end his own life. He could not inflict that additional grief upon his mother, father and wife. So Cain decided to leave, to wander, to try to clear his mind. He wasn't sure where he was going or what he was looking for, he just needed some time away.

"Cain wandered until he came upon a garden…you know the one. He had never seen this place before, but he felt drawn to it. He entered the tropical paradise and felt peace; he felt at *home*, like he belonged there. Do you ever have that feeling when you dream of this place?"

I absentmindedly nodded my head. I longed to dream of this garden because of the sense of calm and tranquility it bestowed upon me, for the sense of contentment I felt after exploring this paradise.

"I thought so. Cain spent time just wandering through the garden, smelling the flowers, listening to the birds, watching the animals, until he was drawn forward by…"

"The sound of water," I murmured.

"Yes. The sound of the water drew Cain forward until he reached a clearing. You know what he saw then, don't you?"

It was apparent Vincent enjoyed telling this story. Or maybe he was enjoying the attention I was now giving him. Either way, the thrill seemed to illuminate his eyes even more.

"Yes, the crazy, misplaced lights glittering from the other side of the garden!" I leaned in.

"Mmm hmm," Vincent replied in an encouraging hum. "Then what?"

"The stranger, I mean Cain, made his way to the tree with the sparkling fruit."

"Yes, but Cain did not realize it was the tree that his parents had eaten from and which had caused them, and all of mankind, to be banished from that garden for all of eternity and denied any chance at eternal life."

"Oh, no," I exclaimed. I didn't realize Vincent's hand was on my shoulder as my dream flashed through my head, clear as day. I saw Cain and the serpent speaking at the tree and I instantly knew what happened as I could now hear the entire conversation, unlike my muted dream. "He was tempted by the serpent, just like his mother!"

"Yes, only this time there were more devastating consequences. After biting the apple, Cain fell to the ground as poison flowed through his veins. The serpent slithered to his side and whispered in his ear that he could save Cain, but only if Cain promised to carry out his work on earth. If he did not agree, Cain would die."

I leaned in closer, as if that would speed the story.

"Cain, fearing death, agreed without knowing all of the details of the contract he was about to sign in his blood. The serpent struck Cain in the neck, the venom permanently changing him, bestowing upon him the eternal life his parents threw away. Only this wasn't the eternal life that the Lord had promised Adam and Eve. This was a damned existence on earth. Sure the serpent and his new disciple could not exercise their persuasion over mankind like the snake had with Adam and Eve...the Lord had prevented that. But that didn't stop the serpent from inflicting pain on mankind, stealing its souls and committing them to eternal damnation."

Vincent paused for effect. I was enamored by the story and the smooth voice that told it. It was quite an interesting tale and if true, clearly apparent why it wasn't included in the Bible. Such truths, if known to man, would inflict vast fear. But then it hit me - this could be just a tall tale. Vincent could be feeding me a line, a piece of fiction conjured up in his mind. But I couldn't imagine why he would do that. I also couldn't imagine what his point was with all of this.

"Well that's a great story," I said, "but what does any of this have to do with me? You said earlier that this was, and I quote, my story." I made air quotes with my fingers for added effect.

"I will get to that; I wanted to give you some time to absorb that piece of history."

I snorted. History, huh? Vincent continued.

"Cain didn't know what he had signed up for at first. He was in so much pain from the poison in his system that he didn't realize the serpent had bitten his neck. Cain lay on the ground for several hours, maybe even days, first turning icy cold," Vincent paused on those words, "then turning fiery hot." He paused again. "When he woke, he felt parched and set out in the garden towards the river to drink the sweet liquid. On his way to the river, a pack of gazelles crossed his path. A sensation rushed over Cain like nothing he ever felt before. It stirred in his stomach like a fireball and spread its way over his entire body. He had no control over his next actions as he broke into a sprint, running as fast as the wind, springing on the slowest creature in the pack. He sunk his teeth into the animal's throat and devoured its blood."

I gasped. Vincent was quite the storyteller, his face animated as he spoke of Cain's urge and how he attacked his prey. He was now on his feet, throwing his arms in the air for added drama.

"The warm liquid provided temporary relief. The dryness that occupied his throat was gone...for the moment, at least. Cain came out of his haze and looked down at the carcass that was his meal. He was confused, unsure of what had just happened. He decided to head home and on his way there, the fire in his belly began to burn again. He sat on a rock to rest, only to look up and see a whitetail deer. The deer did not sense Cain as the creature could not smell him. A now familiar sensation overcame Cain and he sprang and took that creature as he had taken the gazelle.

"Confused by his actions, Cain wandered towards home. As he approached his village, he saw his wife washing laundry in the river. Cain began to run towards her, and then felt the dreaded feeling. The inferno came alive in his core as a sweet perfume – his wife's scent – tickled his nose. This time Cain realized what was about to happen. If he approached his wife, she would surely suffer the same fate as the gazelle and the deer.

"Cain, feeling deeply ashamed, knew he could never return home. He wasn't sure he could keep his wife or the rest of his family safe from the threat he had become. He somehow resisted her sweet scent and exiled himself."

Vincent paused again. He stood still, over the edge of the stone ledge, just the tips of his boots holding him in place, and waited for my response.

"Well if this is true," I started, "I can definitely see why this was kept out of the Bible. This is the stuff horror movies are made of."

"Yes, but unlike fictional Hollywood tales, this is true," Vincent replied matter of factly.

"Great tale, but you've given me no solid proof that vampires exist or how any of this pertains to me."

"I'm getting to the part about you."

"Good," I retorted.

"Cain roamed the earth, realizing that he, once God's creation, was now the devil's masterpiece and only existed to inflict damage on mankind. He tried to subsist himself by feasting on animals alone, to save mankind from his damnation, but soon realized he could not resist that temptation. The smell of humans was too overpowering and Cain could not always control his urges. He quickly realized how much more fulfilled he felt after consuming human blood. It made him stronger, more powerful. Animal blood can sustain a vampire but mortal blood is like a drug – intoxicating and addictive."

The flecks in Vincent's eyes seemed to glisten at the mention of human blood. I wondered if that was lust I could see in his eyes.

"Cain realized he couldn't exist by himself; he craved contact with another individual of the female variety. He needed a companion but could not stand the idea of transforming a mortal without her having full knowledge of what she would become. So Cain staked out village after village, looking for the ideal companion. And one day he found her.

"Ina lived in a small village in what is now known as Poland. She lived a life of poverty where she slaved in the fields and was beaten by her father. She was about to go through with an arranged marriage, and he could see the pain in her life and he wanted to help her. One night, Cain approached Ina and said he could save her, but it would not be without great sacrifice. She would have to forgo everything…her life, her family, her soul. Ina, desperate to escape her miserable existence, jumped at the opportunity and that night, Cain transformed her.

"Cain watched in horror as Ina withered in pain, first turning colder than death, and then hotter than the flames of hell." Vincent stroked my flaming cheek with the back of his fiery fingers, as if trying to make a point. He grabbed my hand and led me deeper into the woods, jumping over crevices and scaling the trail with ease as he continued the tale.

"After several hours, Ina was converted; she was a vampire just like Cain.

"The two of them roamed the earth, happy to have each other. Cain was pleased Ina was willing to join his existence and she was happy that Cain saved her from her desolate life. Together, they

vowed to inflict as little pain on man as possible, even trying to survive on animal blood alone. Of course, there was the occasional
mishap but never any transformations.

"Then, one day Ina disappeared and never returned. Cain was
distraught and searched all over Earth for her. After several decades of trying to find her, and still craving companionship, he took
up with a mortal.

"This mortal in particular was very pleasing to Cain, but he did
not want to transform her. She had a good life, a loving family
and was about to be married. Her name was Amelia. Two weeks
before Amelia was to wed, she discovered she was pregnant. Amelia was mortified, ashamed of her condition, and so she pushed
Cain away, never telling him of the child. She opted instead to get
married and pass the child off as her husband's."

Vincent paused and stared at me. He grabbed my hand and led
me to another clearing where we were surrounded by trees and
rock formations. I searched his face for the next part of the story,
but he was waiting for me to say something.

"So you mean to tell me, Amelia had a child that was half vampire and half human?" I asked in disbelief.

"That's right." Vincent replied, nodding his head. "But Amelia
didn't know what her offspring truly was. Cain never told Amelia
that he was a vampire."

"And how exactly do you know this?"

"Because my brothers, sister and I watched over Cain. We knew
of the affair and the child, though he never knew about us and
never knew anything about the child."

"But that doesn't make sense. You said Cain and Ina survived
on animal blood and killed their human prey, so how were any
other vampires ever created?" I paused, thinking over the words

I had just heard. "Wait. Are you saying…you…Ina…what about your siblings…" I trailed off.

Vincent picked up where my thoughts left off. "Ina converted some humans without Cain ever knowing. She had her reasons for doing this. Of course, she always asked the mortal's permission first, showing them the same consideration Cain showed her. We all consented."

"You consented to eternal damnation?" I asked in disbelief. "But why?"

"We each had our own reasons," Vincent snapped, his voice uncharacteristically irritated. He smoothed his demeanor and continued, "The fact is, Cain conceived a child with a mortal. My siblings and I, we called ourselves the Secret Coven, kept watch over the child, keeping this secret to ourselves. We did not want other vampires to know such an event could happen. We did not want to encourage the behavior because none of us knew what to expect. We wondered if the child would be born at all, and if so, if it would be human, or vampire or something in between. But through the generations, we watched Cain's offspring, looking for signs that the progeny was something other than mortal. No one has ever exhibited signs until…"

"Until what?"

Vincent lowered his head, his eyes glaring at me. He cocked his head to the side like I should know the answer.

"Until me?" I asked in disbelief.

"Yes, Allison, think about it." I tore my hand away from his.

"Think about what?" I shouted. "Your story, although a good one, is just fiction. Vampires do not exist!"

"You heard the story of Cain and Ina's transformation. They turned ice cold, then blazing hot. You have felt my skin. It's cold as ice during the day and hot as the fires of Hell at night. Think about yourself."

Flashes went through my mind of perfectly warm afternoons when I bundled up in jeans and sweatshirts while other people were comfortable in shorts and t-shirts. And at night, my body was usually so hot it prevented me from sleeping. And even tonight, I was so hot I had to press my body against the cool stone for relief.

"That doesn't prove anything."

"You exhibit other signs as well, my darling."

"Like what?" I demanded.

"Your sleeping patterns. You have been getting less and less sleep yet you are full of energy. Vampires need rest but they don't need sleep."

"Great, so my insomnia and body temperature are proof that I'm one of the living dead? I don't think so."

"Have you thought about your appetite? You don't crave human food anymore, do you? When was the last time you ate – and yet your throat aches for relief, doesn't it?"

"Oh come on," I shouted, rage in my voice. "I can be around humans without sinking my teeth into their necks. I don't have any urges for any sort of blood."

"For now," Vincent replied.

"What does that mean?" I asked.

"You're not 100% vampire but have many of the traits. More than any of your ancestors ever had. And your characteristics are materializing quite fast. Not only is it your body temperature, your sleeping habits and lack of diet, but think about it Allison. You were a clumsy girl most of your life but have been remarkably well coordinated as of late. Think about your motorcycle ride here. Did you notice how you took the corners on the wet pavement, your knee just fractions of an inch from the ground? You never had the gusto to ride like that before. And what about your other senses? You have always had a keen sense of smell, but your vision has improved too, hasn't it? And then there's your infertility. The doctors you visited could never diagnose the cause for that because it's something they've never seen before; *you* are something they have never seen before. Female vampires cannot conceive."

My mouth dropped in utter shock. "How dare you! Why are you doing this to me?"

Vincent ignored my question. "But there is one definitive symptom and you know it well. For your whole life, as far back as you can remember, you have had a burning deep inside of you." Vincent placed his hand on my stomach and I smacked it away. "You always thought it was a higher calling, another career path or hobby, but it was something much more than that. It is Cain's seed, burning deep inside of you, telling you that you are something other than mortal. You are a direct descendant of his. Why do you think you have the sense of belonging when you visit the garden in your dreams?"

I shook my head back and forth, tears streaming down my face. "I don't know," I choked out.

"You feel calm and belonging in the garden because that is where your family was created! That is your *home!*"

"I don't believe you," I yelled at the top of my lungs, straining the back of my throat. "I don't believe you," I sobbed in a lower tone as I fell into Vincent's chest.

"I know, I know." Vincent whispered in my ear, rubbing my back. "But I can show you."

I pulled back from his chest and wiped my tears with my arm. "What are you talking about?"

"I can show you and maybe then you will believe. But you need to clear your mind and concentrate."

"What…" I started as Vincent cut me off.

"Can you do that? Concentrate?"

"What are you up to?"

Vincent didn't respond; he only stared into my eyes.

"I suppose I can try."

Vincent grabbed my hands and led me to the middle of the rock platform on which we stood. He gently turned my palms face up and lifted my chin so that my eyes were looking directly into his. It was easy to concentrate staring into the beautiful blue abyss of his eyes. His eyes were hypnotic, the gold raindrops sparkling around his pupils. He placed his hands on top of mine.

I drew a deep breath as I felt a slight shock run through my body. It appeared that I was staring at a white screen and then the visions started. I saw every bit of the story Vincent had just recounted in vivid detail. There was Cain roaming the earth, he found Ina and transformed her. I witnessed the transformation in gory detail which looked extremely painful. I saw the two of them roaming the earth. I felt Cain's grief when he realized he could not find Ina. I saw his first glimpse of Amelia and the attraction he felt. I experienced the love those two shared. I saw the birth of the child, a boy named Grant, and then saw pictures of other people that I did not know. One by one, each picture gave way to another stranger until I saw an image of my great grandfather Peter. The next picture was of my grandmother, Camille, followed by my mother's photo. Then there was an image of me. I realized this was a family tree, Cain's lineage, my family's history.

I pulled out of my daze, Vincent's crystal eyes boring into mine. I dropped my hands to my side, held his gaze and whispered, "What was that? How did you do that?"

"It's a gift," Vincent replied. "You could say it's the dominant trait I carried over from my mortal life. I'm sort of a historian and that was your story."

"I don't understand. Why are you telling me all of this? What do you want from me?" I asked, surprisingly calm. It was as if his story was starting to make sense, starting to sink in with me. This could be true. I could be part vampire. All I could do was wonder what the onset of all of the vampire-like traits meant.

"Allison, you are the first of all of Cain's descendants to exhibit signs of vampirism. I'm not sure what it means, but we, my siblings and I, don't think you are safe."

"I'm not safe? Who's threatening me?"

"You are a danger to yourself. You have been going through changes at an accelerated pace. We're afraid that you may be so frightened of yourself, of what you are turning into, that you will try to hurt yourself if you didn't know the truth, or worse, you would go on a hunt. And an uncontrolled hunt like that is dangerous to all of our existence."

"What are you saying?" I knew where Vincent was going but I needed to hear it to believe it.

"Allison, I need to transform you; you must let me do that. But I need your consent. Either that or we wait until you lose all control and then I would have to destroy you. And believe me, I don't want that."

Any breath left in my lungs now escaped through my parted lips. I knew this was what he was trying to tell me and I thought I needed to hear it. But hearing that ultimatum, if it could be called that, was a shock to my system.

"Wait, you need my consent?" I asked. "Couldn't you just transform me whenever you wanted?"

"No Allison, it's a rule. Consent is needed from the person being transformed and it's a rule that can't be broken without severe consequences."

My head hurt with all of this information. "Great, so my choices are death or eternal damnation?"

"Immortality isn't all that bad," Vincent responded.

"No, just gotta get use to drinking blood and killing humans, eh?" I snickered.

"Our cuisine isn't as bad as it appears. Your instincts take over and you barely taste a thing. Yes, you have to kill the occasional mortal, but we have detailed plans around that. Think about what immortality can offer you, Allison! You will be able to do all the things you could never do in a mortal lifetime, see all the places you always wanted to visit. We could watch every sunrise and sunset together. We could do whatever you want, whenever you want."

"I don't know that I can do this! Any of this," I stammered and turned to walk back the way we came.

My mind was overcome with too much information. The images Vincent had shown me were so vivid and real, there was no denying they were authentic. His explanation for why I felt so comfortable after dreaming about the garden made sense. That was my home. And he could explain all of my ailments; symptoms that mortal doctors couldn't explain now made perfect sense. After starting the night out a non-believer, I now fully believed what Vincent was telling me. I was, to some degree, a vampire. The serpent's venom, the devil's poison, was running through my veins.

"Allison..."

"Really Vincent? Put yourself in my shoes. I'm going about life, the way it should be, and one day this beautiful stranger...you... sweeps me off my feet only to blindside me with information that I am part vampire and need to choose certain death no matter what decision I make. I can't do this." I leapt over a crevice and smoothly started my descent down the rock, this time noticing the gracefulness with which I moved.

"You really don't have a choice, but you do have to consent," Vincent said right behind me. I stopped and whirled around. He raised his index finger to my mouth, stopping me from saying anything further. "But you don't have to consent tonight. You have a lot to absorb. Take some time and think about it. I'm having a Halloween party next week. It's a huge event that my siblings and I throw every year. Come. I'll introduce you to my brothers and sister. You'll see that our life is not as bad as you think."

"I don't really have a choice, do I?"

"About the party? No." Vincent held up my motorcycle key. I hadn't realized we had made it back to the parking lot so quickly. "Now let's get you home." Vincent stared up at the sky. Black clouds rolled over an even blacker sky. "I have no idea how your half mortal riding skills will handle the approaching storm," he said with a smirk.

CHAPTER 8

My mind couldn't stop thinking about *it*. Four days had passed since Vincent had told me that I was a descendant of the first vampire ever created and that the devil's poison ran through my veins. A mere 96 hours ago, I learned that the symptoms that had haunted me for so long were my body's way of telling me that I was one of the eternally damned. Thousands of minutes had passed since I had last seen Vincent and all I could think about was my predicament, for lack of a better word. And yet, I couldn't bring myself to say out loud that I knew what I had to do. All I could do was wonder: why me? Why now after so many generations of others like me?

None of the options Vincent had presented was palatable, but something had to be done with me. I could no longer ignore that something was wrong; this had become more and more painfully obvious since that night at Whipps Ledges. It had been four days since I had slept or eaten a morsel of food, and yet I was neither tired nor hungry. There was, however, a pain in my belly, a deep burning within my core that had slowly grown over the past days. At times it was almost unnoticeable, but at other times I felt the fireball churning away only before it faded back to nothing again. I was constantly thirsty, but so far I had managed to quench this thirst with water. I could only wonder how long that would last.

My decision seemed to change from one second to the next. One minute I was certain that I wanted Vincent to transform me; the next I wanted to take the risk and remain mortal, praying that my symptoms would somehow reverse themselves. Then I would think about how unlikely that scenario was and I was back to consenting, only to suddenly be gripped by the fear of dying and my mind would change once again. It was an exhausting, vicious cycle I didn't know how to break. To make matters worse, always lingering in the back of my mind was the realization that regardless of what I decided, my ultimate destiny was eternal damnation. How ironic that I had wasted all of those years trying to find my true calling, and this was what I got.

I turned on the television in a futile attempt to distract my brain. A football game was on with a news alert banner scrolling at the bottom of the screen. It announced the savage murder of a young couple the night before in Columbus, Ohio. They were to be engaged that night, and worried family members had called the authorities when they didn't hear from them. The couple's bodies were found in a lake, hers drained of blood and his missing his head.

"Vincent, I *need* to talk to you," I said to myself. But I wasn't going to see Vincent until tonight at his Halloween party. Vincent had left four nights ago, saying that he was going out of town on business. But, I knew by the way he had said *business* that he really meant he was looking for food. Or victims. He had mentioned at Whipps Ledges that there was a plan around who was killed and when. All I could do now was wonder if that plan had been executed against these victims in Columbus.

A knock on the door snapped me back to reality. I turned off the television to go and greet my friend. Jenna pushed my front door open as I welcomed her.

"I am sooooo excited about this party," Jenna gushed, her face glowing with enthusiasm. She dropped her overnight bag in the foyer. "I can't wait to thank Vincent for inviting me!"

When Vincent first told me about this party, he had sensed that I was hesitant about attending, so he told me to invite Jenna. He probably also sensed that I wasn't about to put my friend in harm's way by inviting her to a party full of vampires, so he sent her a hand-delivered invitation. He assured me it would be safe for her, that humans and vampires could coexist for an evening without any mayhem and precautions would be taken to ensure that. After initially being angry about the situation, I realized it might be a good idea to include Jenna in something since I had seemingly shut her out of my life for the past three years. And maybe having her here now would help take my mind off other things.

"He seems like a great guy, Ali," Jenna said. "I can't believe you have kept him from me all this time. How long have you two been dating?"

"Um, I wouldn't really say we're dating."

"Well you should snag him. A good looking guy like that won't stay single for very long!"

"Um, yeah I guess." My mind was too occupied to care about this idle chatter but thankfully Jenna's enthusiasm kept her mind clipping along.

"So where are the costumes?" Jenna asked. She searched around my living room and poked her head into the den.

After initially chuckling at the statement that I would dig up an old costume to wear, Vincent assured me that he would take care of this minor detail for both me and Jenna.

"They're not..." I was interrupted by the doorbell. I walked to the front door, Jenna close behind.

I opened the door. A tiny old woman stood on my doorstep holding several large boxes which were almost too big for her short arms to handle. Her skin was dark and creased and her gray hair was pulled back into a tight bun. She wore a plain black pant suit with a crisp white shirt. There was nothing special about her eyes; they didn't glow like Vincent's or have any strange gold flecks, so I assumed she was a mortal.

"Hello, Miss Allison?" the woman spoke in an accent I couldn't decipher.

"Yes," I replied. Jenna had her hand on my shoulder, straining to see our visitor.

"I am Francesca Rousseau. Mr. Vincent sent me to help you and Miss Jenna get ready for tonight's festivities."

"Of course he did," I muttered under my breath as Jenna pushed past me to help Francesca with the boxes. "And please, just call me Ali."

We moved into the living room where Francesca directed Jenna to the boxes intended for her. Jenna anxiously ripped them open like a child on Christmas morning.

"Ali, look at this," Jenna gasped as she pulled her costume from the box. "It's beautiful! Where did Vincent find this?"

"I made it," Francesca responded, a proud smile on her face. "Do you like?"

"Like it? I love it!" Jenna exclaimed.

She pulled an exquisite outfit from the box. Even standing across the small room I could tell the gown was made of real silk.

It was a vibrant shade of blue and looked like it gathered at the waist with extra fabric for draping over the shoulders. The bottom of the gown was stitched with an intricate gold design and embellished with red jewels.

Francesca pointed out in her accented voice that the hem was decorated with genuine gold thread and rubies. She then reached into her bag and retrieved another box.

"Are you kidding me?" Jenna exclaimed. Francesca handed her a beautiful headpiece crafted in gold and covered in jewels, no doubt real ones since the dress was adorned with rubies. She held up a sheer veil of coordinated blue fabric that attached to a gold piece that would cover the lower half of her face.

"Isn't this beautiful, Ali?" Jenna asked.

"Yeah, it's great," I answered honestly.

"Don't you want to see your outfit?"

I wished Jenna's enthusiasm would rub off on me, but my conversation with Vincent from a few nights ago still lingered in my mind. I thought my mind would be clearer after spending so much time over the past few days thinking about everything Vincent had told me, but that unfortunately wasn't the case. I really couldn't wait to see Vincent, and I hoped that he would help put my mind more at ease.

"Ali…"

"Yeah, Jenna, what?"

"Don't you want to see your costume?" she repeated.

"Um, sure."

I walked over to a large box and opened it. "Oh Ali," Jenna exclaimed. "It's out of this world!"

Lying in the box was the most exquisite ball gown I had ever seen. As I lifted the heavy garment out of the box, it became apparent why Francesca was here – I couldn't get dressed by myself. The top of the gown was crafted of deep purple crushed velvet covered with an ornate design sewn in gold thread and speckled with gemstones. White swags of silk fell from the shoulders. Jenna had to help me haul the rest of the garment from the box. The skirt was full and made of white silk, just like the sleeves. The hemline was bordered with a thick band of purple velvet which stretched out into an ornate design of graceful swirls edged in more gold thread.

"It's beautiful!" Jenna exclaimed as she struggled to hold the gown to her body and twirled around, the skirt consuming my living room. "It's fit for a queen."

I was stunned by the costume's beauty. It was clearly custom made and must have taken many hours, even months, to create.

"Ali?" Jenna asked trying to get my attention.

"It's beautiful," I cleared my throat. "It's a bit much though."

"You no like, Miss Allison?" Francesca reemerged, pulling a trunk behind her. "I made it just for you according to Vincent's design."

"Oh Francesca, the dress is exquisite. It's just that when Vincent mentioned a Halloween party, I wasn't expecting such a lavish outfit. I thought I would be dressing up as a witch or pirate, not the queen of England! Did you say Vincent designed this?" I asked as I touched the design on the skirt.

"Yes, Mr. Vincent is very talented. He will be pleased that you like his creation."

Not only was Francesca there to deliver the costumes, but she was there to assist us with our hair and makeup too. We spent all afternoon primping ourselves. Jenna gushed with excitement through the whole process, thoroughly enjoying the pampering. My mind was elsewhere, wondering what this evening would hold.

When it was all said and done, Jenna and I looked like we had walked straight off of a movie set. Jenna's blue dress clung to her tiny frame, wrapped around her neck and draped over her left shoulder and hung down her back. Maybe this was what Vincent had meant when he said there would be precautions. If her neck was wrapped, no vampire could bite it. Francesca placed a black wig on Jenna's head that was parted down the middle and pulled tight in the back. Her head was crowned with the gold ornamentation Francesca had handed her earlier. It fit perfectly into the part in her hair, framing both sides of her hairline, the light catching the rubies, sapphires and diamonds. The face veil was connected to the headpiece and Jenna's look was completed with two matching gold bracelets that wrapped around her arms from wrist to elbow.

"This is so cool!" Jenna exclaimed. "I feel like a genie."

I could hear Jenna downstairs talking to herself as I made my way down the narrow staircase from the loft bedroom.

"Whoa, Ali," Jenna said. "You really do look like a queen."

The ball gown filled the entry way as I walked into the living room.

"This is quite unbelievable if I do say so myself."

The outfit couldn't help but make me feel like royalty. The gown fit perfectly, complete with coordinated purple elbow length satin gloves and lace-up French boots. Francesca had obviously worked for some time on my wig. It was an ornate headpiece with long blonde cascading curls that fell to the small of my back. The sides were picked up and held in place with combs. Of course, no queen would be complete without a crown. Francesca brought several options in her trunk and I selected a dainty yellow gold tiara that peaked inches above my head, crowned with a large amethyst and adorned with diamonds. My head couldn't hold much else under the weight of the wig. Francesca completed my look with a gold lattice necklace speckled with amethyst and an oversized oval ruby gemstone that she placed on my middle finger.

"Ah, that's it," Francesca mused. "Mr. Vincent instructed that I not forget this ring. You must keep this on all night. Understand?"

I nodded my head and wondered momentarily why I would have to wear it all night. I held up my hand and rocked it side to side. The stone reflected the light from the room, rays seemingly shooting out of the center of the stone like a starburst. I held it to my eye for closer inspection and examined the cuts in the stone. There was a diamond-shaped crest, crafted with graceful swooping lines and an etching of a dragon. It was a profile picture of a winged creature which had only two front legs and a pointed tail. It seemed to be a misplaced picture for such a beautiful stone but I didn't say anything.

"I must go now," Francesca announced.

"Thank you, Francesca, for the beautiful dresses," I said.

"Yes, thank you!" Jenna chimed in.

"Miss Allison, Miss Jenna you are most welcome. Enjoy your-selves tonight."

Francesca was out the door, packing her trunk into her car.

"One more question," I yelled after her. "How are we getting to the party?"

"Your ride will be here shortly, do not worry."

"I just hope this ride is large enough for this big skirt," I said to myself as I closed the door. Jenna heard me.

"Your skirt? What about that huge wig? Good luck getting that in a car!"

There was a soft knock at the door. Thankfully I hadn't moved too far, mostly out of fear of knocking something over with my gown.

A chauffeur was at the door. He was a short man dressed in a black suit and a white shirt and had a thick mustache and slightly graying slicked back hair.

"Miss Allison?" he asked in a strongly accented voice.

I nodded my head.

"I am Chadwick, Miss Allison, and I will be taking you and Miss Jenna to the party tonight."

"Please, call me Ali." I responded.

"Mr. Vincent has instructed that I address you as Miss Allison. Are you and Miss Jenna ready?"

I rolled my eyes at the formality. I saw no need for Chadwick to call me Miss anything but I knew not to argue.

"Yes, we are so ready," Jenna responded, full of energy, pushing her way past my gown to the front stoop. "Hey, nice ride."

I squeezed my way through the doorframe to see an exquisite car parked in my driveway, not a vehicle you typically see in rural Ohio. It was long and sleek, and dark as night with equally dark windows and contrastingly bright shiny rims. My jaw dropped when I realized what it was.

"Is that a Maybach?"

"Yes, ma'am," Chadwick responded. "It's a model 62."

"What does that mean?" Jenna whispered in my ear.

"It means the car costs about four times as much as my house," I whispered back.

"Really? Nice," Jenna enthused.

A red carpet had been rolled out for our walk to the car.

"This is unbelievable," I said as Chadwick assisted me and my dress into the car.

"Only the best for Mr. Vincent and his special friend," Chadwick responded with a wink.

Jenna and I were piled into the car. "Special friend?" Jenna asked with a raised eyebrow.

"You heard that, huh?" I responded but quickly changed the subject. "Chadwick, where are you taking us?" I asked through the open partition that separated the front and back of the vehicle.

"Have you heard of Castle Adena?"

"I have heard of it."

Castle Adena was an old ornate castle built in 1803 by one of the richest families the state had ever known. It was about an hour away from Ridge Hollow and located on acres upon acres of land, and the castle was not visible from the street. It had been available for tours but was closed about thirty years ago for major renovations and little was known about its current occupants. That was, until now.

"Isn't that place closed to the public?" Jenna asked.

"Yes, Miss Jenna, you are correct. It is a private residence – the Drake residence. Please, enjoy some champagne as it will be a bit of a drive." Chadwick rolled up the window to allow us some privacy.

"Don't tell me twice," Jenna stated as she grabbed two glasses and poured us some bubbly. I looked at the bottle and chuckled to myself. It was the same champagne Vincent had served me at the cottage. Apparently no expense was being spared for this evening.

We watched the countryside roll by. There wasn't much to stare at on the way to Castle Adena other than rolling hills, bare trees and an occasional farm house. This was truly desolate country, but at least it was finally a nice fall evening. It wasn't raining, for once, and an almost full moon hung in the evening sky, dark purple strips of clouds floating over it.

"Ali, you okay?" Jenna asked. "You're fidgeting."

I looked down. My legs were bouncing and I was playing with my gloved fingers.

"Yeah, I guess I'm a bit nervous."

"About what? Vincent is obviously crazy about you."

"Not that. You know how I am about dancing in front of other people," I lied. I was nervous with anticipation for what this evening would hold.

"You'll be fine. Look – we must be here," Jenna poked a finger towards the outside.

Chadwick turned off the road and we passed under a mammoth steel gate trimmed with a fall leaf garland. Jack-o-lanterns lined a driveway that seemed to stretch on for miles. Nothing was around but flat land. No one would know there was a party here if not for the decorations.

"I wonder who carved all these pumpkins," I murmured.

We passed under a tunnel of trees, completely in the dark except for the tiny purple, orange and black votive candles dangling from the branches. And then we saw it. In the clearing ahead was a massive castle pitted against the sky. The huge structure was several stories high with numerous peaks. Each side was anchored with rectangular mural towers. It appeared to be crafted out of some sort of large, irregularly shaped stone. The stained glass windows were illuminated with a soft candle glow.

"You have to be kidding me," I said aloud.

"My goodness," Jenna whispered, and then exclaimed, "This is going to be one heck of a party!"

Chadwick parked the car and opened the passenger door. Jenna exited first since her costume was easier to navigate in than mine. Chadwick grabbed my hand and pulled me from the car as I attempted to pull my skirt through the narrow opening. I rearranged my dress and made sure everything was in place, then looked up and saw Vincent.

"You look quite lovely this evening, Allison," Vincent said as he took my hand and kissed it. "Quite exquisite."

"Thank you," I said, my mind practically blank as I lost myself in his eyes. I cleared my throat and broke my stare. "And thank you for these wonderful costumes. Francesca did a fabulous job. They're way more than I expected."

Vincent simply smirked. "Hello Jenna," Vincent said. "It is nice to formally meet you."

"Likewise," Jenna responded, seemingly in a trancelike state. "Thank you for the invitation. And the costume. And the cool ride."

Vincent chuckled, amused by Jenna's reaction. "You are quite welcome."

Vincent offered both of his arms to escort us into the party.

"And what are you, Vincent," I asked as I examined his outfit. "Count Dracula?" I asked with a chuckle. Jenna laughed as well, not aware of the inside joke.

Vincent looked quite dashing in a black, no doubt custom, suit that cinched at the waist. He wore a short cape secured around his neck with a large oval ruby, like the one on my finger, with the same crest carved in the stone. Under the cape, was a purple velvet sash with ornate gold scrolling that coordinated with my gown.

"Aren't you silly?" he replied, looking me straight in the eyes as the three of us approached the castle. "Every queen needs a king, does she not?"

"Oh Ali, that's so sweet!" Jenna exclaimed.

"Sweet it is," I said staring back into Vincent's eyes and suddenly overcome with emotion.

We stopped at the entrance. Vincent dropped our arms and turned to face us. "Ladies, there is someone I would like you to meet."

A handsome man, almost as handsome as Vincent, emerged from the castle. His shoulder length blond hair flowed freely and his green eyes were luminescent in the darkness setting in around us.

"Allison, Jenna, this is my brother, Lorenzo," Vincent announced.

Lorenzo approached me and reached for my hand. "Allison, it is nice to formally meet you," he said as he kissed my hand. His eyes had the same gold flecks as Vincent's.

"It is nice to meet you too, Lorenzo." Somehow Lorenzo looked familiar to me, yet I couldn't recall ever meeting him. But there was something about the way he had greeted me that sounded like we had met once before. If we had met before in some informal setting, I certainly didn't remember. I surely would have remembered his sparkling eyes, muscular build and angular jaw.

He gently placed my hand at my side and stood in front of Jenna. "You must be Jenna," he said as he kissed her hand, taking it gently and wrapping her arm under his. "Do you mind if I escort you to the party tonight?" he asked in a smooth voice.

"Um, uh, no, I don't mind," Jenna stammered. She looked back at me as Lorenzo swept her into the castle.

"Bye," I waved. "Have fun!"

After they both disappeared inside the castle, I asked, "She'll be safe with him, right?"

"She will be fine. There is no need to worry. As I told you, precautions were taken. Humans are safe here tonight."

"Those precautions wouldn't have had anything to do with that couple that was killed last night in Columbus, would it?" I couldn't help but ask. The question was at the front of my mind all day.

Vincent stiffened and his eyes clouded over just as they had done when we were in the airplane hangar on Rattlesnake Island. "No," Vincent replied coolly. "*We* had nothing to do with that."

"I'm sorry, Vincent. It's just when you said precautions and I heard that story…"

"It's fine," Vincent replied. "I understand why you would think that. But let's not talk about any of that tonight." Vincent grabbed both of my hands, took a step back and looked me over. "Hmm," he admired. "Absolutely beautiful and I finally have you to myself. Are you ready?"

"As ready as I'll ever be," I responded. I felt my cheeks flush.

We walked into a large room, the great room, Vincent called it. The ceiling was several stories high with exposed chunky wood beams crisscrossing over the room. Fall foliage filled the gaps between the wood beams, giving the effect of a forest canopy. Large iron and aged wood chandeliers had been hung at a safe distance from the wood beams and provided a romantic glow. The walls were covered in sheer black fabric with back lighting reveal- ing bare tree silhouettes. The images, some thick, others pencil thin, appeared to shoot straight up to the leaves in the ceiling, completing the trees. High top tables were scattered around the perimeter of the room covered in long purple silk linens. Center- pieces were crafted of fall flowers, gourds and small pumpkins. A deejay could be heard, although he wasn't visible through the sea of people who were all dressed in costumes equally as extravagant as mine.

"Wow," I said.

"Do you like it?" Vincent asked, his eyes never leaving my face.

"It's beautiful and more than I expected for a simple Halloween party."

"My family doesn't do anything simply," Vincent retorted.

I continued looking around the room, taking in the decora- tions and the other guests. My eyes settled on a doorway that was closed to the party-goers. Above the door, carved into the stone, was a crest like the one etched into my ring.

"I have to ask, what's with the crest?"

"You noticed?" Vincent appeared surprised.

"Of course I did. It's hard to miss. It's the same crest that's in this beautiful ring and your brooch."

"That is the Drake family crest. My siblings and I assumed that as our last name many centuries ago and when we did, we had the crest created. All significant covens have a crest. That was the *thing* several centuries ago."

I pondered that for a moment, but before I had a chance to ask any more questions, the music changed and a slow song wafted through the air. "May I have this dance?" Vincent asked. He bowed, extending his hand out to me.

I shot him a look. Dancing wasn't something I liked doing normally, let alone in this huge dress. I thought I would consume the entire dance floor and didn't want all that attention on me.

"Please, do me the honor," Vincent said as he grabbed my hand and led me to the center of the room.

Vincent twirled me around, our hands interlocked as he caught my waist with his free arm. He pulled me close – very close. We effortlessly waltzed across the room. I didn't give myself much credit as a dancer because I moved smoothly across the floor. Or maybe Vincent was just that good at leading. He stared deep into my eyes. We were so close I could count the gold flecks in his eyes. There where exactly thirteen in each eye, the same number I had in each eye. His body was warm, much warmer than mine, and his breath smelled sweet. We glided across the floor and it felt like others were moving out of our way. I broke my gaze, looked around and soon realized that everyone else was still on the floor, not paying particular attention to us. Vincent placed a finger on my cheek and turned my face back to his. Looking into his eyes, I felt like we were the only two here.

"Enjoying yourself?" Vincent whispered.

"Yes," I breathlessly whispered back.

"We could do this for all eternity, you know." Vincent moved his face forward, resting his forehead on mine.

"I know." I couldn't help the way I felt right now. I was so enthralled with this moment and this man that eternity sounded like the perfect plan.

"Then you know what you have to tell me, right?"

I stared into the blue eyes staring back at me. Vincent picked his head up and moved his lips closer to mine. A rush of desire flowed over me which I quickly suppressed. Seconds before he had asked the question, I would have voluntarily consented to transformation. But the weight of his question snapped me back to reality and kept me from acting on my impulses.

"Not now." I forced myself to say the words.

"But Allison," Vincent stated before I cut him off.

"No. Not now," I sternly replied.

The song ended and not a moment too soon. I pulled myself away from Vincent's body. "I'm thirsty," I said, wanting to change the subject.

"Then let's get you something to drink." Vincent's mouth broke into a crooked, almost devious smile.

"Thank you," I responded, not believing he was giving up this conversation so easily.

Vincent took my arm again, and walked with perfect posture as we glided through the crowd. He held his head high, almost appearing proud to be walking with me. I looked at each party-goer as they moved out of the way of my mammoth skirt. Some had average looking eyes while others had eyes with the now familiar yellow flecks. Vincent had told me the party would have both humans and vampires, but I hadn't believed him until this moment, when I was seeing it for myself. Here I was, in the middle of a dance floor full of vampires and mortals intermingling. I wondered if the humans knew who, or what, company they kept this evening.

"Vincent," I called as we made our way through the crowd. "So the humans really can't tell who is a vampire?"

"What do you mean?"

"The eyes are a dead giveaway, pun intended. The thirteen gold flecks that sometimes revolve around the pupils."

"You can see that?"

"Well yeah. I can tell who in here is mortal or immortal by looking at their eyes."

"Interesting."

"Why is that so interesting?"

"Mortals do not see what we see, what you are seeing. They do not see the tiny specks that swirl around the eyes and increase in intensity when we are hungry. But our eyes are part of our aura, and they're hypnotic to humans. The eyes help draw them in, make us irresistible."

"And since I'm part…"

"Yes," Vincent cut me off. "Watch what you say in public though. Because of what you are, you can see the difference."

Any doubt remaining in my mind about my being part vampire was erased with that statement. My vision was something other than that of a mortal.

We made our way to the glass topped bar. My body was starting to overheat, but I wasn't sure if it was the dress and all the fabric I was lugging around or just my body's vampirey new habit.

"You are feverish," Vincent stated. He stared into my eyes as if he was looking for something.

The bartender approached. "Mr. Vincent, what can I get you and the…" he stuck his nose in the air, as if trying to sniff for something, "…the lady?"

"Isaac, don't be rude. This is Allison Carmichael."

I grabbed Isaac's extended hand, and he, too, kissed my hand. One look into Isaac's eyes was all I needed to tell what he was. A vampire would be serving our drinks.

"Pleasure to meet you, madam," Isaac said.

I nodded my head.

"I'll have the house drink and the lady will have…" Vincent said to Isaac but the music was too loud for me to hear the rest. Isaac dashed around behind the bar grabbing bottles and pouring the liquids into shakers. I saw him grab a familiar bottle – a green one with a black label and crimson colored diamond crest. Upon closer inspection, it appeared the shape that was indiscernible to me at the cottage was that of the dragon that was etched in my ring. Isaac poured the red liquid into both shakers, shook the drinks and dispensed them into glasses. Vincent handed me a wine goblet. I swirled the red liquid and inhaled its scent. It smelled sweet like flowers.

"What is this?" I shouted over the music.

"It's a special drink, just for you," Vincent responded. "Try it."

I raised the glass to my lips and took a sip. The drink was heavenly. It tasted just like it smelled, like a sweet garden filled with flowers and fruit. I nodded my head in approval of the delightful concoction. Vincent grabbed my hand and led me back to the dance floor. Along the way, Vincent introduced me to people, but I could barely hear their names or make conversation because of the loud music. We made our way back to the entrance where it was less chaotic.

"What do you think?" Vincent asked as he waved his hand at the party.

"A bit cliché, don't *you* think?"

Vincent looked puzzled with my response. "What do you mean?"

"Really Vincent? Castle...vampires...Halloween party?" I burst out in laughter and he did too.

A stranger approached Vincent and asked if I would mind if he stole Vincent for a few minutes. Vincent's eyes scanned me and my beverage, as if concerned.

"It's fine," I reassured him. "I need to sit down anyway. This dress is really weighing on me."

Vincent threw his hand up in the air, flagging someone I couldn't see. In a flash, a beautiful angel was at my side, seemingly materializing out of nowhere. She wore a long white Grecian gown, pulled tightly around her tiny waist. Sheer wings sprung from somewhere on her back, and I couldn't tell how they were attached to the costume. A silver halo floated above her long flowing red locks.

I looked at the angel and studied her face for a few seconds.

"Nurse Marlo?" I asked in shock. There was no mistaking the long red cascade of curls and the lavender hued eyes.

"Allison, this is my sister Marlo," Vincent introduced us.

"But how ..." I started.

"I'll tell you later." She wrapped an arm around my waist. "Let's get you somewhere you can sit down."

Vincent grabbed my goblet as Marlo led me to the closed off door I had noticed earlier. I instantly felt at ease with Marlo though we had only spoken a few words. Her face was soothing to look at, almost as if she really were an angel. Marlo tapped something on the wall and a door slid open.

"Can you make it up the stairs?" Marlo asked as she surveyed my bulky costume.

"I think so," I replied. I hiked up my skirt so as not to trip on it and started to ascend the steep, spiral stone staircase. I paused at the top, realizing the stone wall was cool and pressed my body into it for some relief.

Marlo touched my face, "You're boiling hot." She grabbed my arm, her hand a few degrees cooler than my hot flesh. I was starting to feel light headed and my feet were starting to tingle. I should have known I couldn't wear such an elaborate outfit all night.

"Can you walk a bit further down the hall?" Marlo asked, pointing to our destination down the long hallway.

I shook my head. Marlo led me to a chaise in some sort of sitting area off of the hallway.

"Here, have a seat." Marlo touched my head with the back of her hand. "You're really burning up. Do you want something to drink?"

"Please, my stomach and throat are killing me."

Concern washed over Marlo's face. "What does your throat feel like?" The tone in her voice suddenly changed. It wasn't as velvety as before but full of concern.

Realizing where her concern was leading her mind, I lied "It's just a little scratchy. Probably just a sore throat."

She eyed me up and down and appeared to believe my lie. She was gone and back in a second with a tall glass of water.

"Here, drink," Marlo instructed in her smooth voice.

I took a sip of the water and it provided momentary relief to my aching throat. Marlo was watching every move I made.

"Better?" she asked.

"Yes," I lied again. The back of my throat felt like an inferno as did my stomach. The heat had returned and was churning away.

Wanting to get her attention off of me, I changed the subject. "So, um, are you going to tell me why you were at the hospital?"

Marlo stood frozen like a statue, still observing me. I took another sip of water, to prove to her I was okay, though I really wanted to chug the whole glass.

"Thanks for the water," I said, trying to act normally. I didn't want to tip Marlo off that anything was wrong.

Marlo relaxed and sat in a chair across from me. Her eyes never left my face and her stare was most uncomfortable at the moment. She was studying me like a book.

"Vincent called that night. He was on duty watching you. He told you about the Secret Coven, right?" Her demeanor had changed again. She sat there like she was gossiping with an old friend, and truth be told, it felt like I'd known her my whole life.

"He mentioned that you, your brothers, and he together were the Secret Coven that watched over Cain's half mortal, half vampire descendants."

"Yes, well, we took shifts watching you over the past several months. Sometimes one of us would watch you for a week, other times one of us would watch you for several weeks. Vincent looked after you mostly. He is quite protective of you.

"That night, Vincent called and said you were in a very bad car accident and that he wasn't able to remove you from the scene himself. A passing car saw yours on the side of the road and dialed for help. Vincent called to tell me they were taking you to the hospital because you were unconscious. I had to be there to ensure the mortal doctors didn't suspect anything or try to treat you in some way that would harm you."

"Oh," I said. "Well I suppose that makes sense." We sat there in silence for a moment as I sipped my water. Marlo continued studying me.

"So tell me Allison, what has my brother told you about your options?"

"Options? I really don't think I have any options, do I?"

Marlo smiled and glanced at the floor. "Of course you have options." Her eyes returned to mine. "You can't be transformed without giving your consent." She said it as if it were that simple.

"Oh yes, that's right, the vampire rule," I scoffed.

"We have other rules too," Marlo said as she continued staring at me.

"That doesn't surprise me."

"Vincent hasn't told you?"

"No, he hasn't mentioned anything other than my permission is needed to transform me."

"Hmm. Well Allison, like every society, we too have certain rules to live by, punishments in place if the rules are not followed, and a governing body to judge and punish the rule breakers. Our life isn't as glamorous as Vincent might have made it appear to you. We can't just do what we want, when we want to whomever we want or whenever we want just because we're immortal."

Now we're getting somewhere, I thought. Maybe I'll get some answers to the questions I had wanted to ask Vincent.

"You should know these rules, to be fully informed, before you make your choice," Marlo stated smoothly. She stood up as she continued her lesson. She spoke like a professor teaching class.

"We have three simple rules, really. You already know the one."

"Right, you must have permission before transforming anyone; kind of like carrying on Cain's tradition."

Marlo whirled around and studied me as she absorbed my response.

"Well yes, carrying on the tradition, if you want to call it that. But do you know why Cain asked Ina for permission and why she asked all of us?"

I didn't know what to say so I said nothing.

"It avoids the situation of having a disgruntled vampire. You have to know what you are getting into and you have to choose this life. We cannot force anyone into it for fear of not knowing how they will react and the danger they may present to our existence."

I sat there still not knowing what to say. Her words made sense; you cannot damn someone and expect them to act a certain way. They have to want this life.

Marlo looked back at me as she paced the small hallway. "Here's another rule – you can never reveal your true self to *any* mortal."

"That makes sense," I said and shrugged my shoulders.

"It does, but it isn't as easy as you think. There are people in your life, like Jenna, whose life will continue on after your transformation, not aware of the changes in you. She will still want to hang out and be friends, like things never changed. But *you* will have changed. You may not be able to control yourself around her. You may not be able to see her alone, or at all. She will wonder what has happened and will question you. You will not be able to tell her what truly has changed and it will be difficult. She may eventually become despondent with your lack of answers and one day stop calling all together. Do you think you can you handle that?"

I sat there, somewhat stunned at what I just heard. I hadn't thought about how my transformation would affect those around me. I would have to keep my secret and hurt my dearest friend since I couldn't be truthful with her. I didn't answer Marlo's question.

"It's not without basis that we have this rule. Imagine the fear that this truth would impose upon mankind once they realized it was a truth. Think about it; bloodsuckers living among man. Hunter and prey living alongside each other. The two cannot coexist when each have the knowledge of the other's existence. Therefore, for our own self preservation, mortals cannot know we exist. Our kind can only live on in their myths, legends and movies." Marlo paused, allowing me to absorb the rule she just explained.

After a few moments, I asked, "And the third rule?"

Marlo smiled and continued pacing the hallway. "The third rule involves our diet." She turned to see my reaction at her pronouncement. "We adhere to a very strict diet."

"Yes, blood," I stated matter of factly.

"Of course Allison, but it's more than that. You see, our kind tries to limit the damage we inflict on mankind; another of Cain's traditions, as you say, we carry on. We are what we are and of course need human blood to sustain ourselves. However, we do not need it all the time. We have a very strict regimen of what to eat and when. We pursue wild game and raid the occasional blood bank, and only prey on humans to sustain our energy level. And even then, we have very strict rules about who we hunt and where. It can be difficult to stick to, to fight against nature like that, but you do eventually grow accustomed to it."

Marlo paused again for my benefit.

"I've heard 'our kind' more than once. What does that mean? Are there different races of vampires?"

Marlo let out a feathery giggle. "I just told you about our diet, and that's the question you have?" She continued laughing. I felt a bit embarrassed.

Marlo continued after she calmed herself. "We don't have different races per se, but there are others out there that don't abide by our rules. Those vampires fully embrace what they were created to be and do not take pity on mankind. They are quite the opposite of us and only exist to destroy man, as the serpent had intended."

"Why have rules at all?" I asked. "I mean, you said yourself, your diet is difficult to stick to, so why fight it? Why try to limit the damage to humans while making yourself suffer?"

"Good question. We hope that when the end of days – Armageddon, as you may know it – comes that the Lord will see our efforts and He will understand what we were created to be and see that we tried to inflict as little damage on man as possible, limiting the amount of souls we stole. You see, when we kill, we steal the victim's soul, damning that person for eternity. Likewise, when we transform someone, their soul is lost, which is another reason why we give them the choice to transform. Our hope is that the Lord will be merciful and grant us our souls back for limiting the damage the serpent commanded us to do."

"So you are good vampires?" I asked incredulously. "You are vampires with consciences who resist the natural order of things, withholding your desire, to limit the suffering you were created to inflict on mankind so that you might be saved in the end?"

"As good as can be expected," Marlo replied matter of factly.

I scoffed at the concept and then another thought popped into mind. "Wait," I stood up and froze in place. "What did you just say? About your victim's souls?"

"When we kill mortals, we take their souls."

"Why? Why would you do that?" I asked, fear overcoming me.

"We have no choice, Allison. It is what we were created to do. It just happens; there is no way to avoid it."

"So no heaven for those souls? They go to…"

Marlo cut me off. "It is how the serpent designed us. If our kind could prevent it, we would. But we need human blood to survive. There is no other way."

"You know what this means?" I shouted, my voice faltering.

Marlo stared at me.

"I really don't have a choice! My 'ultimatum,' if you can call it that, is for me to give my consent to be transformed to the living dead and lose my soul, or go uncontrollably wild to the point that you have to kill me and I lose my soul – I'll end up eternally damned either way!"

Marlo said nothing. I began to pace the small corridor wracking my brain for another solution.

"Or…" I started.

"Or, what?" Marlo asked.

"Or I can just wait, try to ride this out. There's no guarantee that my symptoms will lead to anything. I don't have fully fledged symptoms, just signs that you all think mean I'm transforming."

"Allison, even if that's true, that you think you won't further transform, what's one of our rules that we just discussed?"

I ran through the three rules in my head and threw myself back on the chaise. "Never reveal yourself to a mortal."

"Right. And now you know what we are."

My mind drifted back to that night at Whipps Ledges when Vincent told me my story, when he revealed that he was a vampire. *Damn it*, I thought to myself. He revealed himself to me and now I know. It's only a matter of time before something is done with me. But I couldn't help but feel that Vincent was somehow trapping me into a decision. "But I promise I won't tell anyone," I pleaded.

"But we already told you. Remember that I said there were punishments in place for those that don't follow the rules?" Marlo asked.

"Yes," I replied, my eyes closed.

"The punishments are in place and we enforce them – our kind enforces them. It's the only way to ensure the rules are strictly followed."

"What's the punishment for breaking *your* laws?" I asked, focusing on Marlo's lavender eyes.

Marlo cocked her head and simply stated, "Death."

"Death?" I asked in disbelief. "But you are immortals, the very nature of the word means you can't die."

"We don't die a natural death, like a mortal. But there is a way, only one way actually, to kill a vampire."

"And how is that? Sunlight? Holy water? Garlic?" I asked sarcastically.

"No, none of that will kill us. Although sunlight is a bit pesky. It makes the venom in our blood boil if we're exposed too long. But the others are just myths. To kill a vampire, you attack our only Achilles heel. The very place where we take a mortal's life is the very place where our existence can be taken."

I lifted my gloved left hand to my neck. "The jugular?"

"That's right. To kill a vampire, you rip out its neck and..." Marlo continued talking but I didn't hear anything else she said.

"Do you hear that?" I asked. I peered down the hall at a door maybe forty feet away, our original destination. I wasn't sure how I could hear anything behind the thick wooden door. "It sounds like there's a scuffle going on down there."

Marlo listened then took off into a graceful sprint down the hall. I followed, not nearly as fast or as graceful.

Marlo flung open the door. The room appeared to be some sort of security center. There were numerous flat screen monitors mounted on the wall which scanned through quadrants of the property and numerous switchboards with blinking lights. Marlo directed me towards a chair.

"What is all of this?" I asked.

"Precautions," Marlo replied. "Our kind can control ourselves, but with a house full of mortals and immortals, you just never know."

"Felix, are you in here?"

"Right here, sis," a man announced as he rolled his chair out from behind a wall of monitors.

"Felix, this is Ali..."

"I know Marlo, I saw Allison arrive."

Felix was average height and build, but like his siblings, his looks were anything but ordinary. His face was accentuated with high cheekbones and an angular square jaw. His hair was a deep brown with blond highlights and was cut short in the back but long and strategically messy on top. He had thick eyebrows perched above eyes the same shade as his hair. Thirteen gold flecks surrounded each pupil.

Felix walked toward me and bent down to shake my hand. "How are you, Allison?"

"I'm well. Nice to meet you, Felix."

"Nice to meet you too," Felix responded in a soft voice. "She is boiling hot," he said.

"I'm fine. Really. It's just this gigantic costume and wig," I said as I fluffed my skirt, revealing the many layers to my audience. "And I'm sure the wine didn't help either."

"Wine? What were you drinking?" questioned Marlo.

"I'm not sure. Vincent ordered it. It was some sort of concoction, like nothing I'd ever tasted before. A mix of things including some of that red wine that Vincent is fond of."

"Hmm," she hummed to herself as she looked me up and down.

"What?" I asked, feeling self conscious.

Marlo looked at Felix who also looked at me and shook his head.

"It's nothing." Marlo stated, walking towards the window beyond the monitors. "But we are quite surprised to see you here tonight, Allison."

"Really, why is that?"

"We're surprised that Vincent was able to get you to forget about your husband so quickly."

"It shouldn't be that much of a surprise. Matt has been gone for three years. That's enough time to mourn and move on."

"Gone? For three years?" Marlo questioned. Felix pushed his chair from around the corner to look at me again.

"What are you...?" Felix started to ask as the door burst open. I didn't see anyone enter as another person materialized in front of me.

"We have a problem," the man announced.

Felix and Marlo rushed to the middle of the room.

"Max," Marlo said, "this is Allison Carmichael," she nodded her head towards me.

"Hi Allison, I'm Vincent's other brother." Just like the other siblings, Max was quite handsome. He wore his hair short, almost a buzz, and had the same chocolate colored eyes as his brother Felix. He was about the same height and build too, but his face had a much softer edge to it. Max and Felix could pass as biological brothers.

"What's the problem?" Felix asked Max.

"Look." Max moved in a flash behind the wall of monitors. I could hear him tapping a keyboard. "*He's* coming and brought *her* with him."

"Who's coming?" I asked. My question was ignored.

"When did you find this out?" Marlo asked.

"I was just out running the perimeter, you know, to ensure no un-wanteds were going to pay us a surprise visit. I could smell *their* scent a hundred miles away," Max stated.

"Who are they?" I asked again. But again, I was ignored.

"Does Vincent know?" Felix asked.

"No, but he will in a minute," Max replied.

Felix sat down behind the wall of monitors and started tapping away on the keyboard. "There's Vincent," he said and pointed at one of the screens.

I got up from the chaise, my legs weak, stomach burning and my throat still haunted with dryness. I walked around the wall where Marlo and Max were hunched over Felix's shoulder, their eyes glued to the monitors.

"Oh no," Marlo said.

The camera panned down the long winding driveway. A black Rolls Royce was slowly making its way towards Castle Adena. "We need to warn Vincent," Felix stated as he reached to grab a phone.

"Too late," Max replied. All faces focused on the monitor that showed Vincent. One moment he was chatting with guests and in the next his demeanor changed, revealing that he could sense something was wrong.

I could see the image, but couldn't hear what Vincent was saying. It appeared he was asking his company to forgive him for having to leave to attend to something else. Vincent looked around the room for someone or something. He stuck his nose in the air as if searching for a scent like a bloodhound.

"What's going on?" I asked again.

Vincent flashed across the screen, too quick for the cameras to keep up with him, but he went unnoticed by the crowd. I saw Lorenzo materialize by his side and the two strode with purpose towards the front door.

"Can you get sound?" Marlo asked Felix.

"I'm trying," Felix responded as he feverishly pounded the keyboard.

Vincent and Lorenzo flashed across the screen again, the cameras unable to keep up with their speed. Max started tapping on buttons to keep up with the visuals as Felix tried to reign in the audio.

The Rolls Royce approached the front of the castle and stopped. Nothing happened for several seconds and then the driver emerged. I squinted and focused on the screen. The driver was a tall, thin man, young with dirty blond hair, a pointy nose and his eyes were the deepest shade of blue I had ever seen.

"I know him," I uttered, although I couldn't place how we had met.

"I doubt you know him," Max replied.

"No, I know him, I just don't know how," I insisted as I strained my mind. There was no mistaking his pointy nose or those eyes.

"Highly unlikely," Max chimed in. "One doesn't usually have long after a run in with Casper."

"Casper?" I looked away from the monitors. "Like the friendly ghost?"

"There's nothing friendly about Casper Devoe," Max retorted. "He's henchman, a scout."

"What are you talking about?"

"For him." Max pointed at the monitor.

Casper walked to the passenger door and opened it. A boot emerged before the immense body that followed it. It was a man, very tall and lean, but with broad shoulders. He was pale, his skin practically glowing against the night sky, and had long black hair that fell to the middle of his back. His eyes were black pits, devoid of all color. He wore a long, black trench coat that fell to his boots and covered the rest of his outfit.

He emerged from the vehicle and looked around, then held out his hand. A pale, white hand emerged from the vehicle, followed by an exotically beautiful woman. She was tall, maybe as tall as the male. Her hair was as long and as dark as his but her eyes glowed like emeralds against the dark night. They were vampires.

"What's going on? Who are they?" I asked again.

"Lucious and Delilah," Max responded.

"Who?"

"Shhhhh," was the response I received from all three of my companions.

"I think I have audio," Felix announced.

There was static but then the words became clear.

"Lucious, Delilah, what a pleasant surprise," Vincent stated in a calm yet sarcastic voice.

"I hardly doubt it's pleasant, but I am sure it is a surprise," Lucious responded coolly in a deep, raspy voice. He coyly eyeballed the castle.

"What brings you here tonight?" Vincent asked.

"Well it is a party, isn't it? We assumed we were invited."

"Well you assumed wrong," Lorenzo snapped.

"Now, now," Vincent stated and placed his hand on Lorenzo's shoulder. "Let's show our guests a bit more graciousness than that."

"So does that mean we can enter?" Delilah asked in a sly tone. She sniffed the air like an animal looking for its next meal.

"She can smell the mortals," Max whispered to those of us in the security room.

"Not exactly," replied Vincent. "What is your business here?"

"No business," Lucious snarled. "Like I said, we assumed we were invited to the party."

"You assumed you had access to an easy meal," Lorenzo seethed.

"Hmm," Lucious purred as he continued to leer at the castle. "I will never understand your kind. Why put yourself through so much suffering by sparing the mortals?"

"So they can be saved in the end," Delilah responded sarcastically as both she and Lucious burst into laughter.

"I doubt the Lord will show sympathy to any of the devil's offspring who steals any of *His* precious souls," Lucious mockingly added.

I had a hard time seeing anything on the monitors over the three other heads. I walked over to the stained glass window and cracked it open, hoping for a better view of our unwanted guests. I slowly cranked the window open wider. A cool breeze rushed past me. It felt welcome against my hot flesh.

"No! What are you doing?" Marlo yelled at me as she hurried to crank the window shut. "Did they sense anything?" Marlo shouted to her brothers.

"No, I don't...wait a minute," Max replied.

The four of us drew closer to the monitors. Vincent and Lucious were still engaged in the conversation, but Delilah's attention was now on something else. The breeze blew past her, throwing her hair wildly into the air. She lifted her nose into the air then snapped her head in the direction of the window I had just opened.

"You have one of them here!" Delilah announced, cutting off the rest of the conversation. She continued to sniff the air and her eyes appeared to become more vibrant. "Smell it, Lucious."

Lucious stuck his nose in the breeze and took a deep breath. "Ahh, it appears you have another treat for us this evening besides all of the mere mortals," Lucious hissed, stepping closer to Vincent and Lorenzo. Casper stood in the background with a look of accomplishment on his face.

"We have nothing for you here," Vincent responded his arms crossed over his chest.

"Oh come on Vincent, don't play your games. There's no mistaking *that* scent."

I strained my neck to see the monitor. "What is he talking about?" I whispered. Max threw up a hand to silence me.

Delilah closed her eyes and took another deep breath. "It's a female," she snarled.

"Oh I see," Lucious said, narrowing his eyes on Vincent. "Shacking up with one of the descendants, are we? Where did you find this one?"

"Oh God," I whispered, "they're talking about me." I pulled myself away from the monitor and found my way back to the chaise. I could still hear the audio and see the scene on a small television near where I sat.

"There is nothing for you here," Lorenzo interjected. "You need to leave."

"Oh, but there is something for us here," Delilah responded. "You think you can protect the mortal, but you can't! Your own rules prevent you from doing that since you can't tell her what you are. That means she doesn't know we exist; she won't even know we're coming for her! What a pity – for her!" Her vicious bellow filled the room.

"I can protect her!" Vincent yelled at the top of his lungs.

Lorenzo stepped in front of Vincent and put a hand on Lucious as he stepped forward. "Leave. Now." Lorenzo directed sternly.

A smirk spread across Lucious's face. "I see someone fancies a descendant," he said as he turned towards his vehicle, Delilah's face still fixated on the window I had opened. "Don't get too attached," Lucious warned.

"Transform her if you must, if she'll even agree, but we'll be back for her either way," Delilah added, winking at Vincent.

Lorenzo had to hold Vincent back from attacking. The duo stepped into the Rolls Royce. Casper slammed the door, his eyes never leaving Vincent's except for a momentary glimpse at the window before he entered the car and pulled away.

"Not good," Felix announced.

"Not at all. We need to keep an eye on Vincent," Max added.

My head was spinning from the ordeal I had just witnessed. I had so many questions in my head that I could barely organize them. The hollow of my throat was distracting me, aching more and more, and the tingling sensation was spreading from my toes up my legs.

"Who are they?" I asked, unable to see the three siblings who were still behind the monitors. "And why do they think I'm just a mortal?"

"You are a mortal, Allison," Marlo responded, emerging from around the corner. "They do not know what you are. Well let me rephrase that. They know you are a descendant of Cain's family; that, they can smell. Only you and your ancestors carry the scent of the garden. They would have to see you to suspect that you are possibly half vampire. That, they could not pick up through your scent."

"So they don't know about Cain's affair with a mortal?"

"No, they don't. No one outside of the Secret Coven knows that. They think you are one of Adam and Eve's descendants."

"Great, another reason I have no choice about my transformation. If they see me, they'll know something is up. See what I mean about not having a choice?"

The room fell silent. The two brothers remained hidden behind the monitors.

"Are you okay," Marlo asked me. "You don't look well."

Max poked his head around the corner.

"No, you don't look good at all," Max added.

"How would you look after learning all this?" I snapped. "So, what's the deal with Lucious and Delilah? Do they have some sort of vendetta out for me?"

Marlo and Max exchanged a glance. "How much did Vincent tell you about your family's beginnings?" Marlo asked.

"He told me about Cain, how he met Ina, she disappeared, he found Amelia and conceived a child," I stated.

"Did he tell you about any of Cain and Ina's transformations or anything about how the Secret Coven was formed?" Max asked. Felix was now peering around the corner.

"Vincent said that Cain never transformed anyone but Ina didn't have the same willpower. They killed as few humans as possible. He never told me how your group was formed, only that you all consented to Ina." My confusion swelled but the feeling wasn't able to compete with the fire in my stomach and throat and the other sensation washing over my body. I started to feel like I was going to shake.

"Wait, wait, wait…he said Cain never transformed anyone?" Felix asked, as he walked to the center of the room. The three of them formed a semicircle around me.

"Is that not right? What's going on?" I demanded. I pulled off my gloves hoping that would cool me.

"Well, it's not true. He must not have wanted you to worry about…" Marlo started, but Max cut her off.

"Maybe he had a reason," Max said.

"Would someone please tell me what you are talking about?" I demanded as I pulled the tiara from my wig.

"Allison, when Cain and Ina were young vampires, they tried to kill as few mortals as possible. But their novice attempts to kill their prey sometimes went in vain. They did transform some mortals without realizing it," Marlo explained.

"And one of those accidental transformations was Lucious," Felix added.

"What?" I asked in disbelief. I reached around my neck to free it from the necklace.

"That's right," Marlo continued. "Lucious emerged from his transformation and was confused. Once he figured out what he had become, he was enraged that his creator had left him for dead and therefore leaving him to fend for himself. He then wondered if his creator knew that he or she had transformed him, so he set off to find them."

"So did Lucious find Cain and Ina?" I asked, now tugging at my wig.

"You are familiar with the story of Noah's Ark, correct?" Felix asked.

"What?" I asked. "Of course. What does Noah's Ark have to do with any of this?"

The door flew open and Vincent emerged, Lorenzo right behind him.

"Allison, are you okay?" Vincent dropped to his knee to inspect me.

I was irritated. "I'm fine." I snapped. "Your brothers and sister are giving me a history lesson, if you don't mind."

Vincent stood up and looked at Marlo, Felix and Max.

"It's fine," Max reassured.

Vincent stepped back and Felix continued the story.

"You see, Cain and Ina roamed the earth and one day came upon a man, Noah, who was building a huge ship on top of a mountain."

"Wait," Vincent interrupted. He looked worried. "Why are we talking about this now?"

"Because I want to hear the story," I snarled. "Felix, please continue."

"Noah was the Lord's favorite descendant of Adam and Eve. The Lord had asked Noah to build the ship and ensure it held a male and female of every species because the Lord was going to create a great flood to wipe out the evil he saw man was doing."

"The evil that the Lord saw, that was Lucious, wasn't it?" I asked.

"Yes, but the holy book doesn't tell you that. Lucious fully embraced his new existence and was wrecking havoc on man.

He didn't care who he hurt, how or where. The Lord knew He
had to stop it and the great flood was the answer."

"Only it wasn't the answer, obviously," I said.

"Right," Max picked up the next part of the story. "Cain watched
Noah for several days as the ark was built, but couldn't understand
why Noah was undertaking such a huge task, especially on the top
of a mountain. Well, a few weeks later, he got his answer.

"One by one, an animal of every species paired up with a mate
and boarded the ark. Cain was still confused until he saw the water
rising up the side of the mountain. He realized that the earth was
being flooded and only one pair of every species was going to be
spared – as long as it was on the ark.

"Cain grabbed Ina as the last animal was about to enter the ves-
sel. They flew over the water and snuck onto the ship. It was
Cain's hope that the flood would destroy the evil he and Ina felt
haunted them. Although they did not know him by name, tales of
Lucious's wrath spread to Cain and Ina's ears.

"The two settled on the lowest level of the ship to ride out the
flood. The great flood lasted several weeks and when it was over,
the ship settled and each animal disembarked. Cain was sure that
any evil he or Ina had created would have been wiped out in the
flood. He was sure no one or nothing could have possibly survived
it. So the animals went on their way to reproduce, as did Noah
and his family. Many descendants of Adam and Eve were born
over time. Unfortunately for them, Lucious created a huge army."

Marlo continued the story. "You see, Lucious survived the flood.
In his vengeful pursuit of Cain, he witnessed him and Ina board
the ark. Unfortunately for Lucious, he did not have time to sneak
on the ship. He was swept away in the flood, but as you now know,
there is only one way to destroy a vampire. Seeing Cain desert
him once again, Lucious was filled with even more rage. He swore

that he would create a following whose sole purpose would be to destroy Cain, Ina and all of Cain's family. This following included vampires like Casper whose sole purpose is to serve as scouts locating descendants for Lucious to destroy."

"Which would include me," I choked out, the heat billowing from my stomach up my throat. The tingly sensation had spread to my upper body and I almost felt like I was going to lose consciousness. I fought the sensations to hear the rest of the story.

"Yes," Felix chimed in. "The Bible documents some of Lucious' evil doings but disguises them as the plagues – water that turned to blood, sick animals, plagues of boils, so many locusts that a black out resulted, darkness for three days – all Lucious; not a natural phenomenon or plague sent by the Lord."

"Allison, are you okay?" Vincent asked, rushing to my side.

"I, uh," I stammered.

"Her history must be too much for her," I heard Marlo say in the background. Her voice sounded so distant to me. "Someone get her some water."

"Wait," Lorenzo warned, holding up a hand to silence the commotion in the room. "Do you hear that?"

I tried to concentrate on what Lorenzo was hearing, but could not overcome the feeling in my body. The others in the room listened as well.

"Who is it?" Felix whispered.

The door slowly creaked open and Jenna's face appeared.

"Hey," Jenna said sheepishly. "I, um, was just looking for Lorenzo. I thought I saw him come up here."

I stood up and glowered at Jenna. I opened my mouth but words escaped me. I clamped my jaw shut and took a deep breath. A scent so fresh and mouthwatering filled my nose. I could smell sweetness and saltiness that was more tantalizing than a candy store. I could hear murmurs all around me but the voices sounded like they were off in the distance. I think I heard Marlo ask me if I was okay yet again and Vincent asking me something as well. But I couldn't hear them because I was concentrating on the scent filling my nostrils. I closed my eyes to concentrate on the smell, stretching my neck to determine the source. It was so clean and pure, like nothing I had experienced before. My mouth began to water yet the liquid that chilled my tongue tasted odd, some-what bitter and numbing like Novocain. I opened my eyes and glared at the source of the scent. I could still hear the murmurs all around me and then a male voice boomed, "Get her out of here!" Lorenzo wrapped his arm around Jenna, the fragrant object of my desire. I twisted my head to analyze her, my mind calculating its next move. Then my mind went blank, my body went numb, and I lunged at my prey.

CHAPTER 9

id-lunge, I was aware my mouth was open and venom dripped from my teeth. My stomach swelled with a burning that quickly turned to desire that clawed its way up my throat. A horrific, ear splitting shriek spilled out of my mouth. I could feel I was about to reach my target and the thought of my teeth sinking into her neck was more than my body could handle. I cocked my head for the kill.

Something wrapped around my waist, stopping my forward momentum and my pursuit of my prey. I came slamming down against the stone floor but felt no pain. My mind was on one thing and one thing only. Her scent filled my nose and created such desire that I trembled for her blood. The venom circled with excitement in my belly and my mouth watered for just the slightest taste of her, but the burning in the back of my throat wanted more – it needed to be quenched.

I sat up but couldn't see a single solid object. Nothing around me had a defined shape; everything had been reduced to bits and specks of color. I inhaled deeply, searching for her, and caught a whiff. Her scent was quickly disappearing but I could hear her voice. "What's happening?" she asked. "Allison isn't feeling well but she'll be okay," a male voice responded. Their voices were growing more distant; she was moving farther away from me. I couldn't let that happen. I had to have her.

I dug my nails into the stone and lunged forward but was stopped by a solid object in front of me. I was trembling. I needed to have her and I needed to find her. I couldn't even imagine what her blood would taste like but I desperately wanted to find out. I tried to move again but was stopped. Vincent's face appeared before mine. Although everything else around me was a swirling pool of color, Vincent's face appeared with perfect clarity. I breathed shallowly, not understanding what he was doing or why he was standing in my way. I shoved his shoulders but he didn't move. I couldn't hear her anymore. I shoved again but Vincent drew closer. He appeared to be saying something to me but I couldn't hear him. My mind was consumed with the need to find *her*!

I opened my mouth but words escaped me. I looked over Vincent's shoulder in an attempt to signal that I needed to go. But instead, Vincent wrapped his arm around my waist and held me securely in place. I couldn't understand what he was doing or why he was keeping me from my mission. Then I saw his mouth open and the tips of his fangs emerge. Then I felt it.

His cold teeth pressed against my neck. I was dumbfounded for only a split second but before I could fight back his venom was in my system and began paralyzing me.

The sensation of his teeth penetrating my skin wasn't painful; in fact, his mouth on my neck felt quite pleasurable. The sensation reminded me of a lover gently kissing his lover's neck. But that warm sensation lasted momentarily. I gasped for breath as I felt two icy cold spots sting my neck under the warmth of Vincent's mouth. The two spots merged into one cold spot and then spread like a spider's web over my neck. The coldness crawled over my face, them my shoulder, then over my chest and immobilized my breathing. I felt it wrap around my waist and up my spine and then down my legs. It felt as though I had just plunged into a frozen lake and my entire body was in shock.

I gasped for air, my eyes wildly scanning the room searching for some explanation as to what was happening to me. I kicked my legs but it did nothing to free me from my attacker. I could hear murmuring around me but it was barely audible. The coldness intensified and it now felt as if every cell in my body was freezing individually. The iciness finally settled in my stomach as my eyes frosted. My body was a solid piece of ice.

My vision was blurred and my hearing muted but I could faintly hear some voices.

"Vincent, no!" a male voice shouted.

"What in the hell are you doing?" another asked.

"You can't! She never consented," a female shouted.

Somehow, the coldness was getting even worse, like I was naked in a blizzard and pieces of snowy ice were striking my flesh. My toes and fingers stung with what I imagined would be frostbite and the sensation spread through all of my appendages. The pressure at my neck disappeared and I fell to the floor. I heard a door slam and more scuffling. I couldn't see what was going on nor could I make sense of the voices. The room was black and spinning. Then, I couldn't see or hear anything at all.

I didn't know how long I lay frozen. It could have been hours or days or a century. Though my body was a cold, hardened block, my mind was still aware – painfully aware – of my frigid surroundings. I couldn't hear or see anything so my mind could only focus on the stinging bitterness. It was incomprehensible. I didn't know if this was what it felt like to be buried alive in an avalanche or to be locked in a meat freezer. All I knew was that it wasn't enjoyable in the least. Every part of my body tingled with a burning coldness and there was nothing I could do about it other than hope it would go away soon.

And then, something shifted in my core. The solid mass of ice slowly began to melt, splinters of ice now swirling in the warming liquid.

Slowly, the iceberg in the pit of my belly began to liquefy and the gentle warmth starting to emanate from my core was welcome relief. The warmth leisurely spread over my chest and through my arms and legs. As my body began to thaw, a new tingly sensation overcame me; it felt like I was dipping my chilled limbs into warm water. The cold had been completely replaced by warmth, to the point that I almost felt normal. My mind was conscious but I still couldn't move, talk, hear or see.

I lay there, trapped in my comatose state, enjoying the welcome warmth. It was comfortable, almost like sitting on a beach, the sun's rays putting me to sleep. This serene feeling lasted for some time, or it at least felt that way. My senses were completely blocked so I had no comprehension of time. Then, the heat began to intensify. I felt it first in my core, like a hot sun in the middle of the universe. My core became hotter and hotter, almost unbearable. Just like the cold, the heat began to spread over my body, but more rapidly than the coldness. It ferociously launched through my chest, down my arms and was particularly painful on the left side of my neck like I was being stabbed in two distinct spots. The heat shot in the opposite direction down my legs. The pain was indescribable; it was as if scalding water was being rammed through my veins with a fire engine hose.

The heat rippled through my body. I could feel it circulate, always seeming to end up at my core where it picked up more heat to spread throughout my body. The heat escalated to an inferno. I was boiling from the inside and I wasn't sure how much more I could take. Just when I thought it couldn't get any hotter, it did. The pit of hell was festering in my stomach, its flames scorching every inch of my body.

I heard a wail. It was the first sound I had heard in what felt like an eternity. It sounded like the source of the sound was in terrible pain and I had to wonder if it came from me. If it wasn't me, the pain in the noise reflected the torture I felt. I started to faintly hear other sounds.

"Hold her down."

"I'm trying but she's boiling hot!"

"She might be coming through."

"Get her something to drink."

My body started to convulse, violently contorting in unnatural ways and something was attempting to restrain me. I could feel my limbs shaking and trembling and thrashing about but this pain paled in comparison to the immense heat.

There was sudden relief in my stomach as the heat backed off a few degrees. As my scorching hot blood returned to my center, it was replaced with a cooler blood. It spread over my entire body giving immediate relief. My body transitioned from inferno, to blazing, to hot, but a hotness like nothing I had ever felt before. The convulsions stopped.

My eyes sprang open. Lorenzo was above me, hands on my shoulders as he straddled my chest. He was apparently the restraint I had felt earlier. Pressure eased from my legs and then I could see Felix peering over Lorenzo's shoulder. Marlo was on my other side. I could see her lips moving but I could barely hear what she was saying.

My breathing was labored. I wasn't sure if that was due to Lorenzo sitting on my chest or because of the ordeal I had just experienced.

"Wha…what…what happened…" I stammered.

"Lorenzo, get off her; she can't breathe," a muted male voice commanded.

Lorenzo removed himself from me and cautiously backed away. I tried to lift myself but had little strength. Marlo laid a hand on me and said something. I closed my eyes and focused my energy on speaking.

"What in the hell was that?" I struggled to ask.

I heard light chuckles, then Marlo scolding her brothers.

"Allison, how are you feeling?" Marlo asked, her head above me observing my face.

"I…I'm not sure."

"Listen to me. You have to drink this. It will make you feel better," she said.

I nodded my head weakly. Felix held up my head as Max rushed to my side with some sort of liquid concealed in a shiny flask.

"Drink," Max instructed.

The thick, cold liquid hit my tongue, washing away the heat. If a fire hose was pushing fire through my body before, this drink was certainly helping to squelch the fire. It slid down my throat and took the heat with it. The reprieve I felt was most welcome. If I could have grabbed the flask myself I would have chugged all of the sweet liquid.

"Easy now," Max said as I drank. Once in my stomach, the relief spread over my body. I felt almost functional, still weak, but I could sense my strength returning.

"You're going to be fine," Max reassured me.

I finished off the flask and lay back, wiping my mouth with my arm.

"Can somebody tell me what happened?" I asked to no one in particular.

I opened my eyes and saw four blank expressions peering over me – Lorenzo, Marlo, Max and Felix. The last time I saw these four, we were at the Halloween party but the costumes were now gone, replaced with everyday looking clothes.

"You, uh," Felix started, trepidation in his voice. "Um, you have been…"

"Transformed," Max finished. "Spit it out Felix. She would have figured it out sooner or later."

"Transformed?" I questioned. My mind drifted to thoughts of my most recent nightmare. The incomprehensible heat I felt, like I was standing in the middle of Hell. And before that, the frigid misery I endured, like I was standing in the middle of Antarctica. Then flashes of Cain and Ina came before me, both withering on the ground in pain as they were…transformed.

"But how?" I questioned. "I never consented. I mean I knew I had no choice, but I wasn't ready. Not now," my voice trailed off. I wanted to cry yet no tears welled.

Marlo sat on the bed next to me. "Vincent changed you," she stared into my eyes.

I stared back, searching Marlo's face for answers. Her eyes were different. They were pallid; not the typical dazzling lavender I was used to. I expanded my search of her face. Her cheeks were sallow and her skin appeared drained of what little color she normally had.

"Vincent?" I questioned. "Why? Why would he do that?"

"At the Halloween party, you almost attacked Jenna," Marlo said.

"I did what?" I exclaimed with what little energy I had.

"Almost," Lorenzo said. "I got Jenna out of there before she could suspect anything. I told her you weren't feeling well."

"So she's not hurt?"

"No, she's fine and she didn't suspect a thing." Lorenzo assured me.

"But why would I have attacked Jenna?" I asked to no one in particular. One of the brothers was about to respond but I cut him off. "Oh Lord," I sighed. "My symptoms. Vincent was right, you all were right. My symptoms got the best of me, making me attack my best friend..." I trailed off, almost not believing what I was saying.

"Vincent feared that we would kill you because of the almost attack," Marlo stated. "Without thinking, he bit you and trans-formed you. You've been out a few days going through the trans-formation."

I gasped. This was not how I wanted this to happen. I knew I had to consent at some point, but at the very least I wanted control over the time and place and wanted to be able to say goodbye to Jenna even if she didn't realize it was goodbye. I would have told her I was traveling the world with Vincent and she wouldn't see me for some time. That lie seemed believable. But Vincent took that away from me. How dare he! How could he have done that? What a selfish bastard to take it upon himself to transform me into a vampire without my consent.

He transformed me, I thought. *He transformed me.* I tried to let the words sink in but it felt so unreal that I was now part of the damned, one of the living dead. I paid particular attention to my body. I wiggled my toes and moved my fingers. Other than feeling weak, I really didn't feel much different. *He transformed me*, I thought again. *I'm a vampire.*

"I'm a vampire," I whispered. My companions didn't say anything as my new reality set in. But the more I thought about Vincent's selfish actions, something dawned on me. He may have damned me but he had actually saved me. I knew that by not immediately consenting, I risked the sort of thing that almost happened. I took the chance that my symptoms would worsen and I wouldn't be able to control myself. And that's precisely what happened. I had almost attacked Jenna. Something had triggered the venom inside of me and I hadn't been able to control myself in her presence. Who knew what would have happened had Lorenzo not gotten her out of the room in time. And who knew what Jenna really saw and if she had believed I simply wasn't feeling well. I almost exposed their secret to a mortal, breaking one of their rules which should have resulted in my death. But Vincent intervened and saved me from that death sentence. He saved me! I was still here! Although I wasn't technically alive any longer, it was better than the alternative. Wasn't it?

And then I realized something else. In saving me, he had damned himself. He had broken his society's cardinal rule by transforming me without my consent, and there was only one punishment for that.

"Where's Vincent?" I demanded.

"We're not sure," Felix replied.

"Does that mean he's still alive?"

"He's not *alive*. None of us are."

"You know what I mean."

"Yes, he still exists," Marlo assured me. "But we don't know where he is."

"We can promise you he won't show his face here though," Max said sternly.

"Why?" I asked, fully aware of the answer I was about to receive.

"Allison," Marlo said, "Vincent broke a rule."

"If he shows here, he's a dead man," Max added.

"What? But he's your brother!" I exclaimed.

"Brother or not, the rules are the rules and if we don't enforce them, then all of our existence is on the line," Marlo explained.

"But this is different, isn't it?" I asked. "You said nothing like me ever existed before so how could your rules apply to me?"

"Simple," Lorenzo coolly replied. "No one outside of this room knows of you and what you were. No vampire suspects that he can conceive with a mortal. Therefore, the rule applies because you are, I should say were, a mere mortal to any other vampire. Therefore, the rule applies."

"Why would anyone have to know that I didn't consent?" I asked. "We could say that I did and everything would be okay. Vincent could come back."

Marlo shook her head. "There were four of us there, Allison. We were all witnesses. Eternity is a long time to hold a secret like that with that type of consequence at stake. There's no telling what the future holds. If one of us lets that secret slip, all of our fates will be sealed."

"We won't seek him out, Allison," Max chimed in. "But Vincent understands what he did. He knows we have no choice but to enforce his punishment if he comes back."

"But—" I started, but Marlo cut me off.

"Enough." She firmly pronounced. "For now that is. There are more important things to discuss at the moment."

"Like what?" I demanded.

"We gotta teach you how to hunt," Max announced. His face lit up with excitement.

I groaned at the thought.

"Gotta get you out there before you drain our stash," Felix said as he shook the empty flask.

"That was blood?" I asked disgustedly. I looked at the sleeve of my shirt where I had wiped my mouth earlier and noticed a red stain. I felt disgusted.

"Of course it was," Marlo replied. "What did you think it was?"

"But it tasted so good. It wasn't what I expected at all," I mulled. "I guess I didn't really think about it."

"Come on; let's go," Max eagerly commanded as he headed for the door. Felix and Lorenzo followed.

I swung my feet over the side of the bed and attempted to stand up.

"Whoa," I exclaimed.

I looked down and the floor was a dizzying sight. I could see every granule that created the stone floor, every flaw and nook and cranny. I looked up at the wall and it appeared to lunge at me and again could see every detail of the stone. I stared at the painting, a framed picture running the length of the wall. I saw all of the individual dots that created the scene but couldn't see the complete painting. It was a mass of varying shades of blue and oddly enough a mass of black dots running through the center in what appeared to be a word. And then there was the noise.

"What is that?" I yelled and covered my ears. I heard nothing but noise, and lots of it. I heard a stereo playing, crickets chirping, the noise of a bird's wings as it flew through the air outside. I heard a vacuum running and a car motoring down a street and a rush of other noises.

"Allison, concentrate," Marlo yelled at me as she pulled my hands from my ears. "You have to concentrate. Look at me."

I gazed into Marlo's eyes. I could see every pore in vivid detail on her face. Her eyes were a blur of lavender and blue and her face was surrounded by a red glow.

"Concentrate," she yelled again. The noise was killing my ears.

I stared into Marlo's eyes deciding to focus on the gold flecks. I counted them; thirteen, just like Vincent, just like me. I repeatedly counted them as Marlo continued to instruct me to concentrate. The noise started to fade as I counted and recounted the flecks in her eyes.

The minute details of her face blended back to reality and the noise faded into the distance. One by one her pores smoothed back into the canvas of her skin. The individual flecks of purple and blue faded to reveal the lavender eyes that were familiar to me.

"What was that?" I asked. I glanced at the painting on the wall and could now see it in perfect clarity. It was a storm over the ocean with menacing waves and ocean spray splashed against a black sky.

"Listen to me," Marlo said seriously, turning my face back to hers. "You need to learn to control that. You have to focus at all times on what is around you so that you aren't distracted by all of the details."

"Okay, but what was that?" I asked, still not understanding.

"That's the hunter in you, your untamed senses. You can see vivid details for miles, allowing you to easily spot the pumping heart of your prey. You can hear miles beyond what you see, expanding your hunting territory. Once you find what you are looking for, your sense of smell will take over and only one thing will be on your mind – your prey. Your sight and hearing will go back to normal after you drink. But lose control of this and you will lose your existence. Understand?"

I nodded, understanding that if I let me senses overtake me – again – I wouldn't be able to control my hunt and that would be the end for me. I didn't like the serious tone Marlo had with me. I missed the jovial spirit she had when we met at the Halloween party. Then again, she was dealing with a lot. Her own brother had committed the most serious of crimes, and she would never see him again or it would result in his death. And me, the new-born vampire she felt the need to babysit so I didn't slip in my ways and subject myself to Vincent's fate.

Marlo stared at me to make sure I understood her explanation.

"Come on," she said as she twirled around and leapt into the hallway.

I started towards the door but my reflection in a full length mirror caught my attention and I took a double take. I stopped in my tracks and inched backwards towards the mirror. I looked at my reflection. It was me but somehow different.

My skin was smooth like porcelain, not a blemish in sight and surprisingly paler than when I was a human. Not a single hair on my head was out of place; it looked like I had just left a salon. My hair was styled with sharp angles framing my chin, and was a vibrant shade of blonde. I should have looked like a mess after the hell I just went through, but I didn't. I looked at the rest of my body which was amazingly fit. I grabbed a bicep and felt a muscle. I was never able to build muscle as a mere mortal but seemed to have developed them through my transformation. I lifted my shirt to see my stomach and to my surprise found chiseled abs. I looked up in shock and then saw my eyes. My naturally blue gray eyes were anything but average. A dark ring of blue bled into a lighter shade which bled into a light gray. And the tiny gold specks, which had been present before, were still there but now circled my pupils.

"Hey," Marlo called from the doorway.

I looked at her and back at my reflection, still not believing what I saw.

"You're even more beautiful now," she whispered.

I continued to stare at myself. I had never considered my mortal self beautiful. Sure I thought I was an attractive woman, but this transformation was something else. No plastic surgeon could have ever achieved such results.

"I don't get it," I whispered.

"What's that?" Marlo reentered the room.

"How? How did this happen?" I waved a hand up and down my body. "Where did the muscles come from?"

Marlo chuckled. "The venom, of course. You are now the perfect hunter. No one will be able to resist you."

Her words stung – *perfect hunter.* More like perfect killer. A wave of revulsion ran over me at the realization of what I had become. I was part of the living dead; a soulless, eternally damned killer whose only purpose was to condemn man just as the devil had wished. I couldn't stand to look at myself any longer.

CHAPTER 10

"Come on," Marlo called out from the hallway.

It wasn't difficult to tear my eyes away from my reflection in the mirror. I imagined that most would have found it easy to stand there and stare at the perfection – the flawlessly sculpted muscles, impeccably coifed hair – but I was very uncomfortable knowing the source of all that perfection was pure evil.

Marlo was heading down the hallway to my left and I followed behind her, keeping her pace. I felt different, as if I were floating over the floor, my feet never touching the cold stone. One glance at me feet told me I was in contact with the ground but I seemed to be moving with a grace and agility, almost an airiness, I never had before.

We arrived at another wooden door down the long hallway.

"The security center?" I asked, sensing this was the room I was in the night of the Halloween party.

"Yes," Marlo replied. "But it's also our command center." Marlo pushed open the door. "Come on in," she beckoned.

The room looked completely different from what I remembered of that night. All of the furniture had been removed from the room including the wall of monitors. I looked around for the couch I had sat on before all of the mayhem broke out that night, but it wasn't there. In fact, there were no signs that my transformation had even happened. I didn't know what I expected to find, but there was nothing there. The only item in the room was one lone computer which sat on top of a small but ornate wooden desk near the wall with the stained glass window, the same window I had opened and unknowingly tipped off my enemies that I was nearby. Felix sat behind the desk typing away.

"What's going on in here?" I asked.

Max appeared out of nowhere behind me. "You'll see," he said, a smile spreading across his face.

A noise, like stone grinding on stone, started from what sounded like the middle of the room. The floor began to mildly vibrate and then felt like it began to move.

"Oh no," I said and covered my ears. "Concentrate, concentrate," I whispered to myself.

The room erupted in laughter. I looked up to see all of my new family there laughing at me.

"No Allison, it's not that. You're fine, it's not your senses," Marlo reassured.

I straightened up and removed my hands from my ears, confused by what was happening. The noise continued and the vibrations intensified.

"Look," Lorenzo commanded and pointed to the middle of the floor.

The center of the stone floor began to shift. A large rectangular piece of stone gave way, dropping several inches beneath the perimeter of the floor where we stood. The piece broke in a straight line down the middle, each half moving to the side. In its place was what looked like a giant piece of Plexiglas that rose to floor level. Lights flickered beneath the surface like a television set being turned on. A world map slowly came into view. At first it was just an outline, yet clearly that of a world map, and it quickly populated with color. Finally, several different colored dots appeared twinkling over the surface.

"What is this?" I asked. I looked up to find four sets of eyes staring back at me, apparently waiting for my reaction.

"This is how we hunt," Max said with a twinkle in his eye.

He walked to the map, glided over its surface and found North America. He tapped it with his foot, and then tapped a few more times until a map of the States was visible. I could see hundreds of colored spots blinking all over the map.

Lorenzo leaned in and said, "Marlo did tell you that Max was the hunter in the family, right?" He smirked as he looked at his brother with a little brotherly pride.

"No she didn't. What does this have to do with hunting?" I asked.

"You see," Max said, taking over the conversation, "the colored dots represent different types of prey. Green represents herbivores, blue is aquatic life, and red is for carnivores. The black dots represent humans. Over the years we realized that we had to be careful how we hunted. Kill too much of one species in one area and people start to become suspicious. We knew we had to balance mortal and animal kills to spread out the damage. We recognized we needed a plan that would meet our dietary needs yet be inconspicuous enough to not reveal our existence. So over hundreds of years, I amassed a group of hunters all over the world. They track the population of various prey and report back to my brother, Felix."

I looked over at Felix who raised his eyebrows at me. "I'm the brain behind this operation," he said jokingly.

"That's right," Max continued, "our resident tech geek. Felix tracks the population sizes and makes recommendations as to which species should be hunted in a particular area. This way, we don't eliminate too many of one breed thereby drawing unwanted attention to ourselves."

"That's very well thought out," I mused.

"I know, right?" Max asked. "But check this out. Say you see a lot of green dots in a particular area; that means there are a lot of herbivores concentrated in one spot. Tap on the grouping of green dots and they'll break out into different shades of green, representing different species. Keep tapping down and you'll eventually get a picture of the animal and the exact location. Then you're all set for the hunt!"

"Huh," I said in amazement. "But you are looking at a forest in St. Lawrence County, New York."

"And..."

"Is that where we're going?"

"Mmm hmm."

"Well, if that's where we're hunting, wouldn't I get thirsty before I got to the destination?" I asked.

The room erupted in laughter again.

"Oh Allison," Lorenzo said, "you still have so much to learn."

"About what?"

"From here to St. Lawrence County," Lorenzo said through chuckles, "you can be there in less than an hour with your speed!"

"Really?" I questioned as if I didn't believe him. I looked down at my body looking for some indication that I would have acquired any degree of speed from my transformation but I didn't see anything. "So do I turn into a bat or something?" I jokingly asked.

There was more laughter which quickly ceased as I grabbed my throat.

"Allison, what's wrong?" Marlo asked, concern apparent in her voice as she glided to my side.

"My throat is getting dry again." The heat in my stomach began to swirl and crawled its way up my throat.

"All right," Max announced. "We would normally run to our destination since it's this close, but we can't chance you encountering a human; not for your first hunt. Felix will fly us there."

"Excuse me?" I questioned. "Fly?"

"Hey, when you have all of eternity, you tend to pick up a hobby or two," Felix said with a wink.

I knocked back another flask of blood, which Marlo ensured would tide me over until I got to New York. I couldn't help but wonder where, or who, it came from. But I didn't dare ask. Some things were better left unsaid. But once the liquid touched my lips, the source didn't matter. This liquid tasted different than what I drank when I first woke from my transformation. It had an earthy flavor but was just as refreshing. It slid down my throat taking the heat, and my urge, with it.

The helipad was on the roof of the castle. Max was decked out in full hunting camouflage...shirt, pants and boots. I couldn't refuse the camo outfit he insisted I wear. It was evident that he loved hunting and the gear meant a lot to him, so not wanting to hurt his feelings, I obliged.

"Hunting gear has come a long way since...well, since I began hunting," Max said.

I grinned and looked down at my jacket, pants and boots. I felt ridiculous. I never hunted in my mortal life and I certainly didn't equate this type of hunting with the need for actual hunting gear.

Felix was already behind the controls of the chopper pushing buttons, sans camo gear; he apparently wasn't hunting with us or somehow resisted Max's pleading to dress the part.

Max helped me get in the back of the chopper and placed headphones over my ears.

"You'll need these so as to not get distracted by the noise of the blades," he yelled over the choppers' swirling blades.

Max hopped in and closed the door.

"Where are Marlo and Lorenzo?" I yelled.

"They're going on a different kind of hunt."

"Different? How so?"

Max returned my question with a stare that meant I should know what he was talking about.

"Oh." I responded. "Where are they, um, who are they, um, going to um…what is their…"

"Marlo is hitting a men's prison and Lorenzo is paying a visit to the club scene in New York City. You know, prison, big city, no one will suspect a thing."

"Oh," I responded flatly. I knew sooner or later I was going to have to face this challenge. Some poor soul out there was eventually going to be my meal and suffer at my hands just so I could survive. This just didn't seem right; it wasn't the natural order of things…or maybe it was in this new world I found myself in.

"How do you know when you need to eat a mortal?" I asked.

"Eat a mortal," Max laughed. "Where do you come up with this stuff?"

I felt embarrassed, again and stared out the window waiting for Max to stop laughing.

"Didn't you notice Marlo's and Lorenzo's eyes?" he asked me.

I thought about how Marlo's eyes had looked when I had stared into them, trying to gain control of my senses. Her eyes had been pale, the lavender faded from its typical vibrant hue. And the spikes of gold twinkled more fervently than I had ever noticed before. I hadn't really studied Lorenzo's face, but now that Max mentioned it, his typical gemstone green eyes had also been quite pale.

"I didn't really think about it, but I guess their eyes had faded in color a bit," I mused.

"And the gold flecks?"

"They were definitely swirling around faster than usual."

"When you're starved of mortal blood, your eyes lose their luster and will fade in color. Of course, only we can see that; the mortals are oblivious. The longer you go without mortal blood, the paler your eyes become. The gold flecks begin to move feverishly around your pupils. We're not really sure why. Maybe it's like how the fruit glimmered on the tree, drawing Eve and Cain towards it. Anyway, our glimmering eyes are mesmerizing to mortals. They don't notice the gold specks but it's exactly that which pulls them in, making it quite easy for us. Well, that along with our scent, our touch and everything else about us. Our whole essence makes a hunt way too easy. But your eyes are an indicator of your hunger; if they fade too much, the pit in your stomach ignites, throwing its fiery flames to your throat until you can't take it and your senses take over and you go on a wild hunt."

"Good grief," I said in horror.

"That's why we hunt like this, Allison," Max reassured me. "It's so well planned that you don't get starved to the point you lose control."

"But then what's wrong with Marlo and Lorenzo?" I questioned.

"This was an unusual week. They didn't have a chance to hunt before the party and they also expended a lot of energy chasing Vincent after he bit you. And they both spent a lot of time with you throughout your transformation, making sure you were fed and were as comfortable as possible."

"Oh," I simply stated. "Wait, they chased after Vincent? Why? Did they find him?"

Max appeared uncomfortable. "It was instinct to go after him, but no, they didn't find him."

"Oh," I said again. "What happens if you don't feed for an extended period? A vampire obviously can't die that way."

"True, it won't kill a vampire, but it's nothing you want to experience. If you go without eating anything your skin eventually petrifies, becoming hard and brittle and discolored. I hear it's very painful. Some other kinds use that as a form of torture. You become entombed in your skin, trapped until you are nourished again. It's a living hell."

"More so than this existence?" I muttered. Max either didn't hear me or ignored my comment.

"What about hunting animals? Can't they fight back, like bite and scratch?"

Max chuckled again. "They can, but it won't do much good against our skin."

"What do you mean?"

"While in pursuit of prey, our skin transforms into a protective barrier. It becomes hardened and impenetrable with the exception of our neck. No animal bite or claw can break the surface. So you just have to protect your neck."

"We're here," Felix's announced.

"Woo hoo, baby!" Max exclaimed.

I looked out the window to my left and could see the pale moonlight reflecting off of the lake below. To my right, I saw treetops. I felt the helicopter descend and could see the water drawing closer and the trees getting bigger.

"Are you ready?" Max looked over at me.

"Where are we landing?" I asked.

"We're not!" Max exclaimed.

"Then how are we getting to the ground?" I asked, sensing another embarrassing moment about to present itself.

"Trust your instincts and you'll be fine." And with that, Max opened the helicopter door and gracefully dove headfirst out of the chopper.

"Ahhhh," I yelled as I gripped the overhead handle.

Felix's voice broke in over my headphones. "Trust me, Allison; you'll be fine. You don't have to showboat like Max. Don't look and just jump. Your instincts will take it from there."

I clung to the grip, determined that I wasn't going to jump out of the helicopter. From my estimation, we were still a good 70 feet or so above the ground. There was no way I could jump and not injure myself.

Felix looked over his shoulder at me, "Allison, you will be fine," he reassured me.

There was something in his eyes that made me believe him when he spoke those words. And besides, I didn't really have another option. I unbuckled my seatbelt, removed my headphones and hesitantly scooted myself over the bench seat. I pushed myself off of the seat Max had just occupied, but my hands lingered behind, gripping the seat as I peered out of the chopper. It was total blackness below. Without the moonlight reflecting off the water, I couldn't see anything. I turned my head and looked back at Felix. He gave me a reassuring nod. I took a deep breath and leapt from the safety of my transportation.

The cool air felt refreshing against my blazing hot skin. Surprisingly, my stomach wasn't in my throat, where I expected it to be. The air blew past me as I descended. In a matter of seconds, I could see the ground closing in on me. I saw every detail of the sand beneath me. My feet landed squarely on the ground, my knees buckling to absorb the impact from the jump. I stood straight up and looked around. I had landed on my feet and unharmed. The mortal version of me would not have been so lucky.

My eyes immediately adjusted. I could clearly see Max standing in the darkness with a huge grin on his face.

"See, that wasn't so bad now was it?"

"I don't understand how I did that."

"You don't have to understand. That's the great thing about our abilities; they take care of us. That was very graceful, by the way."

"Really?" Nothing I had ever done was graceful.

"Really," Max replied. "Now let's go hunt."

Max was off running at full speed into the woods. I took off after him.

Trees whizzed by me with amazing speed. Even in the darkness, I could see every obstacle in my way and was able to avoid it. I caught up to Max in no time and maintained my pace a few steps behind him.

"We're almost there," he said, not even remotely winded from the run. I heard him without a problem despite how quickly we were moving.

We ascended the top of a large hill where the trees and foliage gave way to a clearing. The cloudless sky was full of stars and the air was fresh and intoxicating. Various scents filled my nose and stirred the venom in my stomach.

"Are you ready?" Max asked.

"Do I really have a choice?" I asked in return.

Max gave a quick chuckle. "You remember what Marlo told you about concentrating so that you only see what's right in front of you and hear what's only immediately around you?"

"Yes."

"Well all that goes out the window when you're hunting!" There was that glimmer in Max's eye again. It was apparent that he was completely in his element.

"Really?" I asked, trepidation sweeping over me at the realization of what I was about to do.

"Yep," Max said and walked over to me. He stood close, ignoring the concept of personal space. He grabbed my wrists and straightened my arms at my sides. He stared me straight in the eye.

"Close your eyes," Max commanded.

I stared back into his chocolate brown eyes before resigning to his command.

"Now let your hearing go."

I opened my eyes. "What..."

"Allison, just close your eyes and let your hearing wander."

I closed my eyes again and concentrated on letting my hearing stray, as Max had directed.

"You're trying too hard. Just listen."

I relaxed a bit, my shoulders falling back. I heard crickets chirping throughout the darkness but not much else. I drew in a deep breath and listened more intently. I could hear the grass swaying in the breeze like a melody accompanying the cricket's tune. Then I heard the soft lapping of the lake against the shore though we were miles away. I drew another breath and could hear bat wings fluttering in the air. Another breath and I could hear soft footsteps against the earth. My nose twitched.

"That's it," Max whispered, his hands still clasping my wrists. "What do you hear?"

"Footsteps," I whispered. I drew another breath which greeted my nostrils with a pleasant fragrance. The fire in my belly burned, its flames clawing up my throat. My throat was so hot I felt like I could spit fire if I wanted.

"How many do you hear?"

I listened for a moment. "Eight."

"That's right," Max replied, confirming I had picked up on my prey. "Take another breath," he instructed.

I drew another breath and the scent intensified, making the pit in my stomach roar with desire.

"Where are they?" Max asked of my prey.

I tossed my head over my right shoulder. The herd of deer was to the northeast.

"Mmm hmm," Max responded with approval. "One more breath."

I drew another breath and the scent was stronger yet. My feet began to tingle, the sensation making its way up my legs. I felt the venom begin to flow in my mouth, numbing my tongue.

"Now open your eyes," Max commanded.

My eyes sprang open and I saw Max standing there but only for a brief second. His eyes were illuminated and the gold specks swirled with excitement. Max fled to my left, the opposite of where I was headed.

Every detail of my environment was apparent to me. I could see every leaf, every blade of grass, every piece of bark on the tree trunk. I threw my head over my right shoulder. My vision cut through the trees and foliage and zeroed in on the herd. The sound of their heartbeats filled my ears. I broke into a full sprint, my eyes never leaving the target. I could see their hearts and the luscious blood pumping through their veins. As I approached, I felt an odd sensation overcome my entire body. My skin stiffened forming its body armor to defend itself against my prey. I leapt through the air and pounced on one of the beasts. The poor thing never heard me coming, the fear apparent in its eyes as I held it in my fiery grasp. My lips curled back and my fangs emerged. I saw the vision in my prey's eyes and had to admit, it was quite frightening. Long white spikes protruded from my otherwise delicate lips. I plunged my teeth into the doe's neck, penetrating the flesh with tremendous ease. The animal briefly struggled but then fell still. Warmth filled my mouth, and the liquid was a most pleasant taste. The blood slid down my throat, extinguishing the inferno. My belly filled with precious liquid which cooled the incinerator that otherwise dwelled there.

The ordeal was over in a matter of seconds. I stood above my prey, my breathing rapid. I felt satisfied, but I wanted more. I surveyed my surroundings. The other deer had scattered when I attacked. My vision cut through the forest and my hearing reached out further, seeking more victims.

A slow clap broke through my concentration. I reigned in my hearing and vision. This sound was close and very much misplaced. The details of my surroundings disappeared and I could only see the immediate area where I stood. The clapping got louder as if it were somehow approaching me.

I focused in the direction of the noise. I saw two silvery blue specks among the shadows. I had seen this before. I knew what it was, or rather who it was.

"Vincent," I snarled.

I squinted and concentrated on the two eyes I saw looming in the darkness. The rest of his body appeared as my eyes quickly adjusted. He was leaning against a tree, his right leg crossed at the shin over his left. He was wearing jeans and his motorcycle jacket over a tight black shirt.

My instincts moved me to a crouched, defensive position. I hadn't expected to see anyone out here let alone Vincent. A wave of anger and emotion swelled within me at the sight of the man who had transformed me into the living dead. On one hand I was angry that he took away the last choice I could have made as a human. But in doing so, he also saved me from being killed. Vincent's presence was a shock and I wasn't quite sure how to react to him so I remained frozen like a statue.

"Hello, Allison," Vincent spoke from the shadows. My eyes narrowed, never leaving his. A low hiss escaped through my lips.

"Allison, please don't be angry," he begged. "I came here to see you, not to harm you."

I chuckled to myself. *How could he possibly do me any more harm*, I thought. A growl formed in my belly and crawled up my throat, escaping through my clenched teeth. I burrowed my eyes straight into Vincent's, not wavering. I wanted him to know I wasn't afraid of him and truth be told I wasn't. Yet part of me was somewhat relieved to see him, to know that he was unharmed.

Vincent stepped through the trees, his hands extended as if making a peace offering. "It's okay," he whispered. "Swallow the anger. Don't let it consume you."

My eyes followed his as he slowly approached me. Swallow the anger, he had instructed me. I took a deep breath and smelled the sweet scent that was unmistakably his alone. I looked at his face and his sheer beauty was almost enough to calm me. I felt the anger start to subside and slide down my throat. I slowly stood up to meet his face as he stood just inches from me. I wanted so much to be mad at him for what he had done to me and what he had done to his brothers and sister. I wanted to hit him and unleash my fury upon him; maybe even kill him so as to protect my new family from having to carry out the unthinkable task themselves.

"You looked like a seasoned professional," Vincent whispered with a half smile, referring to my first attack. "Very nice. But these clothes. What did Max do to you?"

"How did you know I would be here?" I asked through my still clenched teeth. I desperately wanted to show him that I was angry.

"Max is quite predictable. He brings all first time hunters to this locale since there's no chance of running into any mortals. I heard the helicopter take off so I ran here."

"You ran here?" I asked in disbelief. Lorenzo had said we could normally run this distance, but hearing Vincent say it, and knowing he ran it as fast as the chopper had flown it was a bit mind boggling.

"Of course I did. I knew it was just you and Max and the others wouldn't pick up my scent since they were heading in a different direction."

"So you know I'm here with Max now, right?"

Vincent ran a finger along my jaw line, stopping at my chin. Part of me wanted so much to smack his hand away; another part of me wanted to pull him close and kiss him. As mad as I was right now, I was still deeply attracted to him.

"I know," he responded.

"And you know what will happen if he finds you here, don't you?"

"There's no need to worry about that. Max is focused on hunting. He knows your instincts will carry you and he doesn't have to worry about you. We have some time before he finishes his hunt." Vincent moved his face closer to mine, still holding my chin.

"Time for what?" I whispered. Vincent, with the slightest touch, dispelled any anger I held for him.

"To talk," he whispered in response, sweeping his lips barely across mine. The slight touch of his lips on mine ignited a new feeling within me. An overwhelming sense of desire washed over me, yet there was a part of me that was somehow able to control myself.

"About…" I pushed myself onto my toes as I waited for his reply. I leaned in hoping for a kiss. Vincent chuckled and stepped back, much to my disappointment.

"Us, Allison. To talk about us."

The disappointment I felt from the lack of a second kiss was quickly washed away. But that brief sense of excitement was replaced with frustration when I thought about our situation.

"Us?" I questioned.

"That's right. Us."

"What about us? There can't possibly be an *us* after what *you* did."

"But there can be an us," Vincent responded with a glimmer in his eye.

"How, Vincent? You transformed me without my permission. You broke your society's law and there's a price to pay for that. So tell me how there can be an us? You ruined all of that."

Vincent chuckled.

"Really," I fumed. "I don't think any of this is funny."

"You're right, it's not. But my dear, there is a way." He placed both of his hands on my cheeks and steadied my face. His touch was magical, sending an electrifying current through my body. He stared deep in my eyes and I stared back into his beautiful, crystalline blue eyes.

"How?" I whispered. His hold on me was astonishing. It was like any time I wanted to feel any anger or ill will towards him, one touch of his hand wiped it away, replacing those feelings with longing.

"Run away with me," Vincent whispered softly touching his lips to mine again. His lips were hot, as were mine, but supple and welcoming. I wanted more and moved my arms around his neck.

Vincent grabbed my arms, stopping my embrace. "Did you hear me?" he asked.

"Uh huh," I muttered. Vincent backed away a few steps, allowing me to clear my head. I took a deep breath and came back to reality. "So how is this supposed to work? I'm just going to run away with you now?"

"No, you can't leave now. Max will be expecting you shortly and if you don't show, he'll suspect something and will come looking for you. It would only be a matter of time before he picked up my scent."

"Then when? How?"

"So you're willing to go? With me? No questions asked?" Vincent peered down at me as if I should have had a few questions.

"Why don't you just tell me what you are getting at so we don't have to play these games?"

"You realize, if you leave with me, we're gone forever. We can never return here."

"Oh," was all I could say. I hadn't really thought about it.

"And you'll never be able to see Jenna again. Or Marlo, or my brothers."

"But why?" I questioned. "I'm not the one that did anything wrong."

"They can never know where I am. They don't want to kill their brother as much as I don't want to be killed. Once they realize you are gone, they'll know you are with me. You being around them will only heighten their awareness of your scent. If they pick that up anywhere near where I am, well they might not be able to stop themselves from finding me."

"So you are asking me to give up the only family I have left in this world for you? You, the person that took from me the last decision of my mortal life?" The anger hiding in my belly was starting to swell again. "Why exactly could you not wait for me to tell you when I was ready? Why couldn't you do that for me?" I yelled. My eyes stung with venom but the tears did not flow.

"Allison, Allison, please," Vincent pleaded. "After you lunged at Jenna, I was afraid one of my siblings was going to kill you. That after all, was the plan all along. We either transformed you with your consent, or we would have to destroy you if you posed a threat to our kind."

"Ugh." I squeezed my eyes shut and what little I could remember from that night filled my mind. "I still can't believe I lunged at my best friend," I muttered.

Vincent began walking in a circle around me. "Your symptoms that night, the night of the Halloween party, they were quite strong. But none of us spent enough time with you throughout the evening to notice the changes. Had I spent more time with you, maybe I would have noticed and we could have avoided this whole situation."

"What changes?"

"Your body temperature was higher than it had ever been before. Marlo said you were light headed and in and out of paying attention to conversations. She also mentioned the tingling sensation you felt in your feet which you attributed to the boots you were wearing. On the contrary, that was the venom building up in your system."

"Oh," I groaned. "You're right. I felt the same sensation as I ran out here tonight."

I paused for a moment.

"How did you know I was about to..." the word hung on my tongue, too painful to say. I couldn't believe I almost attacked my best friend.

Vincent let out a little laugh. "Allison, we're vampires, we can tell when one of our kind is getting ready to attack."

"What did I do? What happened?" Marlo and her brothers had told me what had happened, but I wanted to hear it from Vincent's perspective.

"Jenna crept around the corner, looking for Lorenzo. When you smelled her, you stood up and your expression just changed. The gold flecks danced in your eyes like a hurricane circling over water. Lorenzo noticed and grabbed Jenna and quickly removed her from the room."

"So I didn't attack?"

"Well you did. You leapt through the air just as the door was closing. I caught you midair to stop you."

"I see," I hung my head, ashamed of what I had almost done to Jenna.

"Hey," Vincent said. "Don't beat yourself up. You didn't know what was going on and we were able to control the situation. But now that you are one of us, we can teach you to control your needs. You won't be a threat to Jenna."

"Are you sure Jenna didn't suspect a thing?" I had to ask. If she suspected anything, that could pose a risk to her life.

"No, she doesn't suspect anything."

"What happened after you pulled me out of the air?"

"Allison, you have to believe me," Vincent pleaded, his eyes begging for forgiveness. "I didn't have time to think. All I knew was that you had just almost attacked a mortal, which posed a great risk to exposing us."

"But you said Jenna didn't suspect anything."

"True, but in that moment, I wasn't sure what Jenna had or hadn't seen. All I knew is what you almost did, in front of my siblings, and I was afraid they were going to destroy you. I had no choice Allison. I had to transform you."

"But you did have a choice," I stated. "You didn't have to put yourself at risk for me. You could have let your family do what they had to do with me."

"No, Allison. The thought of this existence without you was too much to bear for me. In my mind, I had no choice; I had to save you."

"Save me," I whispered. The irony of the word *save* struck me. Vincent took my mortal life, destroyed my soul, yet he had saved me from certain death.

"I am sorry," Vincent deliberately stated as he pulled my head up. "Please forgive me?"

I stared into the abyss of his eyes, his finger still holding my chin. There was just something about him I couldn't resist. His rendition of the events on Halloween night made sense. I could understand his fear that his siblings would have acted upon their pact and destroyed me. I could understand his sense of hopelessness at the thought of losing me, because frankly, I felt the same about losing him. The hole that tore through my heart when I learned what he had done, and heard he could never return, was too painful for me to bear. And now he was here, my love, standing in front of me. Yes, he took away my choice, but in doing so gave me something more. He gave me eternity. And I wanted to spend it with him.

"Of course I forgive you," I said. "And I'll go with you. Just tell me when."

Vincent's face lit up. I wasn't sure if his delight was in my forgiveness, or with my agreement to run away with him. Maybe it was both.

"You do? You will?" Vincent questioned.

"Of course, Vincent. I...I'm falling in love with you."

"You are?" he questioned as if he couldn't believe what he was hearing.

"Yeah, I am. The return of my memories of us over the past year has made me realize how good we are together, how much fun we have together. Things may not have gone as planned when you transformed me, but sooner or later I was going to have to consent. And now I'm a vampire and have all eternity. To spend with you."

Vincent smiled. "Oh Allison, you don't know how happy that makes me."

He picked me up and twirled me around. The stars and tree-tops bled into a blur above our heads. Vincent placed me back on the ground and grabbed my face, kissing me again. This time he didn't stop me from wrapping my arms around his neck. He slid his hands down my back, wrapping his muscular arms around my waist and twirled me again. I threw my head back in laughter. I felt such pure joy in that moment.

"Okay," Vincent said as he placed me on the ground again. "Tomorrow, at precisely two minutes before midnight, you need to jump out your window and scale down the side of the castle. I assume they have you in the room with the painting of the ocean, correct?"

"Yes, but why at eleven fifty-eight?"

"The cameras will not be scanning that side of the castle at that time. I'm assuming Felix hasn't changed the configuration as he figures I'm long gone by now and there is no need for such precautions. But you'll have to hurry. You will need to move along the east side of the castle pretty quickly. When you approach the southeastern most part of the castle, break towards the woods, okay?"

"Yeah, got it."

"Run through the woods until you reach the river and follow it north."

"North?"

"Yes, you need to head north but can't head that way from your room; too much exposure running across the front of that place."

"Okay, got it; to the river then head north."

"Right, follow the river until you see a huge boulder; it's unmistakable – you can't miss it. At the boulder, head west and keep running. You'll come upon the lake in your backyard. I'll be there waiting for you and we'll leave from there. Got it?"

"Yeah. What do I need to pack?"

"Nothing, don't worry about that, just bring you."

"No clothes? What about money?"

"I have it all under control Allison. Please trust me. You have to get back; Max's hunt is probably coming to an end and we can't risk his suspicions."

"Okay," I said, my mind whirling with all of these details.

"Now compose yourself so Max doesn't suspect anything."

"Yeah, yeah, I'll be fine."

"Okay," Vincent stated, "I'll see you tomorrow night." He kissed my cheek and then disappeared before my eyes.

I stood still in the darkness absorbing everything that had just happened. I repeated Vincent's directions to help remember them. A huge smile spread across my face. Vincent had just left, but I already couldn't wait to be with him tomorrow night. I took a deep breath to compose myself and looked around. I couldn't remember which way I had come from. I closed my eyes and took another deep breath and allowed my hearing to reach out, to search for my direction. I heard rustling to the west and a helicopter in the distance. I shot open my eyes and took off on foot.

My feet glided over the forest floor. A slight breeze wafted past me and a familiar scent filled my nose. It was Max.

"Whoa, whoa, whoa," Max exclaimed as I ran past him.

I dug my heels into the ground and slid to a stop, pulling up plenty of dirt in my path.

"Oh sorry," I said. I composed myself and was surprised I wasn't winded. "I guess I just latched onto your scent and kept running," I laughed.

"How was your hunt?" Max asked.

"Oh, um, fine," I hastily responded.

"Just fine?" Max looked at me with an inquisitive eye.

"Yeah, fine. I got one doe. It wasn't as bad as I expected. I dreaded this whole experience but it was actually quite amazing. I hadn't really realized what I had done until it was over. And the taste was something I really feared but it was quite refreshing. And the relief I felt was most welcome to my throat and stomach."

"Are you still hungry?"

"No, I don't think so."

"Hmm," Max hummed.

"What?"

"It's your first hunt after your transformation; you should have been hungrier than that."

"Well you all did give me something to drink while I was transforming and after I woke up."

"I suppose, but that typically isn't enough to satisfy a new vampire."

Much to my relief, the helicopter approached, cutting off our conversation.

"How do we get up?" I asked Max, quickly changing the subject.

"The same way you got down," he replied, still studying me. Max was buying my acting skills.

"I'm supposed to jump?" I exclaimed.

"Allison, if there's anything you learned today, it should be to trust your instincts."

"Humph," I replied.

"After you," Max said, waving his hand up at the helicopter.

The chopper descended a bit but was still a good 60 feet up in the air. I looked at Max and he gave me a reassuring nod. I backed up as far as the tree line would allow in order to get a running start.

"Don't take your eye off the target," Max yelled to me.

I took off, taking seven steps. I stared up at the helicopter as I crouched and pushed off the shore. I shot through the air like an arrow at a target, and the cool air rushed past me as it had done on my earlier plunge. I reached the chopper, grabbed the edge of it and flipped myself inside.

"Nice one," Felix mused, giving me a thumbs up.

Max hopped into the helicopter right behind me.

"So how was it?" Felix asked, looking between me and Max before returning his eyes to the cockpit.

"Not too bad," I said, staring out the window.

"Max?" Felix asked.

"I'm not sure. Allison only killed one deer."

"Only one?" Felix craned his neck around his captain's chair to look at me. "What happened?"

"Nothing happened," I replied.

"That's not right Allison. You should have needed more than that. Your instincts should have made you want more, especially since this was your first time out."

I shrugged my shoulders and continued staring out the window. I felt like I was under a microscope. "I wasn't all that hungry after I finished. Maybe I filled up too much back at the castle."

There was a long pause and Max continued analyzing me. Felix maneuvered the chopper to head back to the castle.

"He was there, wasn't he?" Max asked in an accusatory tone.

"What? Who?" I responded.

"Vincent."

"Vincent?" I questioned, turning to look at Max. "No," I curtly replied. "Why would you think that?"

"Vincent!" Felix exclaimed. "Are you sure?"

"Pretty sure," Max said. He pursed his lips and crossed his arms as he studied my every move.

"Well, I don't know why you think Vincent was there, but he wasn't," I responded.

"Why do you think Vincent was there?" Felix asked Max.

I felt Max's eyes burning a hole through the back of my head as I watched the ground and water pass below us.

"Well Allison was *hunting* longer than I expected. So I expanded my hearing to see if she was in trouble."

A chill went up my spine at the realization Max might have heard Vincent. I squeezed my eyes shut.

"And?" Felix asked impatiently.

"I heard something move way too quickly through the woods so I opened my eyes."

"And?" Felix asked again.

"I didn't see anything and I couldn't lock on a scent."

"And so you assumed Vincent was in the woods with me?" I asked incredulously.

"He had to have been. Nothing else could move that fast – no animal, no human. I sensed him! I heard him running through the woods."

"But you didn't see anything?" Felix asked.

"No," Max admitted.

We flew the rest of the way back to Castle Adena in silence. I continued staring out the window and Max eventually gave up staring at me to glare out his window. Though Max hadn't seen or smelled Vincent, it was obvious he was on to something and I wasn't sure how long I could hold up this lie. And if I couldn't keep up the lie, I couldn't expect to keep secret my plans for tomorrow night. My new siblings could not find out about my planned rendezvous with Vincent.

The chopper landed smoothly on the helipad. The three of us exited the aircraft in silence, Max not assisting me as he had when we departed. Both Max and Felix were skimming over the rooftop way ahead of me. I was in no hurry for what was going to happen inside once they told Marlo and Lorenzo what Max suspected.

The door into the castle slammed in front of me. I paused for a second before grabbing the handle. I actually felt exhausted, something I didn't expect with my new existence and after having just fed. I didn't feel like I needed to sleep, but my head felt like it was overloaded and just needed some down time. I definitely wasn't going to get that inside.

I opened the door and took the stairs three at a time. I was certainly enjoying the gracefulness that I had acquired since my transformation. I tried sneaking down the hallway to my room, but luck was not on my side.

"Allison," Marlo called from somewhere downstairs, her voice echoing throughout the hollow hallway. "Can you please come down here?" Her voice was too kind for what I suspected was going to happen. I was not in the mood for an inquisition.

I navigated the stone staircase and crossed through the great room. My senses led me down another hallway to the dining room. It was ironic that my siblings had a full dining room, complete with china and crystal, when such items were superfluous for their lifestyle.

"Hey," I nonchalantly said to Marlo as I entered the room.

"How was your hunt?" she asked, her eyes tense and back to the vibrant shade of lavender I was so accustomed. Max and Felix stood at an opposite corner of the table from Marlo. Lorenzo was seated at the head of the long, wooden dining table, his eyes a sparkling green.

"Max didn't fill you in?" I retorted, hoping to deflect the question.

"He did," Marlo responded matter-of-factly.

"So then you know it went well. It was much easier than I expected."

"Was Vincent there?" Marlo asked cutting to the chase. Her eyes burned into mine. I had to look away.

"No," I sternly stated in my best attempt to sound convincing. "I don't know why Max insists he heard Vincent there."

"He was there!" Max yelled. "It had to be him or another vampire. No mortal or animal could move as fast as what I heard cutting through the forest."

"I doubt it was another vampire," Felix added. "There aren't many of us in this area that would have been hunting in the same spot at the same time."

I burrowed my glare into the floor, unsure of what to say next. I felt all four sets of eyes focused on me.

"Just admit he was there," Lorenzo demanded.

"What did he want?" Felix asked.

Chatter started between the three brothers.

"Do you think he could still be close?" Lorenzo asked.

"Why would he have risked his existence knowing one of us would have been with Allison?" Max asked.

"Where do you think he's heading?" Felix questioned.

"We could probably go back to the forest and pick up his scent," Lorenzo stated.

I couldn't believe what I was hearing. I looked up to see the brothers standing in a tight circle now plotting strategy. The image

I had of these loving siblings, five of them who had been together for thousands of years, whom I thought would be there to look out for each other, were now plotting their brother's demise. I couldn't fathom how they could plot something so horrible after living with someone for so long.

Marlo still stood in the same spot, her arms crossed in a defensive position. Her eyebrows were creased, like she was deep in thought as she scrutinized everything about me. I looked back at the brothers who were still talking about Vincent.

"Wait!" I yelled. "How can you do this?"

The strategic brotherly chatter halted and they all turned their heads to look at me.

"Do what?" Max asked. Agitation was apparent in his voice.

"Vincent is your brother and the three of you are standing there plotting his demise! How can you do that to your own brother? To someone you've known for God only knows how many years?"

The room fell silent as my yelling echoed down the hallways. Everyone continued to stare at me. Lorenzo broke from the group and walked slowly towards me, dragging his hand along the table, his eyes never leaving mine. His blond hair fell over his shoulders and his eyes were red with anger. He stopped inches from me, bent to my height and pushed his face in front of mine.

"There's one thing more important than family," Lorenzo growled at me. His brilliant green eyes illuminated his pale face. His thirteen tear-dropped gold flecks barely moved around his pupils; his breath filled my nostrils. I had never seen this side of Lorenzo before. His anger was apparent as he stood there trembling with clenched fists. A pang of fear stabbed me in the stomach.

"What's that?" I whispered back, holding his stare.

"Self preservation," he snarled. His eyes still focused on me as if he was trying to read my mind. "The one thing that matters most to any vampire," he continued, "is his or her own existence."

"Lorenzo," Felix called out.

Lorenzo stepped back from me and narrowed his eyes one more time before turning around and walking back to his chair at the front of the table.

I stood there in a bit of shock. So Vincent's own brothers *would* turn on him to save their own existence. Sure they had told me there were punishments in place for rule breakers, but I thought they could at least let this slide considering the circumstance. It was apparent that I was wrong and it was a tough pill to swallow. I didn't want to see any harm done to Vincent, but I could also understand their position.

"He...um...he was there," I whispered to the room.

My brothers seemed to relax hearing the truth, but Marlo still stood there in her defensive position, still analyzing me.

"What did he want?" Max hissed at me.

"Uh, um, not much." I wasn't sure what to say. I didn't want them going after Vincent but I also felt guilty keeping the truth from them.

"Not much?" Max asked sarcastically. "You want us to believe that Vincent risked his own existence for nothing much?"

I stared back at my siblings but their return stares were unforgiving. I was going to have to say something, but I couldn't let them know about my secret plans.

"He apologized," I said.

"Apologized? Vincent?" Lorenzo exclaimed as the brothers burst out in laughter.

"For what?" Felix asked through his laughter.

"Why is this so funny?" I asked.

"Because Vincent is the most arrogant person we know. He never apologized for anything in his entire existence!" Max exclaimed.

"Well he did apologize to me," I said sternly. "For transforming me without my permission." At least that was the truth and I hoped I was selling it.

The brothers continued their laughter as Marlo stood there like a mannequin. The amusement of my response eventually wore off.

"Is that all?" Lorenzo asked. "So he just apologized and left?"

"Yes," I replied.

"And did he by chance tell you where he was going?" Max asked.

"No."

"And you have no idea where he is?" Felix asked.

"No, I don't. He apologized and then told me this would be the last time I ever saw him. That he had to flee to save himself from all of you." I pointed an accusing finger at each of them. Tears welled up in my eyes, this time spilling over and burning my face.

"Ouch," I howled as the tears ran over my cheeks.

Marlo snapped out of her stance and was at my side in the blink of an eye.

"You can't let the tears flow, Allison," she said as she dabbed my cheeks with the sleeve of her dress. "The venom will sear your skin."

"What?" I gasped as I jerked my hand to feel my face. I could feel fresh scars on my face where the tears had rolled.

"Don't worry," Marlo reassured me, "you'll heal."

I ran to the nearest mirror hung on the stone wall and examined the fresh, pink flesh exposed on my pale face. I whirled around and looked at Marlo.

"I'm exhausted," I flatly announced. "Why am I tired?"

"I'm sure you are after killing only one deer," she said. "We'll teach you how to rest."

"Teach me to rest?" I questioned.

"Yes, you see, although vampires on a traditional diet need no sleep because of all of the human blood they consume, our kind must meditate, rest the mind, so that we don't go on wild hunts."

"Oh," I replied. Something else about vampire life I didn't know.

"Now which of you buffoons will help me teach Allison?" Marlo asked of her brothers.

Marlo volunteered Lorenzo to assist in teaching me how to meditate. He wouldn't have been my first choice after what had just transpired in the dining room. Maybe that was why Marlo told Lorenzo he was going to help…to smooth over our earlier confrontation.

I followed Marlo and Lorenzo up the staircase and down the hallway. I heard Marlo whispering to Lorenzo that he should apologize to me. Apparently she forgot that my hearing was as good as hers now and I could hear everything she was saying. Or, maybe that was her point.

We entered my room and Marlo closed the door behind the three of us.

"Why do I need two people to teach me?" I asked with my back to the both of them.

"One will demonstrate and the other will tell you what is going on," Marlo replied.

I quite honestly wasn't in the mood for a presentation, but on the other hand I was really exhausted. Max must have been right; I needed more nourishment but didn't get it because of my unexpected visitor. I didn't quite understand what could be so difficult about meditating that two vampires had to show me. I sat on the edge of my bed and waited for my instruction to begin.

"Ahem," Marlo cleared her throat and tossed a glance towards Lorenzo.

"Sorry Allison," Lorenzo said. "Sorry about getting so angry with you before." Lorenzo appeared genuine in apologizing to me but I wondered how truly sorry he was for any plans he had for Vincent.

"Thanks," I muttered.

"Okay, now we can get started," Marlo announced. "So I already told you that our kind needs rest because of our diet."

"Right."

"But we also need rest because of how much energy it takes to reign in our senses. You remember when you awoke from your transformation?"

I nodded my head.

"Remember when you stood up and you could see the tiniest of details around you and you could hear every sound within a hundred miles?"

I nodded my head again. I was hoping Marlo was getting to the point soon because I wasn't sure how much longer I could keep my eyes open.

"Well if you would have let your sight and hearing just wander, you would have been in constant hunting mode. Your hearing would be the first to pick up on prey and then your eyes would focus on that target. After you conquered your prey, your hearing would have taken over again. It's a vicious cycle, but that is what we are in our most natural state; a perpetual hunter."

The thought of that almost turned my stomach. I couldn't imagine doing nothing but hunting for all eternity…conquering one victim just to immediately move on to the next.

"Most vampires don't act like that though," Lorenzo added.

"He's right," Marlo chimed in. "Most vampires control themselves to some degree so that they're not in constant hunting mode."

"Okay," I said. "I get it. Our lifestyle is a drain on our senses. So how do I rejuvenate?"

"Well you meditate," Marlo said. "But of course there are things you need to know."

"Like what?"

"For starters," Lorenzo said, "be careful where you decide to rest."

"When a vampire is in a meditative state," Marlo continued, "he or she is extremely vulnerable."

"Vulnerable to what?"

"To attack or to anything in the outside elements," Lorenzo said.

"I don't get it. Our skin turns into armor when we attack…"

"Right," Marlo said. "But when you meditate, all of your senses are shut down – your sense of hearing, your sense of smell, your sight."

"If you decide to rest in the wrong spot at the wrong time," Lorenzo added, "it could be fatal."

I let out a sigh. "Got it." All of the rules were starting to add up and were becoming quite the annoyance. I thought this existence would be free of rules.

"So you can perch anywhere," Marlo started as she grabbed Lorenzo's shoulders and pushed him to the floor. Lorenzo squatted, one arm resting on his leg, the other steadying him in between his legs.

"Perch?" I asked inquisitively.

"Yes," Marlo replied. "Like a bird…or a bat," she smirked. "You can perch anywhere, even hang upside down if you want."

"Hmm," I replied, letting that thought float through my mind.

"You recall when you went hunting with Max how he told you to let your hearing 'reach out?'" Marlo asked.

"Yeah," I replied.

"Well this time you need to do just the opposite. You need to rein it in with more intensity than you are using now. You pull it in until you hear nothing around you."

I looked at Lorenzo and he appeared to be concentrating on a spot on the wall. His eyes began to narrow.

"See, Lorenzo is pulling in his hearing in now. You can tell because his eyes are closing. Once your hearing is completely shut down, your eyes will close and your sense of smell will be cut off."

Lorenzo's eyes slowly closed and his shoulders relaxed. His face looked tranquil; quite the opposite from the incensed scene downstairs.

"Look," Marlo said as she waved a flask under Lorenzo's nose. "See, all senses shut off."

"What's in the flask?"

"Human blood."

"Oh." I felt silly for asking that question. "So how do you wake from this state?"

"You wake when your mind has had enough. It's similar to how you slept as a mortal. You'll just open your eyes, but you need to be cognizant of your senses to not let them run wild."

"Got it."

"There is one other way you can wake," Marlo added.

"What's that?"

"If someone wakes you," Marlo said with a glimmer in her eye. "You see, if you are attacked in this state, you will wake. Wanna give it a try?"

"You want me to attack Lorenzo?" I questioned.

"Well not attack him to hurt him, but maybe a good shove just to wake him." Marlo winked at me. "You know, a little pay back for earlier."

I let out a chuckle. "Ha, gottcha!"

I crouched on top of my bed and a big smile spread across my face. I was going to enjoy what I was about to do. I leapt off of the bed, grabbed the wood and iron chandelier, flipped myself into the air and planted a firm kick in Lorenzo's side.

I didn't realize my own strength. Lorenzo went crashing into the wall on the opposite side of the room, rattling the picture which hung there.

"What in the heck was that?" Lorenzo shouted as he sprang to his feet ready for a fight.

"Calm down, big boy," Marlo said patting him on the shoulder. "You deserved it."

Lorenzo looked over at me. I still had a smirk on my face.

"You kicked me like that?" he asked, breaking into a chuckle. I nodded my head in agreement and began to laugh with him. "You're much stronger than I thought you would be for an infant!"

We laughed a bit longer and then Marlo cut off our fun. "Rest Allison, you need it. We'll go hunting tomorrow, okay?"

"Okay."

Marlo and Lorenzo headed for the door.

"Hey," I shouted. "Thanks for the lesson. I appreciate it."

"No problem," Lorenzo responded. Marlo smiled an approving smile. Apparently she had accomplished everything she set out to do this evening.

CHAPTER 11

Meditating was quite easy. After controlling my sense of hearing on my first day as a vampire, it was simple enough to rein it in and get some rest. And just as Marlo had promised, once my hearing was silenced, my eyes shut instinctively, as if my body knew what to do even though I didn't. Everything went black and perfectly silent as my mind drifted until I thought of nothing at all.

My eyes shot open and my hearing quickly spread out over the castle. My ears were filled with a commotion of noises and my vision was blurred. I remembered Marlo telling me to reign in my senses as soon as I woke, and I did just that. My vision and hearing came into sharp focus. I saw everything in perfect clarity and heard only the ticking of a nearby clock. I looked down and found myself perched on the wooden foot board which had served as my meditating spot. I felt refreshed, like I had rested for hours.

I hopped off of the bed and walked over to the vanity. The clock showed that it was ten twenty-three in the evening. I had rested almost an entire day. But more importantly, there was little over an hour until I would make my escape to see Vincent and start our new existence together. My heart fluttered at the thought of seeing him again. I wondered which great exotic location he would take me to. I wondered where we would live and how we would get there. I couldn't wait to get out of this castle and start this new phase of my life.

Someone must have been in my room while I rested because a large pitcher and goblet had found its way to my night stand. Remarkably, I hadn't heard anyone enter or leave the room while I was meditating, just as Marlo had said would happen. It was kind of a scary thought that someone had entered the room without my noticing, and it absolutely reinforced Marlo's admonition to always rest in a secure spot. I poured a glass of the thick liquid and slowly sipped it, savoring every drop. I swished it around in my mouth as if drinking a fine wine and enjoyed it as it slid down my throat and into my belly where the liquid extinguished the smoldering embers.

The huge picture on the wall grabbed my attention. I set the goblet on the table and walked to the wall for a closer inspection. It was a beautiful image of the ocean that spanned the length of the wall. The waves were immense and deep in color…blues, greens, even some black. The swells were topped with foamy white caps that were anything but delicate. Fierce brush strokes had made the masterpiece and the artist's anger was apparent in the soaring waves. This was the ocean in the midst of a violent storm.

I continued staring at the picture, losing myself in the crashing waves. Then it struck me that I had briefly looked at the painting when I had first woken from my transformation. I had been able to see every paint drop and brush stroke when I had lost control of my senses. Though it was a blur of color, I swore I saw black letters scrawled across the middle of the painting.

I raised my hand and touched the painting as if that would make the words appear. I found nothing. Whatever it was that I thought I saw yesterday must have been a figment of my imagination.

I walked over to the vanity and sat on the chair. The mirror revealed perfectly soft and smooth skin. The scars from my prior day's tears were completely gone. I pulled at the skin gently, searching for the jagged ruts that were visible yesterday, but found nothing.

I examined the rest of my face in great detail, the first time I had really done so since becoming a vampire. My skin was smooth, all of my mortal imperfections gone. My complexion was now that of a fashion model, supple and perfect. My hair was perfectly styled, as if I hadn't run miles through the woods yesterday and attacked an animal. The blonde color was more vibrant than it had ever been in my mortal life.

My complexion, though pale, needed no makeup. My skin shone as if I was full of life; ironic considering I was now part of the living dead. My lips were a rosy red, as if colored with gloss, and the hollows of my cheekbones radiated the slightest bit of color. The coloring of my eyes, though a mix of dark and light, was vibrant, like a light was illuminating from behind them. *This is good*, I thought. *I must be well nourished.*

All of it – my complexion, eyes, hair – was part of my arsenal. This was what would attract a mortal to me. I had never considered my mortal self remotely beautiful. In fact, I had thought I was pretty average looking. But now, I was just the opposite. There was nothing average about me. I could rival some of the most beautiful people in the world. But I knew I had an advantage over them because I was something they were not…the perfect killer.

I stood up and walked over to the large wooden wardrobe. I pulled open the doors and was surprised to find a large collection of clothes and shoes. I flipped through the hangers and was quite impressed. Someone knew me, knew my style. In my mortal life, I didn't spend much money on clothes. I had invested in an expensive work wardrobe, but didn't see the need to spend a lot of money on casual attire. But if I had, this was exactly what I would have bought.

There were hangers full of jeans in every shade of blue, black and some white, even a few pairs of leather pants. I grabbed the waist of one, searching for a label but found none. At least 30 t-shirts were folded on the top shelf, some plain, others adorned with Celtic crosses or tribal looking designs, none of which had labels. There were fancier tops too made of fine fabrics such as silk and cashmere and there were boots – lots of boots!

I mulled over the options, changing outfits several times, wondering what I should wear to meet Vincent. I settled on a pair of tight, red leather pants, a black blouse and black high heeled boots. I changed with amazing speed, with almost the snap of a finger, and looked in the full length mirror. Something was missing. I went back to the vanity and flipped open the top where I found an assortment of necklaces, earrings and bracelets. I put on a leather cuff and a necklace made of black, copper and silver chains. I looked for something else to wear and spotted the oval ruby ring I had worn the night of the Halloween party. The stone matched the color of my pants so I slipped it on my middle finger and went back to the mirror. *Perfect*, I thought. And not a hair out of place.

I glanced at the clock and realized it was time to go. I walked to my bedroom door and gently opened it, careful not to make a noise that the others might hear. I stuck my head out the door but no one seemed to be around. I gently closed it and tiptoed across the room.

Once at the window, I leaned into the crank to muffle any noise it might make and opened it. I hopped on the edge and turned to look one last time at my room. I wasn't going to miss this place. I hadn't stayed here long enough to feel nostalgic about it. But my siblings on the other hand, I would miss. Especially Marlo. She had been the sister I never had. I would miss my brothers also, but I had something much better to look forward to – my new existence with Vincent.

I scaled the wall of the castle with ease, my high heeled boots proving to be no obstacle. I reached the ground and looked up. It was pitch black, the sky blanketed in voluminous gray clouds that rolled over the full moon. I ran down the side of the castle and rounded the corner, speeding along the back of the building as Vincent had instructed. I turned to look behind me, but no one was there. I briefly glanced up and saw that Vincent was right; the cameras were facing elsewhere at this moment. If they hadn't been, my siblings surely would have stopped me to see what I was up to.

I approached the corner of the castle and broke for the woods. I glided across the dewy grass, the cool fall air pleasant against my hot skin. My eyes narrowed on my entrance into the dense woods. I attacked the branches and foliage as I pushed my body through the foilage, fluidly navigating my way around the obstacles. I came upon a rock, pounced on it like it was a diving board and threw myself into the air. I grabbed a branch and vaulted over it, as polished as a trained gymnast, landing on another and bounding to another branch and then another. I leapt from branch to branch, having fun with my newfound skills until I thought better of it. I needed to stop playing around and focus on the task at hand. I jumped to the ground and concentrated on finding the river. I could hear it in the distance.

After several more yards I came upon water and stopped. Vincent had told me to head north. I looked up the river, then down it. Something inside of me told me to turn left. I dug my heels into the soft earth and took off.

"Going somewhere?"

A familiar voice floated through the chilly air and stopped me in my tracks. I looked in the direction of the voice but I couldn't see Marlo. I only saw a streak of black and gray moving amongst the thick shrubbery and soaring trees. I must have imagined Marlo's voice. I examined my surroundings one more time and still didn't see her. I took a step forward and heard it again.

"Going somewhere, Allison?"

I looked in the direction of the voice but only saw swaying branches as if someone had just run past the trees. "Marlo?" I called out.

A pair of lavender crystalline eyes emerged from the blackness of the forest. The red hair followed and then the familiar pale face. She wore black pants and a gray sweater that nicely showed off her toned arms.

"Marlo, what are you doing out here?" I asked.

"I could ask you the same thing."

"I was just going out for some fresh air," I replied.

"Really? And what was wrong with the front door?"

"I decided to try out my new vampire athleticism." This lying thing was really starting to get easy for me.

"Mmm hmm," Marlo hummed as she approached me. She looked me up and down. "Nice outfit for a walk in the woods."

I looked down at what I was wearing. It really wasn't appropriate for a stroll in the woods.

"I uh, woke up from my meditation and decided to check out the new wardrobe. I couldn't resist wearing something new. Did you pick this out for me?"

"Don't change the subject. What are you doing out here?"

"I was going for a hunt," I lied again, knowing I couldn't hunt this close to home.

"You're going to see *him*, aren't you?" Marlo questioned, ignoring my response.

"See who?"

"Come on, Allison!" Marlo yelled with slight agitation in her voice. "Stop playing these games. You're going to see Vincent, aren't you?"

"Marlo, I told you I was just taking a run; nothing more." I stared her straight in her eyes wishing I could make her believe my excuse.

"Which is it? A walk in the woods or hunting? They're all lies!" Marlo shouted. "My brothers were too blind to see it. But I can't blame them; men don't pick up on such emotions."

"What are you talking about?" I asked, completely confused as to what Marlo was referencing.

"You're in love with Vincent," Marlo simply replied, arching her eyebrows.

The words hit me like a brick wall. How could Marlo have known that? No one, besides Max, had been in the vicinity when I had confessed my love for Vincent. My face must have given away something yesterday when my siblings had grilled me over my Vincent sighting. Maybe I wasn't as good of a liar as I thought.

"I, uh, I don't know what you are talking about. I'm just going…"

"Stop," Marlo instructed. "There are things you need to know about your precious Vincent before you run off with him."

"I'm not running off with Vincent!"

"Vincent isn't the man you think he is. He's not the man I thought he was and I've known him for a really long time."

Marlo now had my attention but I didn't want my interest to show. I had no idea what she could possibly be talking about or when she had learned it. I wondered if Vincent had made contact with his siblings or if he had left something behind at the castle.

"Marlo, if this is about Vincent transforming me without my consent, I told you that it's okay, I forgave him for that."

"No," Marlo said. "It's not that. What if I told you that he did something to speed along your symptoms? That he didn't quite leave things completely up to nature?"

"What? What are you talking about?" I demanded.

"The night of the Halloween party, the drink that Vincent gave you wasn't just wine."

I thought back to that night and recalled going to the bar with Vincent where he had leaned into the bartender to order our drinks. The music had cut in just in time for me not to hear what he had ordered. I remembered the bottles the bartender had grabbed including the green bottle with the strange label that I had seen at the cottage. I recalled the taste of the sweet liquid as it tickled my tongue. The drink tasted like wine yet was different somehow. It had been quite refreshing, so much so it actually took away the burning in my throat. Sort of like the blood of my first prey.

"Really?" I questioned sarcastically. "Then what was it?" I couldn't wait to hear the story Marlo was about to deliver.

"It was some sort of concoction. It was mostly wine but not real wine." Marlo shut her eyes and shook her head as if confused.

"Marlo, you're not making any sense. It was wine but it wasn't wine? Which is it?"

"It was a wine made by gypsies. It's a mix of red wines and human and animal blood. Vincent had been drinking it for weeks and wouldn't share it with us. I don't understand it and it doesn't make sense. Gypsies and vampires are enemies so I have no idea how Vincent got the wine or why he was drinking it."

I stared at Marlo. I couldn't believe what I was hearing. At the cottage on Rattlesnake Island, Vincent had drunk that wine but wouldn't let me have any. He had said that I didn't like that kind of wine. If he wouldn't let me drink it then, why would he trick me into drinking it at the party? Vincent couldn't be that vindictive. Or could he? I glanced down at my ring which had the same dragon crest – the Drake family crest – on it that the wine bottle bore but couldn't make sense of any of it. "Are you trying to tell me that Vincent fed me blood with my wine?"

"Yes, that's exactly what I'm telling you."

"Okay, suppose that is true, why would he do that to me? He knew I would have to consent at some point."

"Vincent gave you the concoction hoping it would accelerate your symptoms and that you would agree to the transformation sooner rather than later."

"Oh come on," I said in disbelief.

"Haven't you noticed Vincent's penchant for unique things?" Marlo shouted.

I jerked back at her question.

"His motorcycle, for one," Marlo pointed out.

"So, it's an Agusta…"

"A custom made, one-of-a-kind bike, Allison."

"And your point is?"

"And his car – it's a custom Maybach. That's just one of many expensive or rare cars he owns. And then there's the castle. He went ahead and bought it without consulting any of us. Like we really needed a castle."

I couldn't understand where Marlo was going.

"And his clothes, custom made by Francesca," Marlo carried on. "Your clothes, too. He had those made for you, you know."

"What's your point, Marlo?" I asked, my voice full of frustration, my mind not knowing what to think.

"My point is that my brother has a fondness for things no one else has. Things that are rare, one of a kind. Sound like anyone you know?"

I couldn't believe what I was hearing. Was Marlo trying to tell me that Vincent only loved me because of what I was...a mortal descendant of Cain who was morphing into a vampire? That I was something so rare and unique that otherwise he wouldn't love me? That I was just another prized possession he wanted to add to his collection?

"He had to have you," Marlo said. "It's not that he *couldn't* wait for you to consent – he didn't *want* to wait."

Her words lingered in the air for a moment. "I don't believe you," I said, shaking my head from side to side. "Vincent loves me. He wouldn't hurt me like that."

"Vincent only loves himself," Marlo yelled. "He had no regard for you and your choice. He grew impatient waiting for you to give your consent. So when an opportunity arose, he took advantage of it...and you. And now he wants to run off with you and have you all to himself, his precious little trophy that no one else has."

"How dare you," I shouted. "Why are you saying this? Are you jealous that your brother has found love? Are you jealous of me?" I felt the pit of my stomach begin to churn with venom. The anger I felt was building and about to spread through the rest of my body.

"Why do you want to run off with him?" Marlo shouted at me. "Knowing what I just told you, why would you want to go to him? He only wants you because of what you are, because you're a descendant of Cain. The first of your kind to show signs of vampirism."

"I don't believe you," I hissed through clenched teeth. "What I do know is that Vincent loves me and I love him. Besides, I believe you made all this up in some desperate attempt to stop me from being happy. Well you know what? I thought you were the sister I always wanted, but I'm through with you. If you can't be happy for me, well then that's too bad for you. But I'm going to find Vincent and we are going to disappear and be happy together for eternity."

I threw all of my rage into a full sprint, ready to run off and find Vincent, hoping the cool air would erase the lies Marlo had just spoken. But as I took off, her next words stopped me dead in my tracks.

"Matthew is alive," Marlo shouted. Her words were clear though my back was to her.

My boots stuck in the ground and brought me to a dead stop. I froze trying to comprehend what I just heard.

"It's true," she said.

"Excuse me," I questioned, turning my head to look over my shoulder.

Marlo stepped closer to me. "Matthew is alive."

"Matt died three years ago," I whispered, still looking over my shoulder.

"No Allison, that's what Vincent made you believe."

"What are you talking about?"

"The night of your accident, Matt was with you."

"No, no, no," I stuttered. "I woke up thinking that Matt was with me, but Jenna corrected me; she reminded me that he had died years before. Doctor Frid said the accident report showed me as the only passenger that night."

"I'm afraid you're wrong, Allison. You were driving your Jeep and Matthew was in the passenger seat. Another driver t-boned your car through an intersection and your car flipped and landed in a ditch."

"There was no other driver. The police report said I lost control on the wet pavement and that I was the only one in the vehicle."

"That's because Vincent removed Matthew before anyone could get there."

"Right. And what exactly did Vincent do with Matt? And what about the other car? And how is it that Jenna and my other friends all know that Matt died in an accident three years ago?" Fury was building in me with each ridiculous claim.

"Vincent learned to manipulate his gift. I didn't know this until the night of your transformation."

"What?" I growled.

Marlo let out a huge sigh. "After Vincent bit you at the party, I ran after him. I wanted to know why he did it. He claimed that after you lunged at Jenna, he feared for your life and thought that the rest of the Secret Coven would kill you since you hadn't consented to your transformation. He knew the incident was a risk to our existence."

"You aren't telling me anything I don't know already," I coldly stated.

"I questioned Vincent as to why he thought that. We suspected that Jenna hadn't seen anything since Lorenzo was able to get her out of the room so quickly. And in fact, Lorenzo confirmed afterwards that Jenna hadn't suspected anything out of the ordinary. She believed that you were feeling ill. Allison, you are an exception to all of our rules. We wouldn't have killed you, but you definitely would have needed to consent very soon thereafter. We would have transformed you. So to me, Vincent's excuse didn't make sense, especially considering the penalty he would pay for transforming you without your permission."

"His own death; yes, I questioned the same thing."

"And as I said earlier, Vincent is one of the most selfish people I know. I couldn't see him risking his own existence just to transform another mortal." Marlo paused before continuing. "But you weren't just any other mortal."

I narrowed my eyes. "No, I'm a descendant."

"Exactly," Marlo replied. "And the first of all descendants to show signs of vampirism."

I didn't like what I was hearing, but what Marlo was saying was starting to make sense, even if I couldn't bring myself to admit it.

"You are something that none of our kind has ever seen before. Allison, you truly are one of kind. Knowing Vincent's affinity for rare things, I started putting things together. I thought back to the day you were born."

"What? Why?"

Marlo sighed again. "Vincent insisted that he needed to be in the delivery room, that he had to see you. At that time, we didn't think too much of it. After all, we had watched over the births of descendants for centuries, watching for any abnormalities. But on the day you were born, Lorenzo was going to observe. Vincent insisted that he observe instead, and Lorenzo agreed. After you were born, Vincent was in such a good mood. It had been years, maybe decades, since any of us had seen Vincent so elated. When asked about the cause of his jubilation, he only said that he knew you were going to be special, that he could see it in your eyes."

"He said what?" My jaw dropped and I looked away from Marlo. Vincent had helped deliver me. Vincent was the doctor who had handed me to my parents and told them that I was going to be special. He uttered those words which lodged in my parent's minds, the words that they repeated to me throughout my life. Those words that haunted me and kept me searching for my true calling were first spoken by him. Those words which wouldn't just allow me to enjoy the life I had. Those words which forced me to keep looking for my true calling and led me to this.

"He must have noticed the thirteen gold flecks in each of your eyes," Marlo muttered. "No other descendant had ever had thirteen in each eye. We didn't know then that it meant anything, that it would lead to this. But that's not all."

I looked back at Marlo but didn't know what to say. My mind couldn't process that Vincent was present in the delivery room with me and my parents and that he was the original source of the angst I had experienced all of my life.

"Do you remember how shocked Felix and I were at the party when you said Matthew had been dead for three years? Well we knew that wasn't true. Allison, I was watching over you just a few weeks earlier and Matthew was alive and well."

My mind went blank. Although I heard the words, I couldn't comprehend them. Marlo was standing here telling me she saw Matt just weeks earlier. I wasn't sure how that was possible as I'd had a flood of memories in recent days telling me the opposite was true. Matt hadn't been in my life for some time. He was dead and I had grieved for him and moved on and then I met Vincent and started dating him and fell in love.

"That doesn't make any sense. Jenna confirmed Matt's death. She had all of the details of what happened. And I'm living in a different house that I've been in for almost three years. My other friends have abandoned me because of the self-induced exhile I plunged myself into after Matt's death."

"No Allison, none of that is true. When I confronted Vincent in the woods, he stuck to his story that he feared for your life and wanted me to believe that he understood his sacrifice. So I asked him about Matthew and how he was able to separate you so quickly from him. Vincent became enraged as I pressed the topic. His reaction seemed strange to me, especially if he had been able to get you to leave your husband so easily. When he was good and angry and thinking about nothing else other than how he had separated you two, I touched him."

My mouth dropped open when I realized what Marlo tried doing in the woods with Vincent. "You saw it, didn't you? You saw the truth? You saw his visions?"

"Yes. You see, Vincent's gift as a historian is not only to record stories, either seen firsthand or through another, but also to retell them."

"I know. He showed me Cain's story using his gift."

"Well, he manipulated this gift. Allison, I promise you that Matthew was in the car with you the night of the accident. I saw it in Vincent's vision. Vincent was driving the vehicle that hit yours and spun you out of control. He pulled your vehicle out of the ditch. He wanted to take you, that was his plan, but he had no time to get you out of the car as an ambulance was quickly approaching. So he took Matt instead."

"And then what?" I asked, feeling defeated.

"He called me and asked me to go to the hospital to watch you and make sure the mortal doctors didn't suspect anything."

"I don't remember this. Why don't I remember the accident or the ambulance ride or Vincent at the scene?"

"Because Vincent didn't want you to remember any of it."

"What?" I asked in disbelief. But I didn't really care to hear the answer. I wanted to know what had happened to my husband. "So what happened to Matt? Where did Vincent take him? And what about Jenna's memory and that of my other friends?"

"As for your friends, Vincent was quite busy the few days you were in the hospital. He used his gift to erase their memories of you and Matt over the past three years and replaced them with new memories."

"He did what?"

"He must have concocted a story in his own mind and fed it to your friends as the truth. That's the only thing I can think of. He had all the time in the world to do this when you were in the hospital."

"And what about Matt?"

"I don't know."

"What do you mean you don't know?" I yelled. "You saw his memories, how could you not see what he did with Matt?"

"Allison," Marlo pleaded. "Vincent knew what I was doing; he knew I was trying to see the events in his mind's eye. He pulled away as quickly as he could. I didn't have a chance to see what happened to Matthew."

"Then how do you know he's alive?"

"Because Vincent said so."

"And you believe him?" I asked incredulously.

"I actually do on this one."

"Why?"

"Honestly, I think he knows it would have hurt you too much if you learned that he had killed Matthew. I think in Vincent's mind, he thinks you will forgive him and still move on with him since Matthew is alive."

"Oh does he now?" I muttered to myself. My mind was processing everything I had just learned. "Well, tell me this Marlo. Why didn't you figure any of this out while I was in the hospital? Didn't you think it strange that I was in a car accident and my husband wasn't at the hospital to visit me?"

"Vincent told me that Matthew was taken to a different hospital. He said that he was following you home that night but that you were in an accident. He said you were being taken to Medina General but Matthew was being life flighted to another hospital. I didn't think anything of it, honestly. I was concerned about getting to the hospital in time to see you. Vincent had said that he knocked you out so the EMS workers weren't suspicious that you made it out of an accident that bad unscathed. With your symptoms accelerating, it was no surprise to us that you escaped that accident. But I had to get to the hospital and keep you unconscious for a few days while the doctors ran their tests. I had to make sure they didn't suspect anything with you. And knowing Matthew was taken elsewhere, well, I didn't expect to see him at Medina General."

"What about after I woke? I was screaming for my husband. Your vampire ears didn't hear that?"

"After I woke you, I got Doctor Frid. I assumed all would be well. I had to call Vincent and let him know that you were awake; he insisted on it. I was on the phone with Vincent when Jenna and the doctor were in the room with you. I was in the nurse's locker room, far away from your room. I heard nothing; I wasn't trying to hear anything because nothing should have been wrong. When I got back to the floor, Nurse Gail just said that you were hysterical and she gave you something to sleep. She said nothing about you looking for your husband or that he was dead. Allison, you have to believe me, at that point, I had no reason to suspect Vincent of anything. He played me for a fool in all of this, too."

"Apparently he played us all, now, didn't he?"

2442Kelley Grealis

"He did. I am so sorry; I wish I would have seen this earlier. I wish I somehow could have stopped it."

"Don't apologize for Vincent's actions. But thank you, Marlo."

"For what?"

"For telling me the truth."

"Of course, Allison." Marlo grabbed my hand and gave me a soft smile. "Now let's go back to the castle."

"No," I said. "You go to the castle. I have something to take care of."

"Allison, you can't seriously be running off with Vincent after what I just told you."

"No, I'm not running off with Vincent," I replied sarcastically. "But he is the only person who knows where Matt is and I need know what he did with him."

"But..." Marlo started.

"Stop," I commanded. "I have to do this Marlo." I held her gaze for a few seconds. "Matt was my world. He was my husband and I loved him, still love him, more than anything. I can't let Vincent get away with all of this – the lying and the manipulation. My symptoms aside, Matt was innocent in all of this and whatever has happened to him isn't fair."

"I understand," Marlo replied. "Please be careful though. Vincent is older than you and therefore stronger."

"Well hopefully it won't have to get to that." I twirled around and headed into the woods, preparing myself for what I would say to the man who had ruined my life.

CHAPTER 12

An immense, irregularly shaped rock protruded from the river's shore and formed a sharp point at the top. I slowed my pace to a walk as I approached it. There was no mistaking the landmark Vincent had given me. The outcroppings on the west side were bigger than those on the east, almost as if the boulder was directing me to where I needed to go.

I took a giant leap and landed on the point, balancing there on one foot as I looked up at the sky. It was a perfect fall night complete with a clear, black sky and an almost full moon. Every star in the sky was visible. My enhanced vision revealed things my mortal eyes had never seen. The sky was filled with so many stars, so much so that it looked like someone had spilled salt across a black table cloth.

I took a deep breath and thought about the course my life had taken over the past few weeks. As I did, a pang of heat bubbled from my stomach and scorched the back of my throat. I sighed and tried to swallow the heat back down. I couldn't help but wonder that maybe my course began to change earlier than the past few weeks and I had just been blind to it. Maybe my destiny had been set from the time I was born. This burning deep inside of me had always been with me. I had thought it was my conscience telling me I had to do something more meaningful with my life. After all, there simply had to be more to my simple, average life other than the same old routine. I had never been able to give up the feeling that my body knew something my mind couldn't comprehend. Little did I know that I had the devil's poison running through my veins. Maybe it was my constant curiosity and yearning to figure out my true calling that caused the venom to bring about my symptoms. Maybe my mid-life crisis, as I had called it, caused my symptoms to go into overdrive. Something had to do it; something that had never happened to any of my ancestors.

But even if I had unknowingly set my symptoms in motion, it was no excuse for what Vincent had done. I went from being happily married to a widow to falling in love with someone new who in turn had done nothing but completely manipulate me for his own selfish reasons. And I had been blind to all of it. After realizing Matt had supposedly died three years ago, my mind was suddenly filled with new memories of a new love – memories I had never questioned. The memories came back quite swiftly, the amnesia wore off, or so I thought. Day after day, a new memory of Vincent had emerged in my mind, yet nothing of the prior three years, and I had never asked any questions. I didn't know how I could have been so gullible.

And then there was Matt. I couldn't fathom why Vincent would have crafted such an elaborate plan. He intentionally caused our accident without regard for Matt's life or my own. Then he stole Matt and hid him. But where? And why? Why not just kidnap me if he feared me transforming and going on a wild hunt? Or why not just kill Matt? I shuddered at the thought, but if Vincent was as selfish as his siblings said he was, why would he go through the trouble of kidnapping Matt and transplanting him somewhere else? It seemed it would have been easier to just permanently remove one of us from the situation.

Anger swelled inside of me as these thoughts ran through my head. If only I had known what that burning was deep in my core, my true lineage, maybe I wouldn't have looked so hard to discover what it meant. But what I was really having a hard time dealing with were the never ending questions: why me and why now? Was it possible that my ancestors had been happy enough with their lives that they ignored the burning inferno at the center of their being? And I just couldn't ignore it and kept searching for an answer which brought about the symptoms even faster? And look where that got me. Vincent stole my husband, manipulated my friends' minds, manipulated my mind and now I was one of the living dead – soulless and eternally damned. I should have listened to Matt when he told me to watch what I wished for. Was he ever right! What I wouldn't do to go back to that life I thought was so average and ordinary and, dare I say, boring.

I came out of my daze and breathed in the cool air. My skin was hot but my blood was boiling even hotter with anger and contempt for Vincent. He wasn't going to get his precious trophy this time.

I leapt from my perch and headed west. The thought of Vincent not knowing what was coming made me smile.

It took just a few minutes at the speed I was traveling to reach the lake in my backyard. I slowed to a jog and focused my eyes. Vincent was sitting on the bench by the lake. Even from this distance I could see how handsome he was. His silhouette was flawless, each feature in perfect proportion. I couldn't let his looks or his charisma faze me this time. I slowed to a walk as I approached him.

"Allison," Vincent uttered as he stood and walked towards me. He grabbed my face with both of his hands and kissed my lips which sent an electrifying current through my body. I didn't reciprocate. "You look beautiful," Vincent stated as he stepped back and eyed my outfit. "Do you like the clothes? Francesca made them just for you."

"They're nice," I responded bluntly.

"Nice?" He appeared surprised at my response or lack thereof. "That's not the word I would have chosen to describe a custom wardrobe made exclusively for you."

"I never liked clothes all that much."

Vincent didn't respond. He stared at me as if trying to read my mind. I was sure he was wondering why I wasn't over the moon with my new wardrobe and my lack of enthusiasm must have had him stumped. He was still holding my hands and I made sure not to concentrate too long on any one image so he couldn't pick up on my thoughts.

"What took you so long to get here?" A different expression washed over Vincent's face. It appeared that he was worried but I wasn't sure if he was worried about me or worried that something wasn't going according to his plan. Or maybe he was truly suspicious about my long commute.

"I stopped by the river to take in the view," I said, trying to hold back my anger. I shook my hands loose from Vincent's grip and placed my arms firmly by my sides. Vincent combed my face with his eyes.

"Okay," he reluctantly said, apparently believing me or ignoring the obvious. "Are you ready to go?"

I was in awe of his response but showed no emotion. I couldn't believe that he could clearly tell something was wrong with me and he wasn't going to ask. Maybe he really was as self-centered as his siblings had said.

I scoffed. "No," I replied, narrowing my eyes directly into his.

"No?" Vincent questioned, cocking his head to the side.

"You have to answer a few questions first."

"Allison, we really have to get going. We have a flight to catch."

"Don't worry," I replied, "this won't take long."

Vincent looked me over one more time and finally resigned. "What is it that you would like to ask?"

I looked down at the ground and then back up into his eyes. "What did you say to me before you bit me? I recall seeing your lips moving but I couldn't hear anything. What did you say?"

Vincent smiled and appeared relieved, maybe by the nature of my question. "I said that I've always known how special you were."

My heart dropped and if my face could still flush, my cheeks had to be bright red. "You son of a bitch," I cursed.

"Excuse me?"

Looking at Vincent now, I felt nothing – no love, no desire, nothing. Actually I felt something. I felt hatred and abhorrence and revulsion.

"You," I hissed, "uttered those words to my parents on the day I was born and somehow engrained in their minds the need to constantly remind me just how *special* I was. Those damned words have haunted me my entire life, forcing me to look for my true calling and lead me to this! Lead me to you! You had no right to do that to them."

"What I said to your parents on the day you were born was the truth, Allison. How they choose to deal with those words was their choice alone. I can't be held accountable for that."

"No, you don't get to blame this on them." I pushed his shoulders forcing him backwards and onto the bench.

"Why don't you tell me what's really bothering you, Allison. This attitude can't all be about a silly little phrase I uttered thirty-two years ago."

"Humph," I shook my head in disbelief and whispered to myself, "silly little phrase." That silly little phrase had had an unbelievable impact on me for my entire life, an impact which he apparently couldn't see. I leaned in over Vincent and placed both hands on the back of the bench, blocking him in with my arms. "Where is Matt?" I whispered.

Vincent's head jerked back at the sound of Matt's name.

"Allison, Matthew is dead. Remember…"

"Cut it out, Vincent!" I yelled, anger seething through my clenched teeth. "I know everything. Where is he?"

Vincent took a moment before he responded. A cocky grimace spread across his face. "And what exactly do you think you know, Allison?" His voice was cool and calm. He pushed both of my shoulders, backing me away from the bench, as he stood up.

"I know that you bit me the night of the Halloween party and Marlo ran after you. She saw the accident in your mind; she saw you take Matt." My voice broke and venomous tears began to roll down my face at the thought of Matt. The anger that had been building in my core was now overflowing. "She saw the visions you fabricated in your mind and fed me as the truth. You used your gift to record and replay stories to manipulate my mind and that of my friends. You helped accelerate my symptoms by feeding me blood and passing it off as wine. Do I need to go on?"

"Hmm," Vincent mulled his thoughts for a moment, stroking his chin. "You've been talking to Marlo." He was coy in his response.

"It doesn't matter who I've been talking to. I know the truth and now I want answers from you. Where…is…Matt?" I demanded.

Vincent turned his back to me and walked around the bench, seemingly taking his sweet time in selecting his next words. His calmness angered me.

"Even if I told you where Matthew is, what good would that do you? You can't see him. Or rather," Vincent paused, "he can't see you." Vincent waived his hand up and down, insinuating Matt couldn't see me because of my post- transformation appearance. "You can't openly reveal who you really are to him, unless…"

"Unless, what?" I shouted.

"Or maybe you would reveal yourself to Matthew," he said in a taunting voice, "yes, and then you would be in the same situation I am. A rule breaker, damned to death."

"You would like that wouldn't you?" I snarled. "You would like it if I broke a rule just like you, and faced death, just like you. What? Then I would be left with no other choice than to run off with you so we could exist happily ever after?"

"It did cross my mind," Vincent replied arching his eyebrows.

"You bastard," I roared. Anger piled up in my belly and I could barely hold it back. The urge to leap over the bench and rip out his throat was so tempting. "After all you have done to me, you still think I would run away with *you*?" My voice echoed through the hollow ridges below us.

Vincent ignored my question. "You know, Allison, even if I did tell you where Matthew is, it wouldn't matter." He stopped pacing and squared himself to me. He twisted his face into mine and said, "He wouldn't know who you are." His lip curled up at the edge, the tips of his fangs visible and an arrogant grin stretched his mouth.

"You erased all memory of me?" I was disgusted by the thought. Not only was it bad enough that he had kidnapped Matt and transplanted him somewhere, but he had erased the past eight years of his memory and our life together.

"I had to, Allison. It was for his own good."

"What is wrong with you?" I shouted. "You think you can just go around manipulating other peoples' lives for your own benefit?"

"Our kinds shouldn't intermingle anyways."

"What in the hell does that mean?"

"Allison," Vincent stated calmly. "I don't understand why you are so angry. If anything, you should be thanking me."

"Thanking you?" I yelled. "And what exactly should I be thanking you for?"

"Think about it, I saved Matthew's life." Vincent was sincere in his response.

"You can't be serious?"

"Your symptoms were there and they were real; you know that now. I removed Matthew from a very dangerous situation before you transformed on your own and possibly harmed him, maybe even killed him. How could you be mad at me for that? I saved him from certain death and eternal damnation."

Vincent's siblings were right, he was selfish and self-centered and lived in his own world.

"You stole him from me, hid him and then basically drugged me to accelerate my symptoms and you expect me not to be mad? And not only that, you expect me to thank you for destroying my life and Matt's?"

"I only nudged your symptoms along. It was inevitable that you were going to have to transform. I did what I had to do to get you to finally see what you really were."

"You did what you had to do?"

"Yes, Allison. You certainly didn't pick up on any of the more subtle hints that I had left for you."

"And what kind of subtle hints did you leave for me?"

"I knew you were dreaming about the garden, of course."

"Because you planted those dreams!"

"No. I did not plant those dreams." He said the words with such sincerity that I believed him. "That was the venom in your system trying to tell you your history. I heard you talk about the dream and that's when I knew you were more than just a descendant with thirteen gold flecks in each eye. But you couldn't interpret the dream on your own so I left some books to help you piece it all together."

"Books? What books?"

Vincent sighed. "In your den, Allison. At your house." He tossed his head over his shoulder and nudged it towards my house. "All of those leather bound books detail your family's history. I recorded everything that I had learned from your ancestors or witnessed with my own eyes and wrote them down on those pages. I even left the Bible open to the story of the Garden of Eden thinking it would catch your attention and make you want to read but it didn't."

No wonder Vincent had been so persistent for me to read the night I came home from the hospital. He had wanted me to figure everything out on my own.

"And when you obviously weren't going to read the books I thought I'd try something else."

"And what was that?"

"I wanted to plant a different sort of dream. Not one of the garden because I didn't want to tamper with that. But I figured since I knew you could dream, why not plant one that directly told you that you were a vampire."

"You planted that nightmare that I had on Rattlesnake Island? What were you thinking?"

"Allison, believe me, that wasn't the dream I envisioned. I dreamt up a romanticized story, something you would see in the movies, something that would have made you want to become a vampire, not scare you from it."

"Well then what happened?"

"I don't really know. Maybe the venom…"

"Enough. Enough!" I yelled. I couldn't take this anymore. Vincent was avoiding anything having to do with Matt. "You could have approached me and left Matt out of this!"

"Oh yes, because when I told you on our trip home from the island that you were part vampire, you really believed me," Vincent sarcastically replied. "If I would have told you that, you would have run back to Matthew and told him about the conversation and I couldn't have that."

"You could have faked my death! Didn't you think of that? You could have left Matt and my friends alone and just faked my death."

"Events may not have unfolded the way I wanted them to, but what's done is done," Vincent replied.

"And you think you have what you want. Me."

"I would still like you to go away with me, yes."

"You have to be kidding me! Never! I never want to see you again," I said through labored breath, tears scorching my face. "You stole my husband, manipulated my friends and cursed me. If I ever see you again, I'll kill you myself and save my siblings from having to do it!"

Vincent snorted. "Your siblings," he stated.

"Well they certainly aren't yours anymore."

"And they certainly can't protect you! Caz was hot on your trail and Lorenzo wanted to have a family meeting to discuss how to handle the situation!"

"Caz?"

"Yes, Casper Devoe, Luscious' henchman. You remember him from the Halloween party don't you? He was getting closer to you.

He scouted out descendants in Cocoa Beach, then Tennessee, then that young couple in Columbus. I knew he was at the hospital the day before your accident; I could smell him all over you. And then he showed up at Jordana's party. And what did *your* siblings want to do? They wanted to talk. Well there was no time to talk. If Caz was that close, then Lucious and Delilah weren't too far behind, and I was right, wasn't I? I did what I had to do to protect you!"

"Leave," I yelled, pointing a finger out over the valleys. "And never, ever return."

Vincent paused and eyed me from head to toe. "It's too bad you don't want to join me. We really could have enjoyed eternity together."

"Leave!"

Vincent took a deep breath and sighed. "Your wish," he placed one arm in front of him and the other in back and took a bow, his eyes never leaving mine, "my command." With that, he stood up and in two huge leaps he was out of sight.

I stared out over the lake and into the ridge where he had just disappeared. Everything had happened so quickly I had to wonder if it had happened at all. I took a deep breath and swallowed the cool air into the pit of my stomach. The anger still churned, but now that he had left, it seemed to subside. Could he really be gone, just like that? I expected more of a fight from him. I thought he would try harder to convince me to go with him. If I was such a prized possession, how could he just go? The depth of my anger must have shown through so much that he knew he couldn't convince me tonight. Or was there something else?

I walked to the edge of the ridge and looked down. Fog rolled up over the jagged landscape like a bubbling caldron. I hopped off the ledge and descended into the darkness. I had to see for myself if Vincent was gone or up to something else. I landed on an outcropping and searched through the fog in the three directions around me but saw no sign of him. I took a step off the ledge and descended several hundred feet below to the river's edge. The riverbank was smooth dirt dotted with rocks. There were no foot prints. I took a deep breath but could only smell the crisp fall air. Vincent's scent was nowhere to be found. He must have moved so fast that I couldn't pick up his scent.

I looked around again. The moon had moved towards the west and reflected brightly off of the stream. *What am I doing*, I thought to myself. I told Vincent to leave yet I was down here looking for him. I should have known better. He wasn't going to stick around and be humiliated by my rejection. His ego wouldn't allow that.

I looked into the stream and saw my reflection staring back at me. The tears had stopped but trails of blistered flesh were temporarily left in its place, some already starting to heal. I looked sad and felt confused. I didn't know what I was supposed to do now. I desperately wanted to look for Matt but had no idea where to even start or what to say to him if I found him. I wasn't sure if I wanted to go back to the castle or just leave and start fresh someplace new. Something in my reflection caught my attention. Something was different. I examined my mirror image trying to identify what was off. My eyes. They were a pale version of the vibrant rings I was accustomed to seeing. My belly let out a growl that snuck up to my throat. The back of my throat felt like it was on fire. I needed to feed.

I turned toward the wall of rock that I needed to scale to get back to the lake and my house. From there, I would run back to the castle so that I could hunt with one of my siblings.

I leapt towards the ravine, aiming for a rock jutting out of the side but as I approached the rock, I missed it. I expected to land on my two feet on top of the rock, but my new found agility failed me. I wrapped my arms around the rock as my legs dangled below. "What was that all about," I muttered to myself. I swung my legs back and forth until I had enough momentum to swing myself up and around, where I landed on my original target. I took a deep breath and pondered what had just happened. After relaxing for a minute, I realized I was drained. It must be a combination of not eating enough on my first hunt and my argument with Vincent that had zapped me of all my energy. I wondered again what I should do – run back to the castle and hunt or rest first. A flare of heat ignited in the back of my throat...eat, I need to eat.

I set my sights on another rock, several feet above me. If I could make it to that rock, then it would be just a short jump to the top and I could head back to the castle. I dug down to find some energy and sprang towards my target but missed again. I didn't land anywhere near where I wanted. I hit the side of the ravine and slid down, rocks and brush scratching my skin.

I slid down the side finally resting on another jagged outcropping, small rocks and other debris hitting me on their way to the river. I realized I needed to take smaller jumps to get to the top; I just didn't have the energy for anything more than that.

I took small leaps, expending all of my energy, and eventually made it back to the lake. I bent over and grabbed my knees taking in a much needed breath. I surveyed my body. My blouse was ripped and several scrapes appeared on my arms. I had a hole in the knee of my pants and even broke a heel off of my boot. I sat on the bench and took my boots off; they were of no use to me broken. I hung my head and decided I needed rest first before hunting. There was no way I had the stamina to run back to Castle Adena.

I got up and walked towards my house, remembering the important rule Marlo had taught me when it came to meditating...find a safe place. I grabbed the handle of the backdoor but it was locked. I formed an open palmed fist with my right hand and pushed it through the glass. I apparently had enough strength for that because it broke on my first attempt. I pulled my hand back and it was a bloody mess and stung with venom, but at least it would heal itself. I unlocked the door and walked in.

It felt like I was home, like I had really lived here for the three years Vincent had said I did. Everything was familiar to me, but that was probably due to Vincent's contrived, and quite convincing, images. I walked through the living room and came upon the sofa table where the framed photographs were displayed. I picked up one of me and Jenna. I felt the sting of a tear touch my eye but I fought off the tears as I did not want to deal with the fiery pain. I missed my best friend Jenna so much and wondered if I'd ever be able to see her again. I then grabbed the photo of Matt on his motorcycle and stared at it before holding it to my chest as if hugging his photo would make me feel better. It didn't. I set down that picture and picked up the next. This one was of me and Vincent on the Lake Erie shoreline at sunset. We were sitting on the beach with the bright orange sky behind us. We had our arms wrapped around each other in a playful embrace. We both looked so happy.

I felt disgusted. I slammed the frame down against the table shattering the glass. I flipped over every other framed photo of the two of us. I didn't want to see him, even in a photo, after what he had done to me.

After breaking all of the picture frames, and throwing a few across the room, I stomped up the stairs to the loft bedroom. I threw myself on the bed and stared up at the ceiling. The bed was soft and feathery like a cloud, but I wasn't comfortable and this wasn't going to help me rest. I sprang from the bed and landed on the wall overlooking the living room. I surveyed the rooms below me and decided this would be the best place to rest.

I crouched down, assuming my meditation position. I pulled back my hearing but was having a difficult time. This morning's events were still running through my head like a marathon runner. I took a deep breath and tried again. The sounds of the cricket's chirping and the soft breeze began to fade. Slowly, my eyes began to close. I heard a noise from below, it sounded like something moving over broken glass, but I fought to keep my concentration. I had to rest before my run back to my family and my next hunting trip. My hearing turned to deafness and my vision faded to blackness. As my sense of smell cut off, I caught a tiny whiff of something pungent. My mind went blank and I was out.

I wasn't sure how long I perched there but the next thing I knew I was falling off the wall and sailing across the living room. I landed with a great deal of force against the fireplace. My senses were all over the place. Every nook and cranny of the brick was visible to me. I could see every grain of wood in the floor. Sounds flooded my ears as if thousands of radios were blasting at the same time. I looked up to the loft and saw a shadow move amongst all of the fine details I was trying to comprehend.

I used all of my will power to pull in my senses, to gain some self control. Pretty quickly all of the minute details faded into complete pictures and the ruckus in my ears was replaced with the breeze and crickets, and another noise. Heavy footsteps were clunking down my staircase at a slow pace. I stuck my nose in the air and caught a whiff of a pungent, earthy smell. It was the same scent I had picked up right before I slipped into meditation.

"Well, well, well," a raspy voice rang from the stairs, one heavy footstep following another. "Look who I found."

The figure emerged from the foyer, his black, glass-like eyes leading the way.

"Lucious," I hissed. His menacing figure stood at the edge of the foyer, his bitter scent filled my nostrils. His long black hair cascaded over his shoulders which were cloaked in a long black coat. He stepped forward and a glimmer of the rising sun illuminated his silhouette. His build was strong and muscular and tall, an ominous combination considering the feral expression his face wore. His eyes were a frightening shade of black, like coal. It was like looking into the depths of nothingness.

"You know who I am?" Lucious asked sarcastically.

I stood up, fireplace bricks crumbling around me. The scrapes on my arms from my fall down the ravine were gone except for a few pink scars which were rapidly disappearing. Venom from my fresh cuts from my trip into the fireplace, courtesy of my uninvited guest, was stinging in their place. But I felt better than I had before; I had some of my strength back, so I must have gotten just enough rest. But looking at Lucious, I wasn't sure if I would have enough stamina to outrun him or the strength to take him on in a fight.

This visit couldn't be good news for me after the promise he and his mate, Delilah, announced at the Halloween party. He was here for me. He was going to kill me.

"I would ask what you want," I boldly stated, trying to give the impression I wasn't afraid, "but I already know."

Lucious chuckled. He stepped down into the living room and walked towards the kitchen. "I am surprised to find you here alone, Allison. That is your name, right?" He threw his head over his shoulder when he said my name and then looked away like he wasn't the least bit interested in me.

I turned my body as Lucious walked into the kitchen but didn't respond to his question.

"You have my sincerest regret that we were not formally introduced before, well," he turned to face me across the kitchen counter, "before all this." Lucious pointed at the fireplace.

I said nothing, not knowing where Lucious was going with this conversation. Instead, my mind clicked ahead, assessing my situation. How was I going to fight Lucious? He was so much bigger than me. And not only that, I hadn't been in a fight since becoming a vampire. Heck I was never in a fight as a mortal, how was I going to know what to do?

Lucious walked out of the kitchen and back into the living room. As he walked in front of me, the couch the only separation between us, he stuck his nose in the air and took a long sniff.

"You smell even sweeter since he changed you." Lucious walked next to me and grabbed my chin. "Tell me Allison, why did Vincent transform you?"

I stared down at the ground, wishing my body would go into attack mode so my armored skin would protect me.

"Answer the question!" Lucious yelled, his voice thundering through my tiny house.

I jerked my head up. "I don't know," I said with a surprising amount of calmness.

Lucious stepped closer and pressed his face next to mine. "I'll tell you why," he snarled. He grabbed my throat with his left hand and slowly, effortlessly, hoisted me in the air. My body clenched in fear and all I could think was that I was going to die in this moment. I grabbed his one hand with both of mine hoping for some relief.

"Because he knew you had no chance against me as a mortal," Lucious snarled. I grabbed at his leather cloaked arm, hitting it, hoping it would release me. Lucious chuckled, maybe at my feeble effort or maybe at the thoughts running through his head.

"And by changing you, he thought you might have a chance to fight me off!" Lucious exclaimed as he threw me across the room into the wall. His laughter filled the house.

I landed on the ground and gasped for air. I grabbed my neck, rubbing it for relief. I scanned the room looking for a way out of the house. I had to get Lucious out in the open if I wanted any chance at winning this battle. But with my last trip across the room, I was further away from the door, my only escape.

Lucious bent lower, his head even with mine though he was still across the room. "Where is your dear boyfriend Vincent?" he growled.

"He isn't my boyfriend," I choked out.

"Oh, I see. Trouble in paradise?" Lucious walked slowly towards me, kicking a framed picture of me and Vincent that I had thrown earlier.

"Something like that," I said. Springing to my feet, I grabbed the fireplace poker that was lying on the ground and charged Lucious. I drew my right hand back, holding the poker like a spear, and aimed for my enemy's throat. I leapt in the air and as I did, Lucious let out an evil laugh. He caught the spear with me still holding on to it and tossed me into the kitchen.

"Is that all you have?" he cackled through his laughter. "Allison, you are going to have to try harder than that."

Lucious continued laughing as I darted out the broken door. The cool morning air was not welcome against my icy flesh. The sun was starting to rise in the east so I headed west, where it was still a bit darker. I leapt over the shrubs that bordered the woods, ran a few paces and came upon a huge tree. I scaled it and perched myself on a branch. I couldn't see Lucious but I could still smell him. I stooped there in silence for what seemed like an eternity until his harsh voice broke through the morning air.

"Come out, come out where ever you are," Lucious sang in a slow, wicked tone.

I closed my eyes to allow my ears to concentrate on the sounds in the woods. I heard a branch snap to my left and turned to look. I strained my eyes but couldn't see anything. I closed my eyes again hoping to concentrate like Max had taught me on our hunting trip. I let my ears concentrate on my surroundings. I could hear his footsteps in the distance. There was no mistaking it was Lucious; no one else lived remotely close to my house. I kept my eyes closed and could hear each slow and methodical step he took looking for his prey; looking for me. Then he stopped. I kept my eyes closed. He wasn't moving but I could hear his breathing. He must be trying to trick me, to make me believe he left the woods so I would come out. I slowly opened my eyes, each diminutive detail of my surroundings presented in front of me. It was the visual equivalent of the thousands of radios I had heard when Lucious woke me from my mediation. I let my sense of smell guide my eyes to my target. There he was off in the distance. Lucious was casually leaning against a tree picking at his nails. He either wasn't taking this seriously or was overly confident that his ploy was going to work.

I pushed myself to the edge of the branch, my eyes never leaving my attacker. I gingerly pushed myself from the branch, and landed on another branch on the tree in front of me. Lucious didn't move. I did it again, quietly moving to a tree closer to my target and again, he didn't hear me. I repeated this a few times until I was closer to Lucious, yet still too far away for my normal vision to see him. I quietly scaled down the tree. I was going to have to do something here. I couldn't run because Lucious would hear that and besides, he could pick up my scent and follow me. There was no escape; I had to face my enemy head on.

I felt the pit in my stomach flare up and the back of my throat burn with desire for another meal. Nothing seemingly wanted to go my way. Not only did I have to escape Lucious and his planned demise for my existence, but I also had the need for another hunt. Nice timing.

I paused at the base of the tree, readying myself for the attack and then his voice cut through the morning air.

"You smell just like him, you know," Lucious stated.

I froze. Lucious stood by the tree playing with his nails like he was uninterested in the situation. "Just like Cain and the rest of his family. Did your new friends tell you about your long lost ancestors?" He looked up and appeared to look straight at me though I had no way of knowing if he could actually see me. "But your scent is stronger. Why is that, Allison?"

A chill went down my spine as my enemy spoke my name.

"It's a shame really," he continued, standing straight up, "that you are one of his. It's such a shame to have to rid this world of such a beautiful vampire." A half hearted smile spread across his lips and he leapt out of view. My eyes scanned the woods for him but I couldn't find him. I could smell him, so I knew he was still near.

"You don't have to kill me, Lucious," I yelled, hoping for a reply so I could determine the direction he had gone. "I have no issue with you." Part of me was really hoping that Lucious would just take me up on that and leave me alone, but I knew better.

His wicked laughter rang through the forest. "You may not have issue with me," his voice sounded like it was coming from all directions, "but I have issue with your great ancestor that left me for dead…twice," he sneered. "And for that, all of his descendants must pay the ultimate price."

Two feet landed with a heavy thud several yards behind me. I whirled around. Lucious stood there, his jacket gone. He wore a high necked, skin tight white t-shirt over tight black denim pants. His arms were covered in tattoos which caught my attention but I didn't have time to analyze them. I instinctively crouched, a low growl grumbling in my stomach. Lucious assumed the same stance; his upper lip curled back revealing his teeth which glistened with venom. I dug deep for some energy and pushed off the ground and ran towards Lucious. He ran towards me as well. The growl in my belly bubbled up my through my throat and out of my mouth which coincided with a giant leap off the ground. Lucious leapt in the air as well. Mid-jump, I felt my skin harden into my protective armor.

I collided with Lucious in mid-air. It sounded like two cars crashing into each other, metal on metal. The clanking rang throughout the forest and the valley below us. I wrapped my hands around his neck as we fell to the ground and quickly realized this was no ordinary t-shirt that Lucious was wearing. The high necked collar was made of metal, a protective covering for his Achilles heel.

We rolled over the forest floor. Lucious rolled on top of me and straddled my chest. He easily pulled my hands from around his neck and pinned my arms to my side. He laughed a sinister laugh as he read the expression on my face at my realization of what was around his neck. He slowly wrapped his left hand around my neck and sneered, "You really didn't think it would be that easy, now did you?"

I gasped for air as I flailed my legs trying any way to get Lucious off of me. He threw his head back in laughter, the sound clattering through the valley. He calmed down and dropped his head to look at me. Something in his eyes had changed. They weren't coal black. His eyes had a red tint to them and gleamed like gems. It took me a moment but I realized I had seen these eyes before. They were the same as those of the serpent in the garden. The black turned into red, a harrowing sight against Lucious's ghastly expression and stark black hair. He drew his lips back and the long fangs slowly protruded. I could now understand how my prey felt before an attack.

Lucious threw his head back and lunged for my neck and in doing so loosened his stance. I shook my arms free, grabbed his arms and kicked him over my head. He landed against a thick tree with a thunderous sound and slid down the trunk, bark falling around him. I sprang to my feet and assumed my fighting stance.

"Oh," he purred. "You do have a little fight in you."

"Come on," I hissed, curling the fingers on both of my hands, inviting him forward. "Let's get on with this."

We both let out growls as we charged each other. This time I lifted Lucious overhead and heaved him into a boulder. Another deafening sound echoed through the air. My strength surprised me and apparently surprised Lucious too.

"You are much stronger than I expected," he said as he lifted a hand to touch his bloody lip. "Especially for an infant."

I charged at him and lunged in the air, one leg extended at my target. But before I could deliver the kick to his chest, Lucious grabbed my leg. It was as if I had frozen in midair for the briefest of moments, and then fell crashing to the forest floor on my back. The fallen leaves didn't provide much of a cushion.

Lucious pounced on top of me and we rolled around in the dirt and leaves. He again pinned me on my back, his red eyes blazing with hatred and the venom flowing through his veins. He shoved his hand towards my neck so I shifted my head to cover the only vulnerable part on my body. I used my left hand to push on Lucious's neck. I clawed at the metal collar, barely able to discern it from Lucious' armored skin. I knew that I had to remove this contraption if I had any hope of seeing nightfall.

Lucious grabbed both of my hands, stood up and whipped me across the forest. I somersaulted through the air and landed flat footed on the ground. It seemed I was getting more coordinated as this fight progressed. Lucious looked perplexed as I stared through the trees at him. I ran towards him, leapt towards a branch, flipped myself around it and planted a kick square in his chest. I amazed myself with my power after seeing how far I had kicked him. I ran towards him again and sat on his chest, pinning him to the ground. Lucious hissed and writhed beneath me as I tried removing the metal brace, the only thing between me and my existence.

"You'll never get that off," Lucious uttered through labored breath. "You aren't strong enough for that."

"Never say never," I replied and winked at him as I pulled a chunk of the metal loose.

Lucious looked shocked that I had the strength to break through what he thought was an impenetrable collar. I shoved my hand towards his neck to take another piece, my confidence growing at the realization that I could defeat him, and as I did, he let out a deep growl and shoved me off of him. I went sailing through the air and as I landed on the ground, Lucious landed on top of me. He threw his head back letting out another snarl and I responded with a deep rumble of my own. Our roars echoed through the ridge like clapping thunder. Lucious turned his head to look at me, his lips curled back, his fangs protruding from his mouth. I held his chin with my left hand as I used my right to claw at the band around his neck. I pulled off another chunk and tauntingly waved it in his face. Another growl bellowed from deep within him; his eyes more piercing than before.

I kicked Lucious off me and he landed in a clearing where the rising sun covered half of the forest floor. I walked over to him

and planted a foot into his jaw which sent blood and venom flying. His venom hit the dry leaves, instantly igniting a smoldering
fire. I grabbed Lucious by what was left of his protective collar and
dragged him to the part of the clearing where the sun was shining.
I knew the sun wouldn't kill him, but it would inflict some serious
pain, maybe even give me the upper hand in this fight.

I sat on his chest and slowly pushed his upper body into the
sun's rays. Lucious rolled his eyes back to look at what was coming
and panic washed over his face.

"Noooooooooooo," he yelled. He knew what was about to happen and it wasn't going to be pleasant.

The sun slowly washed over his ashen face and as it did, pain
became apparent. Lucious' body shook violently. He tried to
buck me off of him but I held steadfast. I grabbed the collar and
yanked on it. A growl billowed from my stomach as I exerted my
energy in attempting to free the collar from his neck. Lucious
thrashed with pain as the sun boiled the venom in his blood. His
body jerked violently and he was cursing me in a language I didn't
understand. But I focused all of my attention on the collar wondering if it would ever come free. The sun burned my hands as
well; I felt the venom beginning to simmer underneath my icy
skin. I eased my grip for the slightest of moments trying to muster
more strength and then tugged on it again.

A loud snap rang through the air. As the collar gave, I tumbled
backwards from the amount of power I had used to break the protective shield. Lucious rolled out of the sunlight and gasped for
breath, trying to recover from his boiling blood. I sprang to my
feet. I had Lucious where I wanted him.

I lunged at him, flying effortlessly through the air. As I was
about to land on him, he pulled his knees to his chest and threw a
kick with both legs that hit me in the chest, reeling me back from

where I had just come. I crashed into a fallen tree but immediately popped back up ready to fight. Lucious was crouched across the clearing from me.

"Let's go little girl," Lucious summoned.

"You're all mine old man," I hissed in return.

We ran towards each other, clashing in the air again like two metal boulders colliding. Our hands interlocked and we twisted each other's hands outwards like we were playing a game of mercy. Both of our arms shook as we tried to overpower the other but I was gaining the upper hand. I was overpowering Lucious.

Lucious fell to his knees as I twisted harder. He wrinkled his nose in pain as he continued to quiver. I briefly turned his wrists up, providing momentary relief for him, and then sharply twisted them back, snapping both. Lucious let out an agonizing howl. I pulled him to his feet and towards me and head butted him, sending him into a tree. Lucious was dazed. I could see in his eyes the reflection of the fire burning behind me. It was like looking into the fiery depths of hell. I marched up to him and grabbed him by the neck, as he had done earlier to me. I hoisted him high above me.

"Good riddance," I snarled and dug my nails into his neck. His venomous blood spilled over my hand and stung my skin. The pain was too much to bear so I dropped his limp body to the ground; he struggled for breath as he choked on his own blood. I hovered over him and finished the job. I sunk my teeth into his neck and took a bite, ripping his life line from his body. Venom spilled over onto the ground, singeing the fall leaves.

I stood and backed away a few steps, not really believing what I had just done. It was not disbelief for having killed Lucious; I had to do that to ensure my existence. It was incredulity that I was actually able to overpower Lucious so easily; as if my agility and skill advanced the longer I fought him.

I walked over to Lucious's lifeless body and kicked his leg. There was no reaction. I tilted my head and stared at his face. His eyes, an abyss of black and red earlier, were now dull and lifeless.

I felt the heat of the fire behind me and turned towards it. The flames would take over our battle ground in a bit. The smoldering leaves on the other side of Lucious would also ignite shortly. The smoke would eventually send a signal to someone to call the fire department. I figured it would be best to leave. With the condition my house was in, someone would assume there was a break in and then would find Lucious's body in the woods. He would be blamed for the whole thing.

I leapt over the flames to head back to Castle Adena.

CHAPTER 13

It felt like an eternity, but I managed my way back to the castle. The fight with Lucious had drained me and I didn't think I'd have the strength to keep my senses in check to prevent me from going on a wild hunt. Any unfortunate rabbit, pheasant, turkey or fox that came within one hundred feet of me became a meal. It was a good thing that this land was owned by the Drake's, otherwise my trail of carcasses would have sent off bells and whistles with the mortals. The food was good but not enough to satiate me.

Castle Adena's security cameras must have picked me up because Lorenzo and Max rushed to the edge of the woods to help. My appearance must have been alarming considering all of the healing scrapes on my body and all of the tears in my clothing. Lorenzo grabbed one arm and Max grabbed the other to support me.

"My God, Allison! What happened?" Lorenzo asked.

"What did Vincent do to you?" Max questioned.

I was too exhausted and too famished to speak. "It wasn't Vincent," I muttered.

Lorenzo and Max looked inquisitively at each other and then back at me.

"Then what happened? Who was it?" Lorenzo asked.

"Lucious," I choked out.

"Lucious!" They shouted in unison. We approached a door at the rear of the castle that had been left ajar. Max opened it with his foot and my brothers escorted me inside. Lorenzo and Max peppered me with question after question.

"What was Lucious doing there?"

"How did he find you?"

"What happened?"

"Where is he now?"

We walked down a long hallway and into the dining room. I waved my hand trying to call off their verbal assault.

"Allison?" an angelic voice rang out. "Oh my, what happened?"

It was Marlo, my ever thoughtful sister, with a goblet in hand just for me.

I grabbed the cup and chugged the sweet liquid. The concoction was enough to relinquish the burning in my throat, but the relief would only be temporary. Hunger, it seemed, was a vicious cycle. I circled my tongue around the inside of the cup desperate for every last drop then feebly pushed the cup away once it was licked clean.

"It was Lucious," one of my brothers stated.

"Lucious?" Felix questioned as he entered the room.

Another barrage of questions was tossed at me but I didn't have the energy to deal with them at the moment. I threw my hands on the table and rolled my head back.

"He's gone," I muttered.

A hush fell over the room as four sets of stunned eyes looked at me.

"Gone?" Lorenzo questioned.

"Dead," I responded.

"You killed Lucious?" Felix asked.

I nodded my head in affirmation which sent off another round of questions.

"But how? You are just an infant!"

"Did he put up a good fight?"

"Did you rip his throat out?"

"How did you finish him? What did you use?"

"Guys," Marlo interrupted. "Not now. Can't you see Allison is exhausted? Here, drink this," Marlo instructed as she pushed another cup in front of me. "Let her rest," she pointed a finger at our brothers. "Allison can fill us in on all of the details later."

I was thankful for Marlo's interjection. All I wanted was to sit in my room, meditate and be alone for awhile. And I did just that.

As I pulled out of my meditative trance, I heard my siblings talking somewhere on the first level of the castle but I ignored their chatter. I was pretty sure they were still talking about the day's events, something I would much rather forget. I examined myself in the mirror. My scars were all healed, as if I had never been in a fight hours earlier. I changed into a pair of black tights, a long burgundy sweater which coordinated nicely with my oval ring and black boots. I walked to the window and sat and stared at the late afternoon sun. For starting out like Hell, a truly beautiful autumn day had unfolded. For the first time in many weeks the sun was out in full view, no rain or gray or clouds in sight. The leaves were losing their vibrant colors, turning brown and falling from the trees. I was entranced with them as they blew over the vast yard behind the castle. The air smelled clean and felt crisp against my warm skin. After taking in the scenery for some time, I decided to eavesdrop on my siblings.

"Are you sure he's dead?" I heard Lorenzo ask.

"Lorenzo, the forest was completely charred," Marlo replied. "There's no way anyone survived that."

"But what if he wasn't dead before the fire consumed the area?" Felix questioned.

"I'm sure he's dead," Marlo reassured her brothers. "I told Allison everything she needed to know about how to kill a vampire."

"And you're sure she understood?" Max asked.

"Yes!" Marlo exclaimed. "Allison is quite smart. I'm sure she remembered."

"I just don't get it," Lorenzo announced. "She's only an infant! How could she have destroyed someone of his age and skill? How could she be that strong?"

"Maybe that was her trait from her mortal life that was enhanced through her transformation," Felix offered up.

"Yeah, you know how it goes," Max chimed in, "no one ever knows what mortal strength will be augmented when someone is transformed, if they get a special gift at all."

"I guess that's a possibility," Lorenzo resigned.

I crept down the spiral staircase and moved into the dining room. I wasn't fooling anyone; I couldn't sneak up on a group of vampires who were keenly aware that I was on the premises and who desperately wanted to hear my tale.

"Allison!" Lorenzo exclaimed. "Tell us what happened."

"Come on Lorenzo," Marlo pleaded. "Allison has been through a great ordeal today; she'll tell us in time."

"No, Marlo," I stated. "It's okay. What do you want to know?" I really didn't feel like talking about this but figured I needed to get it out of the way sooner rather than later.

"Where did he come from? How did he sneak up on you?" Max inquired.

I sighed as I felt the heat climbing its way up my throat. "Can someone please get me another cocktail? I'm thirsty."

"Sure, no problem," Marlo responded and disappeared from the room.

"I don't know where he came from," I started. "I'm sure by now Marlo filled you in on why I was at my house – to confront Vincent."

"Actually, I think we forgot about Vincent after you mentioned Lucious," Felix stated. All three of my brothers nodded their heads in unison. A snarl crossed over Lorenzo's lips at the mention of Vincent's name. "Marlo mentioned that you were going to meet Vincent. What happened?" Felix asked. "Did you get the answers you were looking for?"

"No," I curtly replied. "You all were right and I didn't see it. Vincent is completely and totally selfish. He wouldn't tell me where Matt is or why he went to such lengths to kidnap him and hide him. In fact, he thought I should have been thanking him."

"Thanking him?" Lorenzo questioned. "For what?"

"For removing Matt from our home before my symptoms advanced to the point where I possibly would have attacked or killed Matt."

"You have to be kidding me!" Max exclaimed. "He knows we wouldn't have let it get to that point."

"Yeah, well, apparently Vincent couldn't wait. He wanted me and was going to do whatever he had to in order to get me to run away with him. I told him that would never happen after what Marlo told me she discovered the night Vincent transformed me. It's unfathomable what he did to me and Matt and my friends and he still expected me to run off with him! I told him to leave and never return or I'd kill him myself."

Silence fell over the room as my last words settled on my brother's ears. I continued after a brief pause.

"Vincent actually listened to me and left. I figure his bruised ego wouldn't allow him to beg for my forgiveness. After he left I was exhausted and hunger was starting to set in. I knew I didn't have enough energy to make the trek back to the castle so I decided to meditate. And I remembered the first rule of mediation – make sure to pick a safe spot. So I picked a safe spot, or so I thought."

"Your house," Max quipped. "That normally would have been a good choice."

"Right," I concurred. "So I perched myself in the loft and went to sleep and the next thing I knew I was being attacked. Lucious somehow knew I was there; I'm not really sure how he knew."

"He probably kept tabs on you after Jordana's party and tracked you," Felix suggested.

"And then what?" Lorenzo eagerly asked.

"Then there was a fight. It felt like it lasted forever. I doubted my skills initially but the longer we fought, the stronger I seemed to become."

"Interesting," Felix mused.

"Yeah well, thankfully I was able to overpower Lucious and I finished him off. He'll never be able to torment me or any of my kin ever again."

"How did you 'finish him off'?" Max asked.

Marlo entered the room with a goblet and pitcher and poured me a drink. "Max," Marlo snapped. "Not now. Why do you need all of the details? Can't you see Allison is tired and doesn't want to talk about this?" She cast a glance in my direction and I returned it with an appreciative smile before sipping my drink. "Lucious is dead and that's all that matters."

My brothers stood in silence, obviously disappointed with my abbreviated, detail-lacking rendition. But Marlo was right; I didn't want to rehash what I had just lived through.

"Do you want to go back to your room?" Marlo gently asked me.

"Actually, I want to see the sunset."

Marlo gave me directions to one of the highest peaks in Ridge Hollow. She offered to accompany me but I declined. I wanted to be alone with my thoughts and figure out what I was going to do next.

I sat high above the valley, the sun a bright orange ball against the purple sky. An oak tree served as a chair and an umbrella, shielding me from the sun's rays. Enormous buzzards filled the hollowed ridge, their silver trimmed wings spanning the emptiness. I chuckled at the irony of it; buzzards circle over dead carcasses – their next meal. Maybe they were circling me for a better view.

My thoughts drifted back over the past several weeks. I couldn't believe how much my life had changed. I went from being just any other mortal to…well, to this, whatever you want to call it. The accident changed my life forever, for eternity. In a blink of an eye, life as I had known it was gone.

It still angered me that I hadn't seen what was going on around me, especially that Vincent had caused my car accident. After all, it was his crystalline eyes I had seen in the blackness of the windshield as his truck plowed into my vehicle. I had seen those shimmery eyes so many times before. When he followed me to Whipps Ledges, it was his eyes that emerged first from the darkness. Then there was the time in my backyard, before the accident, when I fell asleep on the hammock after another sleepless night. I thought I saw lightening bugs disappearing into the woods, but now I knew otherwise.

That was Vincent keeping a close eye on me, watching my symptoms. He was waiting for the slightest sign that my symptoms were accelerating so that he could intervene for his own selfish purposes; so he could have me, a mortal descendant of Cain and part vampire, something that had never existed before, for himself.

Vincent got what he wanted. Something in me had changed and he noticed it. Had it been my cyclical body temperature – cold during the day and hot at night – or my infertility, or my change in diet, or my insomnia, or a combination of everything? Whatever it was, Vincent took it upon himself to steal my husband and his memories and hid him somewhere; where, I didn't know. And if that wasn't bad enough, Vincent had altered my friends' and coworkers' memories, making them believe his fictional tale that Matt had died and I had struggled over the past three years to come to terms with it. He had essentially cut everyone out of my life so he could act on his plan. Only a cold and vile person could do something like that.

Anger bubbled in my stomach and I let out a long yell. It felt good to release the anger. I listened to my voice echo through the empty abyss as venom began to pour over my cheeks. I wiped my face so my tears wouldn't stain my skin but instead began sobbing uncontrollably. I had no idea what I was going to do with my life and bit my lip when I thought about the word *life*. Life? What life? I had no life. That was taken from me and I was left with this existence I had no idea what to do with.

I heard a twig snap but didn't move. I could have cared less about who or what was approaching.

"Allison," a soft voice called. "It's Marlo."

"Go away," I yelled. "I told you I wanted to be alone."

Marlo didn't listen and walked closer. "I thought you might want someone to talk to."

I stood, crossed my arms and stared at Marlo. What a good sister she had been to me over these past few weeks. She took care of me in the hospital, risking her own existence by surrounding herself with all of those mortals. If she had slipped, taking just one life, her existence would have been over. I couldn't understand how she had so much self control to not lose it. She also forewarned me about this life when her brother, Vincent, was trying to convince me it was something grandiose. She ran after Vincent to learn the truth after he transformed me and she took me under her wing. I felt the need to repay her but couldn't think of something to do or say to someone who had been around for thousands of years.

I broke down in tears and wrapped my arms around Marlo.

"What has happened to me?" I moaned into her shoulder. "Just a few weeks ago, life was normal. And now what?"

"I know, I know," Marlo cooed in my ear. She pulled away from me and wiped my tears with her jacket sleeve. My tears singed the fabric.

"You need to stop crying," Marlo said as she grabbed my chin. "Before you set me on fire!"

We both chuckled as I finished wiping my tears and tried to compose myself.

"Do you want to talk about it?" Marlo asked.

"I don't know what to talk about. I mean, I don't even know where to begin, Marlo. What happened? Why me? And where am I supposed to go from here?"

"I don't know why it happened to you, Allison. But look at it this way, you are still here. Lucious didn't win and you still have an existence to fill."

An existence to fill. No longer a life to live.

I scoffed. Her explanation wasn't enough to satisfy me. I wanted to know why my symptoms had come about and what I had done to bring this upon me and why this had all happened now. These were questions I would probably never know the answers to.

"The grass is always greener, isn't it?" I whispered.

"What was that?"

"It's something Matt used to always say to me when I told him how frustrated I was in not finding my true calling. He would say 'the grass is always greener until you get to the other side.' I can't help but feel that he was right. I feel that I somehow brought this upon me in my never ending search to leave a mark on this world. A lot of good that did me. A lot of good that did Matt."

"You have left your mark on this world, Allison. You destroyed Lucious. He's gone. Forever! He can never, ever harm any other descendants again. Think about how many people you saved. It's one life sacrificed to save so many."

I let the words sink in. How many people – descendants – were out there that didn't know their bloodline dated back to Adam and Eve and Noah and Cain's other relatives? They didn't know that they had been born with targets on their backs. They didn't know they had a mortal enemy whose sole purpose was their demise. Yes, by transforming, I had somehow acquired enough skill and strength that I was able to destroy their adversary and in doing so, ensured my relatives, people that I had never met, could live out their lives in peace.

I should have felt better about my situation, but I didn't. I was now part of the undead. I had no soul. I was a killer. There was nothing glamorous about this existence. That boring, average life I complained about only weeks ago…I wanted it back.

"I want Matt," I stated.

Marlo let out a sigh. "We don't know where Matthew is," she gently stated.

"We can look!"

"Where would we start?"

"I don't know. Maybe one of Matt's favorite places."

"Do you really think Vincent would have been thoughtful enough to place Matthew somewhere where he wanted to be? Some place where you might look for him?"

Marlo had a good point. I picked up a baseball sized rock and heaved it over the edge of the cliff. We both waited several seconds as it descended into the darkness, finally clunking into the river.

"I have to say something that I don't think you are going to like," Marlo said, breaking our silence. I had a hunch I knew what she was about to say and she was right, I didn't want to hear it.

"You need to give up on the idea of finding Matthew."

The words stung worse than the venomous tears and worse than any pain Lucious inflicted upon me. I dropped my head and turned away, as if not seeing Marlo would make her words go away.

"You know I'm right, Allison." Marlo's voice was smooth and gentle, sympathetic. "Even if you did find Matthew, what would you do? What would you say?"

"I can try to make him remember me. Remember us," I desperately replied.

"Okay, and if by some miracle he did remember, how would you explain…you? How would you explain who you are – what you are – today?"

I felt the tears well up again in my eyes. Marlo was speaking the truth and I didn't like it. My life with Matt was over. I would never find him and if I did, I couldn't reveal myself to him.

"He has a new life Allison, whether you like it or not. He doesn't remember you. Matthew doesn't even know what happened to him. Just let him live his life."

I squeezed my eyes shut trying to trap the tears. The venom stung my eyes.

"You're right," I whispered. "You are right."

"It's not about me being right."

We stood there in silence and watched the sun dip behind the ridge. Puffy clouds reflected the sun's rays though the orange ball had disappeared.

"Come on," Marlo said. "Let's go back to the castle."

I stood there, frozen, peering down into the ridge below me. The temptation to just fall over the edge was overwhelming but it wouldn't solve anything. Thoughts filled my head as to what I should do with my existence from here.

"No," I coolly replied.

"Allison…"

"I don't want to go back to the castle."

"Then where do you want to go?"

"I don't know Marlo." I replied. "I need to get away though. Away from here."

"All right," Marlo replied looking confused. "Do you want to go on vacation somewhere?"

"I don't know where I want to go but I am going by myself."

"But Allison, we talked about this…Matthew…"

"I'm not going to search for Matt. You're right. I need to leave him alone. That's probably best. But I need to get away, clear my head, figure out what I want to do with this…" I paused, "…existence. I need to figure this out on my own."

"But you are just an infant. You really shouldn't be on your own yet."

"Listen, I have never been on my own. I lived with my parents until I married Matt. My life has completely changed and for the first time in thirty-two years, I am on my own. I want some time to myself."

"But you need to learn how to hunt humans," Marlo pleaded in an attempt to change my mind. "Max must teach you that before you go anywhere on your own."

"Really?" I winked. "I'll be fine," I promised. "I think I proved that with Lucious, didn't I? If I could take him down I think I can figure out how to kill a human."

"True," Marlo resigned. "It's really not that difficult considering what you've been through. But you do have to come back to the castle for one thing."

"What's that?"

"This," Marlo said as she pulled a device from her jacket pocket.

"A phone?"

"It's not just any phone. It has all the information on it you could ever need – all of our properties throughout the world, bank accounts, hunting locations – you name it."

"And why all that on a phone?"

"We've been around a few years. It gets kind of hard keeping track of everything we've amassed. Come on! Felix is programming a phone for you as we speak." Marlo tucked the phone back into her pocket.

"Okay, I'll come back for that but then I'm gone."

"Fine," Marlo said, obviously pleased that she convinced me to not run off for the moment. "I'll show you some of my favorite properties and you can choose."

"Sounds good," I said. "But I need a few more minutes out here alone if you don't mind, just to clear my head a bit more."

Marlo eyed me but resigned. "Okay, but don't be long."

I walked over to Marlo and hugged her. "Thank you for everything." I pulled away from her. "I promise I won't be long."

Marlo turned on her heels and was gone in a flash. I closed my eyes and took in a deep breath. I heard her enter the castle. I turned my hand over and looked at the black phone I had taken from Marlo's pocket. It would only be a matter of time before she realized I wasn't returning to the castle.

AUTHOR'S NOTE

I didn't grow up thinking that I wanted to be a writer. It was a culmination of events in my personal life in 2009 that caused me to rediscover my passion for creative writing. Ever since then, writing has been my escape, my release, the one thing that has kept me sane and has given me purpose.

Thank you for reading The Descendant. I hope you have enjoyed the first book in the series. I've always enjoyed fictional tales that were able to weave historical and biblical elements and that's why I've chosen to do that with this series. Quite honestly, this story is the vampire story that I had always wanted to read, and since I never found it, I decided to write it.

If you've read the book and enjoyed it, please consider leaving a review on Amazon, Barnes + Noble, Goodreads, or wherever you purchased the book. Reviews are a tremendous help to authors to help spread the word about their books. The review can be as simple as a few sentences or as long as you want it to be and you can paste the same review on each site. If you do write a review, I thank you in advance for taking the time to do that.

If you'd like to connect with me, you can find me at http://www.KelleyGrealis.com. All of my social media links are available on my website.

Stay tuned…

The Search

The Descendant Vampire Series

Book 2

Coming Fall 2013

Made in the USA
Middletown, DE
30 December 2021